THE STOBES TRILOGY

Book One

The Time Table

NJ Rayner

First Published in 2014
NJ Rayner, 27 Second Ave, Kent ME7 2HY
nigelrayner@hotmail.co.uk

njrayner.com

For Valerie, Ben and Hayley.

Preface

THE LONDON UNDERGROUND WAS THE world's first underground railway. It opened in January 1863.

It is over two hundred and fifty miles in length, and has two hundred and seventy stations. There are four hundred and twenty six escalators, sixty-four lifts, and the deepest section is over one hundred and ninety feet underground. There are also hundreds of miles of ventilation shafts and stairwells.

It closes at around midnight each day, and opens again at around 5.30am the next morning, and there are over 2.7 million journey's made every day.

What you might not know, is that there are forty disused and abandoned stations, and over fifty miles of disused and abandoned tunnels.

There are also rumours of other 'hidden' stations and tunnels that the general public knows nothing about.

So if you're ever travelling on it, maybe, as you speed through the twisting dark tunnels, you might find yourself wondering whether there could be anything strange living down there.

After all, it would seem to be the perfect environment, with its old abandoned stations, miles of disused tunnels and ventilation shafts, and a labyrinth of decaying stairwells and passages.

However, the chances are, if there is anything lurking in the shadows down in the subterranean depths, it is nothing more than the ghosts of the workers who built it and the odd big rat.

But then again…?

Chapter One

A SOUND, SIMILAR TO A SOCK filled with loose change hitting the side of an old tin bath filled with empty soup cans, echoed around a dimly lit room somewhere deep in the bowels of the London Underground.

It was followed two seconds later by an explosion.

The stench of rotten eggs, burnt fish and sulphur filled the air.

The blast hurled large amounts of old Victorian tiling, bricks and rubble across the room. Most of it landed on top of a strange looking creature, which was huddled on the floor in the far corner making whimpering noises.

The creature slowly picked up its extremely tall, extremely thin body from the floor. Shaking bits of rubble off an old, badly fitting beige cardigan, it stared across at the clouds of smoke on the other side of the room.

It continued to stare across the room; the expression on its face resembling someone with a bout of constipation. Its eyes narrowed as they tried to focus through the smoke and dust, most of which was coming from its own clothing.

Then, a look of horror spread across its long, elfin face. The old stone table, which a few seconds earlier had stood in the opposite corner of the room, was no longer there.

With one enormous hand it picked bits of dirt and soot from its short, pointed, stubby red beard. With its other even bigger hand, it reached up and began to pull various pieces of cement and rubble out of a huge column of wild, spiky red hair.

The creature continued to look across at the empty space in the corner of the room where the table had been and tried to work out what had happened.

It knew it shouldn't have removed the old tattered blanket from the stone table in the first place.

It also knew that it shouldn't have pulled out the strange looking gold peg, from the red hole on the right hand side of the tabletop.

But it couldn't help itself.

When the table had begun to make a low humming noise, it immediately put it back. Only it hadn't put it back into the red hole, but into one of the six black holes on the strange looking diagram in the centre of the tabletop.

This had caused the table to vibrate even louder, and the gold peg, along with an identical silver one, which was already in one of the other black holes, had started to glow and pulse brightly, accompanied by a deep humming sound.

The creature had known that kicking it to try to stop it vibrating and humming was something it certainly shouldn't do.

But it kicked it anyway.

The creature couldn't remember what had happened after the loud bang that followed, because it had been too busy running across to the opposite side of the room with its fingers in its ears.

As the clouds of dust finally settled, the creature began to realise exactly how much trouble it was in.

"Furtling twazlets!" it exclaimed loudly, "Wattage is going to be well furtled this time!"

Closing its eyes and hunching up its shoulders, the creature prepared to do what it always did when things went wrong - panic, and run away.

It did this a lot. And it was good at it. Well, they say practice makes perfect, and no one had more practice than this creature. In fact, it was the undisputed master of panicking and running away. Given a decent stretch of tunnel, it could get from 'oops' to eighty miles an hour in less than three seconds. On one occasion, when it accidentally blew up an old lighting generator, it managed to cover the two-mile distance from Warren Street to Oxford Circus via the Victoria Line in a minute flat.

However, on this occasion there was a problem. The room was small. Thanks to the explosion, it was also now filled with bricks, tiling and other assorted rubble.

Yet despite this the creature started to run, on the spot at first, its skinny legs with ridiculously oversized knees pumping up and down. Then it began to run round in circles, getting faster and faster, its enormous size nineteen feet stamping up huge clouds of dust and debris. Finally, it started to run up and down the length of the room. Back and forth it went, narrowly missing a collision with the walls each time. Soon it was hurtling around the entire room until it was just a shadowy blur.

As it ran, it began to repeat over and over to itself a simple chant. "Silly Spoogemige, silly furtling Stobe, silly Spoogemige, silly furtling Stobe!"

It wasn't long, however, before disaster struck again.

As the creature sped round the room, all of a sudden it suffered a blowout in one of its ancient sandals. One second it was upright, the next it was flying sideways with all the grace of a drunk staggering across a floor covered in marbles.

The creature's body hit the ground with a dull thud then bounced and slid into the wall, accompanied by a high-pitched scream and a sickening crunching sound.

There was a moment of silence as the stunned creature stared around the room, its head flopping from side to side. It was just about to get to its feet, when a large brick fell from the roof and landed on top of its head.

"Furtling twazlets," were the creature's last words before it passed out.

***** *

In the garden of a terraced house in Knightsbridge, retired bank manager Norman Beswick and his wife Florrie were enjoying a nice pot of tea.

They were suddenly disturbed, by the sound of their potting shed exploding, and the equally sudden appearance of a stone table in its place.

The stench of rotten eggs, burnt fish and sulphur filled the air.

"The teapot Florrie, the teapot!" were Norman Beswick's last words before he passed out.

***** *

On Platform Two of Knightsbridge Tube Station, a young busker was disturbed by a rumbling vibration in the wall he was leaning against. He looked down the platform in the direction of the tunnel, expecting a train to emerge, but one did not. Rubbing his tired eyes and brushing the scruffy strands of his fringe away from his forehead, he settled back down on his bench and continued to clean the spit and flem from the mouthpiece of his saxophone, using an old damp rag.

One of the problems with a reed instrument, especially one that has been played for five hours in a warm and sweaty underground passage, is that it gathers a lot of saliva in the mouthpiece.

He finally finished, and after putting the mouthpiece back inside the old battered case he laid his head back against the wall, and started dozing.

However, as he did so, he could hear what sounded like a voice. Leaning forward he looked down at the platform once more, but apart from one other person way down at the far end, there was no one else around.

Resting his head on the wall once more, he stared across at a poster on the opposite side of the tunnel that was advertising 'Prince Phillip - The Musical'.

His eyelids began to close, but as he was drifting off into sleep, he was jolted awake yet again. This time he could definitely hear a vibration and a low humming noise. Pressing his ear against the tiles, he heard what sounded like a muffled explosion followed by a dull thud. He jumped up, startled. A blast of stale air swept down from the far end of the platform. Hurriedly picking up his saxophone case with one trembling hand and grabbing his old battered holdall with the other, he ran off down the platform.

There was another rumbling noise. He leapt back again. However, this time it was the sound of a train pulling into the station, much to his relief.

As it came to a halt, he rushed onto it. The doors closed behind him. As the train pulled away, he stared through the windows at the wall where he had been sitting. Soon the darkness of the tunnel and his own reflection in the train windows were all he could see staring back at him.

* * * * *

Doreen Fudge sat on a bench on Platform One of Edgeware Road Tube Station. Glancing around she noticed that unusually, she was the only person there. She smiled to herself, and took a family-sized bar of chocolate out of her handbag. *Breakfast time*, she grinned.

She was eighteen-years-old and a bit on the fat side. This was probably due to her fondness for crisps and chocolate, and an awful lot of it. However, according to Doreen, all the women on her mothers' side of the family were big-boned so it was genetics, not crisps and chocolate, that were to blame for her size.

She worked in the accounts department of Johnson, Pratt & Livingston, a small firm of car mechanics that was conveniently situated a short walk from the underground station at West Brompton, which meant a straightforward commute on the District Line.

She had worked there for nearly a year. It wasn't a fun job. In fact, it was rubbish. The offices were like something from a Charles Dickens novel, and so was her boss. Still, it was a job. After leaving school with only two GCSE's and the school record for most detentions in a term, she was lucky to have one at all.

The reason Doreen got the job though was not that she was the best candidate. It was because she was the only candidate who managed to complete the journey from the front door to the interview room.

* * * * *

Reaching the offices of Johnson Pratt & Livingston involves one or two obstacles. Firstly, there is the front door. This involves the use of a doorbell. However, this is not your average doorbell.

This is the doorbell of death!

At least fifty years old, and held onto the rotting wooden doorframe by two bare electric wires, using it at all is a high-risk strategy. Using it in the rain is nothing less than a suicide attempt.

If you manage to get past the front door without getting electrocuted, you reach the corridor. Looking like something from Indiana Jones, it is narrow and dimly lit. Covering the walls is the most gut-wrenchingly hideous wallpaper imaginable. It is impossible to say what is covering the floor. It could be carpet, it could be tiling, or it could even be linoleum. Trying to work it out would take a team of scientists several years, and to describe it in any more detail would only make you feel sick. Let's just say, if you think of the most horrible thing you've ever seen and then double it, you might be half way there.

For those brave enough to survive the corridor, there is a final sting in the tail.

The Stairs!

Even narrower than the corridor, they are lit by a single light bulb which dangles from an old piece of frayed wire. It flickers constantly, and makes a strange hissing sound. The steps are covered in bits of rotting carpet and rusting nails. To add to the fun, they all slope in different directions, and when stood on, wobble violently from side to side. The walls at the top have dozens of scratches on them. They resemble the aftermath of an angry tiger's rampage, but they are in fact fingernail marks left by visitors, mainly postmen, who have lost their balance and tried to stop themselves falling all the way back down..

Finally, at the top of the stairs is a dirty blue door on which hangs a battered black sign held on by sticky tape. It reads SON RAT & LINGO.

There were actually three candidates for Doreen's job. The doorbell, rather predictably, electrocuted the first, whilst the second collapsed in convulsions halfway down the corridor.

Doreen however, had been too busy stuffing her face with crisps to notice the grotesque surroundings, and, apart from a slight delay near the top of the stairs when her bag swung sideways and jammed her across both walls, negotiated the journey successfully, and therefore got the job.

* * * * *

As Doreen waited for her train, she happily munched her way through the entire bar of chocolate in slightly less time than it takes the average person to eat one piece.

Still hungry, she reached into her handbag and pulled out a jumbo-sized packet of cheese & onion crisps - her second that morning.

The bag of crisps was soon finished, but another rummage in her handbag produced three Crème eggs and a Snickers bar. As she began to unwrap all four at once, she heard the sound of whistling coming from the direction of the tunnel. She was, however, too busy stuffing them all into her mouth to look up and see what it was. Only when she had finally crammed them all in, did she look down the platform to see where the whistling was coming from.

Doreen began to listen to the tune more closely. Although she couldn't put a name to it at that moment, it was certainly familiar. As she continued to stare down the platform, she noticed that little puffs of green smoke were now floating out of the tunnel. They seemed to be in time with the whistling.

As she listened more and more intently, she began to recognise the tune. *La la la, la la la la la, la la la, la la la la, I just can't get you out of my head.*

"Yes!" exclaimed Doreen, spitting out a huge stream of chocolate-coloured saliva at the same time. "I Can't Get You Out of my Head, by Kylie Minogue!"

She smiled and started to whistle along to it, bits of Crème Egg dribbling out of her mouth. It was not a pretty sight.

The whistling got louder.

Suddenly, out of the tunnel entrance, appeared something incredible, prompting Doreen to stop whistling.

In fact, it was so incredible it achieved something very rare. It made her stop eating too!

She watched, open-mouthed, as out of the tunnel walked a small, orange dragon-like creature. It was about three feet tall, and wearing a black Kaiser Chiefs 'I Predict a Riot' t-shirt, and carrying a plastic carrier bag.

It climbed onto the platform, and then began to walk slowly down, swinging its hips from side to side, until it drew level with her, and stopped. Turning to face her, it put down the carrier bag, smiled, and then pulled what looked like an earphone out of one of its long pointed ears.

It looked at Doreen for a few moments, and then with a loud belch, blew a big puff of green smoke into the air. Bending down, it proceeded to pull a pair of old grey carpet slippers out of the carrier bag. Looking up and pushing a long, pointed purple tongue up inside its left nostril, it began to put them on its long clawed feet one at a time.

Doreen sat motionless, her gaping mouth resembling one of the tunnels. A steady stream of brown, yellow and white goo was running down the front of her blouse, and down onto her skirt.

In a control room somewhere else in the Underground, the man responsible for monitoring the security cameras on that section of the Bakerloo line sat with an amused expression on his face as he watched Doreen. For some strange reason, the small orange dragon-like creature didn't show up on his cameras.

The dragon finished putting on the carpet slippers, then started to rummage about in the carrier bag. After a few seconds, it pulled out a loaf of bread. It grinned excitedly at the loaf and then at Doreen, before putting the loaf back in the carrier bag. Grabbing the handles of the bag with its stumpy little orange claws, it picked it up then put the earphone back in its ear. Looking once more at Doreen, whilst pushing its tongue this time up its right nostril, the dragon lifted one leg in the air and farted loudly.

Then, accompanied by wisps of brown coloured trumpy smoke, it began to whistle again, before strolling off down the platform.

Doreen continued to watch in a mixture of fear and amazement, as the creature disappeared into the darkness of the tunnel at the far end of the platform.

The muffled sound of a strange voice singing completely out of tune echoed inside the tunnel.

"*Boy, your lovin' is all I think about,*" were the last words Doreen heard before she passed out.

✦

Chapter Two

ROD HEATH HAD BEEN BUSKING in the London Underground for just over a year, after dropping out of school early. This came as a great shock to his parents, who had spent a huge amount of money on his education. Money they could not really afford. However, despite this, Rod had decided he wanted to be a musician. Their son standing in a corridor playing 'Baker Street' for loose change down in the underground was not exactly what his parents saw as a great career move. Yet despite this, they always tried to make sure he had enough money to live on. Even if it meant they themselves rarely did.

Once the train pulled into Hammersmith Station he got off and made his way out towards the escalators, still trying to work out exactly what he had heard back at Knightsbridge station.

He walked out onto the busy street outside, weaved his way through the familiar conveyor belt of people rushing about their business whilst texting or updating their social media, and headed down the road to the Dog & Trumpet pub.

This was just around the corner from the flat he shared with two other school dropouts, Charlie and Wedge. Charlie was from Surrey and had a calm, tranquil manner about him. Wedge on the other hand, was a highly animated and at times decidedly odd character from Ruthin in Wales. Charlie, like Rod, had dropped out of school early. Wedge however, had been expelled from his, after setting fire to the rugby posts during sports day.

Wedge was now working for Finchley Council as a bin man, whilst Charlie delivered pizzas for a local take-away.

The Dog & Trumpet was just the same as it was most lunchtimes. Two tattooed young men in white overalls were swearing aggressively at a grinning Chris Tarrant on a slot machine. A couple of old East End boys were having an argument about which of them was most closely related to the Kray Twins, and a group of art students were complaining about the price of Aldi's spaghetti whilst playing Angry Birds on their iPads and Smartphones.

Rod made his way around to the other side of the bar, to where Wedge and Charlie were sat. He explained what had happened earlier in the Underground, then sat back and waited for the ridicule to start.

"I've had a similar experience down at Knightsbridge myself," said Charlie. "I'm sure I once heard someone being chased by a lawnmower!"

"Me too," said Wedge. "Last week for instance, I was coming back from a gig in Camden. It was late at night, and I was waiting for the last train out, when I'm sure I caught a glimpse of this shadowy blur hurtling through the station."

"Very funny," said Rod sarcastically.

"I'm being serious," replied Wedge. "There could be anything down there. Look how old it is. Some parts are over a hundred years old."

"Exactly," said Charlie, "There are old abandoned stations, old ventilation and lift shafts, and miles of disused tunnels. Perfect hiding places…"

Charlie's voice dropped deeper, and took on an almost patronising tone. "…For whatever you want to imagine, young man!"

Wedge and Charlie burst into laughter, Rod too began to laugh, as he realised it was more than likely his imagination.

"MORE BEER!" shouted Wedge suddenly, doing a poor imitation of Brian Blessed. He jumped out of his chair and rushed off to the bar with a manic grin on his face. "Another three pints of your lukewarm beer please, landlord. And three packets of out-of-date crisps."

"Very amusing Wedge," replied the rather fearsome looking barman. "And would you like a slap round the head to go with that?"

The landlord was momentarily distracted from serving Wedge by the two young lads in overalls, who were now threatening Chris Tarrant with physical violence.

"Oi, you two muppets!" shouted the landlord angrily. "One more peep out of you, and I'll introduce your heads to the internal mechanism of that machine!"

One of the old East End boys looked across at the two lads, and then turned to the other one.

"I'll tell you somefing, tweacle, they wouldn't ave behaved like that if Won and Weggie were still wunnin this manor,"

"Too true Arry," replied the other one.

The two lads in overalls quickly finished their pints and left rather quickly and sheepishly, whilst the landlord finished serving Wedge.

Wedge returned from the bar carrying three pints of lukewarm beer, and three packets of crisps, which surprisingly for The Dog & Trumpet were not out-of-date until next Thursday.

The rest of the evening was spent discussing more serious matters, such as how were they going to pay this month's rent, finding a new bass player for the band, and replacing Wedge's missing drumkit. Last, but not least, was Wedge's recent run-in with the Police for setting fire to a wheelie bin in the car park at Asda.

* * * * *

Rod had first met Charlie and Wedge at Glastonbury two years earlier.

Queuing up in the pouring rain for a burger, after the Kaiser Chiefs' set, he had been fascinated by the antics of a big guy with spiky ginger hair. He was wearing a huge, badly fitting green woollen jumper that came all the way down to his knees, some old ripped brown trousers and a pair of very old blue Wellingtons, which he seemed to be having a conversation with. The other thing Rod noticed was his strong Welsh accent.

Charlie, on the other hand, seemed quite ordinary by comparison. Dressed in jeans and a blue waterproof jacket, he was somewhat smaller than Wedge. He had a stocky, muscular build, with a shock of long black hair and a rounded, young looking face. His eyes were vivid blue. Unlike Wedge, Charlie's accent was very upper class, almost aristocratic, yet at the same time soft and friendly.

As they waited in the squelching mud and incessant rain the three of them found an instant rapport, cracking jokes and discovering that they had a lot in common — other than being soaked to the skin.

They were all musicians dreaming of being in a successful band.

Charlie played keyboards, Wedge the drums, whilst Rod played both guitar and saxophone. All three were also struggling to make ends meet in badly paid jobs, or in Wedge's case, a succession of badly paid jobs. This was due to his disturbing ability for setting things on fire. In particular, wheelie bins. Whilst some of the fires were accidents, there were a number, which plainly were not. Whichever way you looked at it, Wedge undoubtedly had a latent tendency towards pyromania, and leaving him alone with matches and combustible material was not a good idea.

By the end of the day, Rod had not only found two new friends but also two new flatmates and, as an added bonus, the nucleus for a band. All they needed was a bass player, and they were ready to take the world, well maybe not the world, but certainly the local pubs and gig venues, by storm.

At first, they had difficulty coming up with a name for the band. Sturgeon and the Pikes, Muddy and the Wellingtons, Rift Raft, and the highly inappropriate Douglas Baader Meinhof and the Spitfires were all considered, until they finally settled on 'The Rent Dodgers' because they spent most of their time avoiding the landlord, especially towards the end of each month.

Charlie was very good at getting gigs in the local pubs and bars in the area. This was because he was hopeless at negotiating payment terms, so they ended up playing most of them for free.

However, both finding, and then keeping hold of, a decent bass player was proving to be a real problem.

The first one to join the band was a great player, but had a slight drinking problem. This meant that by the time they got to the third or fourth song, he would start to stagger backwards, eventually crashing into Wedge's drum kit, then stagger forward, tripping over his own guitar lead, then falling off the front of the stage, dragging his amplifier behind him.

The second one was an even better player, with the added advantage that he only drank coke. The disadvantage was that his mother, a big brash woman, accompanied him to each gig, and insisted that he was finished by 10.30pm. She would point to her watch at exactly that time, then walk round to the side of the stage, unplug his amplifier, and drag him home.

Number three was undoubtedly strange even compared to Wedge. He hardly ever spoke, and always wore a navy blue pinstripe suit, white shirt and red tie. He also wore the most dazzlingly polished black shoes this side of an army parade ground. Nevertheless, he was a great bass player. One day however he suddenly announced at the end of a gig, that he was going to Australia the next day to paint electricity pylons.

Then of course, there was Eddie, the most recent one. They met him whilst playing a gig at a particularly rough bar in Bethnal Green. Here the locals were more interested in watching TV than the band, and apart from hurling insults or, if it was Friday night, the odd bottle, paid little attention to who was playing.

They were half way through a song when one of the men leaning at the bar, turned round and shouted over to them.

"You know it would all sound a hell of a lot better with a bass player."

He was tall, with badly fitting stained jeans and an even more badly fitting stained shirt. To round his image off perfectly, he also had a set of badly fitting stained teeth. Sitting on the floor next to him and growling, was a small rough-haired dog similar to a Jack Russell Terrier. Its teeth were also badly fitting and stained.

"Well why don't you join us?" replied Charlie with a hint of sarcasm.

With that the man walked out of the bar, leaving the dog behind, still growling.

A couple of minutes later he returned. He was carrying a battered guitar case in one hand, and an equally battered amplifier in the other.

Pausing at the bar long enough to pull his dog away from the throat of an old man who had foolishly bent down to stroke it, he made his way to the stage.

Opening up the guitar case, he pulled out a bright red Fender bass, covered in dints and scratches. Heaving the ancient looking amplifier onto the stage, he plugged in the guitar, and slung it around his neck like a gunslinger. Then he just stood there, his hands resting on the fret board.

"Hi, I'm Eddie, what we gonna play?"

"Can you read music?" replied Charlie.

"No,"

"Do you know 'I Predict a Riot' by the Kaiser Chiefs?"

"You mean this one?"

He started to play the opening bass lines of the song. Wedge, then Rod, then Charlie watched in amazement, as the most jaw-

dropping baselines thundered out of the amplifier. This bloke could certainly play.

Wedge, grinning like a man possessed, kicked the drums in. Charlie and Rod followed suit, and soon the sound coming from the stage had attracted everyone's attention.

The rest of the gig was the best they had ever played. Eddie didn't read music because he didn't need to.

No matter what they played, Eddie knew it. Even when towards the end, they played one of their own songs; it only took him a couple of bars to work out how the bassline should go. He even added some improvisation to make it sound even better.

They finished to rapturous applause and whoops for more. They even got paid!

Eddie joined the band. The gigs got better and better, and they started to get a growing reputation as a great live act.

There was however, a slight problem with their new bass player.

The problem was not actually with him. No, it was his dog, which was the problem. Everywhere they played, Eddie's dog always tried to bite someone. Not just a playful nip either. Oh no, Eddies dog was a killer. It went for people's throats.

And so it was, on a fateful night at the Coach and Horses in Fulham, that it all went horribly wrong. As the band began setting up their gear in the lounge bar, Eddie's dog, for no reason whatsoever, began attacking the landlord in the snug bar.

During the panic and carnage that followed, Eddie punched the landlord after he had kicked the dog, whilst trying to shake it off his leg. Then, just as the police walked in, the dog leapt across the bar and tried to bite one of the barmaids in the throat.

It took four policemen to pin the dog down. As the landlord, his wife, and the barmaid were led sobbing and bleeding to a waiting ambulance, Eddie and his dog were led away to a police van, the dog still growling and trying to bite the arresting officer in his privates.

To round the evening off perfectly, Wedge loaded his drum kit into the back of the wrong van.

* * * * *

By the end of the evening, Rod, Charlie and Wedge were no nearer to finding the weeks rent, a new bass player or a new set of drums for Wedge. They were however, slightly drunk.

"You know, being serious…" slurred Wedge, falling over the sofa back at the flat and landing in a crumpled heap, "…I really do believe there are strange things down in the Underground."

The sound of Rod and Charlie snoring was the last thing Wedge heard, before he drifted off into a drunken slumber.

Chapter Three

DOWN IN A DARK, DUSTY room deep in the London Underground, Spoogemige felt hot breath blowing through his tall column of spiky red hair, followed by a sharp prod in his side. He opened his eyes to see puffs of green smoke rising in the air, and a small orange dragon chewing on a piece of burnt toast staring down at him. It was tapping its right foot slowly.

"Oh, Scorchington. it's you,"

"Want some toast, Spoogy?"

The dragon pulled a piece of bread out of a plastic carrier bag. Holding it up to his mouth, he blew three short bursts of fire onto it. Spoogemige looked up at the burnt offering and shook his head.

"Still not mastered how to toast bread yet, have you Scorchington?"

"Nope," replied the dragon with a smile, his hips swaying and feet still tapping.

"And it doesn't look like you've mastered how to go in a room without blowing it up either," continued the dragon sarcastically.

The dragon looked down at Spoogemige, smiled, farted loudly, and leaving wisps of brown trumpy smoke behind him walked over to where the stone table usually stood.

"Go on, give us a clue then - what have you done to the table?"

"It wasn't my fault. I didn't do anything."

"So what happened?"

"I don't know what happened to it. It just exploded."

"Just exploded... all by itself eh?" the dragon sniggered.

* * * * *

In Knightsbridge, Norman Beswick sat in the back of an ambulance with a blanket round his shoulders. As his wife Florrie wiped tea stains from the front of his shirt, a paramedic tried to remove the lid of a teapot from a large gash on his head.

Out in the garden, two police officers were examining the stone table standing in the ruins of the potting shed.

Despite having destroyed most of the potting shed, there appeared to be no damage to the table. It just sat there with smoke coming off it, making a low humming noise.

As PC Walton stood there nervously, PC Meredith bent down and looked at the front of the table. There was what looked like a drawer, and there was a piece of wool hanging off an iron lever on the drawer front with what looked like a button fastened to it. It was badly singed, but looked as if it might have once been beige.

"What do you make of this?" said PC Meredith, holding up the piece of singed wool.

PC Walton ignored him, and continued to stare nervously at the table.

"Well...did you hear me?"

PC Walton turned his head for a fraction of second to look. "Looks like a piece of old clothing," he replied, before returning his attention to the table.

"What do you think it is, and where did it come from?"

"Haven't a clue, I'm more concerned about that humming noise."

"What do you make of these two gold and silver pegs too?" said PC Meredith with a very puzzled expression on his face. "And is this some kind of diagram on the tabletop?"

"I actually think you should stop messing about with this table," said an increasingly agitated PC Walton. "I don't like this one bit – there's something decidedly spooky going on here."

"Oh you big Jessie, where's your sense of adventure?"

"In the same place as your common sense."

As PC Walton shifted uneasily from foot to foot, PC Meredith continued to do what PC Walton didn't want him to do, and carried on fiddling with the table.

"I don't suppose you've got a magnifying glass on you?"

PC Walton looked across.

"Of course I have, it's in the same pocket as my Napoleonic spanners and spare horseshoes!"

"Alright keep your shirt on, I was only asking."

"Well honestly, who do you think I am, Sherlock chuffing Holmes? Anyway, what do you want one for?"

"To try and make out this small writing underneath each of these six holes on the table top."

"What does it say?"

"I can't make it out. That's why I need a magnifying glass!"

"It probably says – do not continue to mess with this table unless you want to be seriously injured or killed."

"Oh, don't be such a wimp!"

PC Meredith was beginning to enjoy himself. PC Walton on the other-hand had a very bad feeling about the whole situation. It was the same feeling he always got just before something bad happened. Like the time the brakes on his bike had failed while approaching a set of roadworks going down Boxhill, or the time he jumped over a garden fence while chasing a robber, and found himself inside a kennel containing three very bad-tempered Dobermans.

"I wonder if the old couple have got one? Think I'll go and see," continued PC Meredith.

As PC Meredith made his way up to the house, PC Walton continued to stare at the table, and waited for something bad to happen.

PC Meredith knocked on the door. Florrie Beswick answered. "Oh do come in, Sergeant Meredith."

"It's Constable Meredith actually, Mrs Beswick."

As he walked in behind her, he noticed that she seemed to be limping. Closer inspection revealed that it was because the heel on one of her shoes was missing. He also noticed that there were still pieces of burnt wood stuck to the back of her sweater, and that her hair was sticking up in the air and badly singed.

"Norman, it's Sergeant Meredith."

"It's Constable Meredith, actually."

"Hello Sergeant," said Norman Beswick, wearily. He was now sitting in an armchair in the front room, a large bandage wrapped round his head. His shirt was still covered in tea stains, and he had a tartan rug over his knees. Cradled in his lap were the remains of a teapot.

"Do you know, Sergeant Meredith, this teapot has been in our family for over three generations."

PC Meredith looked down at the teapot.

"Three generations!" he continued. "It's survived two world wars, including the blitz, four house moves and eight grandchildren. It has been dropped, kicked, and on one occasion, fallen down an entire flight of stairs. My

24

sister who was carrying it, broke both her legs, but the teapot? Not a scratch! Blooming indestructible it was. Now look at it!"

PC Meredith found it difficult to offer commiserations to a teapot.

"Perhaps you could glue it back together."

"There you go, Norman," said Florrie. "What a good idea, Sergeant Meredith."

"Glue it back together? Oh yes, that's a wonderful idea. And I suppose when I've finished, I can rebuild the potting shed using matchsticks,"

"I am sorry, Sergeant Meredith," said Florrie "He always gets grumpy when something's gone a bit wrong."

"Gone a bit wrong? So that's how you'd describe today's events then is it?" replied Norman angrily.

"Well, these things do happen every now and then, Norman."

"Oh do they, Florrie? So today's events are normal, are they? So it's normal for potting sheds to suddenly explode? And I suppose it's perfectly normal for stone tables to appear suddenly from nowhere? And I bet lots of people have nearly been killed by flying teapot lids as well?"

PC Meredith and Florrie Beswick looked at each other. He did have a point.

"I think I'd better put the kettle on," said Florrie.

"Oh that's right, you put the kettle on. That'll solve everything won't it? If in doubt, put the kettle on." said Norman sarcastically.

PC Meredith followed Florrie into the kitchen.

"He seems upset,"

"Oh don't worry; he'll be fine once he's had a nice cup of tea. There's not a lot that can't be sorted out with a nice cup of tea."

PC Meredith looked at her. He couldn't work out whether her matter-of-fact reaction to the day's events was down to stoicism, or a slight touch of insanity.

"Mrs Beswick, I don't suppose you've got a magnifying glass?"

"Magnifying glass? Hmm, let me see... You know, I think Norman might have one. He used to go fishing."

PC Meredith tried to work out what a magnifying glass had to do with fishing.

"Norman, have you still got that old magnifying glass? You know, the one you used to use when you went fishing?"

"It should be in the cupboard under the clock,"

Florrie opened the cupboard under the clock. A large pile of newspapers fell out onto the floor, followed by some eggcups and a hot water bottle. She bent down, and proceeded to climb inside the cupboard until just her legs were sticking out. It was not a pretty sight. Her skirt was pushed up, revealing an assortment of undergarments, which would not have looked out of place on Mary Queen of Scots. They were ripped in several places, and had what looked like burn marks all over them. In fact, they bore more than a passing resemblance to a World War II parachute, which had been deployed rather too early by the pilot of a burning Spitfire.

After a few minutes of searching and a great deal of grunting, she climbed back out and stood up. Her hair was even more dishevelled than before and all the exertion had dislodged her false teeth, so that the top set was now jammed sideways between the roof of her mouth and her tongue.

"Heel yoo are Slergeant Meweditlh," she said, handing him a brown envelope with an address on the front.

PC Meredith tried not to stare, as she tried to chew her teeth back into position. She looked like a horse trying to eat raw squid. She suddenly started to choke. Her face turned blue and she started shaking violently, before collapsing back against the sink. PC Meredith grabbed hold of her from behind and, squeezing her tightly round the waist, proceeded to apply the Heimlich manoeuvre. It did not work. The teeth wouldn't budge. As her face turned from blue to a frightening shade of purple, her legs gave way and she slumped into his arms, now barely conscious. In a last act of desperation, he managed to prop her up against the wall with his knees, and using a spoon and a tea towel, finally wrench the teeth out.

A few moments later, she regained both her breath and her composure, and straightened herself up.

"Oh goodness me," She panted. "That was a silly thing to happen wasn't it?"

"Are you alright?" enquired PC Meredith, concerned.

"Oh I'm fine, these things happen you know."

PC Meredith shook his head in disbelief.

After checking yet again that she was all right, he transferred his attention back to the envelope and pulled out a small brass magnifying glass. Meanwhile, Florrie Beswick had put her teeth back in place and was climbing back into the cupboard once more and starting to put everything back inside. When she came to the hot water bottle however, she stopped. Standing back up once more, she held it in front of her and smiled.

"I wonder whether I can still do it?"

"Do what?" replied PC Meredith nervously.

"Well Sergeant Meredith, when I was a small girl, I was the village champion at blowing up hot water bottles,"

PC Meredith wasn't sure what 'blowing up' meant exactly, and became rather worried.

"Oh yes," she continued. "I could blow up three in under a minute. Big lungs you see. I could also swim two lengths underwater."

PC Meredith's expression changed from worry to genuine concern.

"How old were you?"

"Fourteen,"

"And if I may ask a delicate question, how old are you now?"

"Eighty Seven!"

"I don't wish to interfere, but isn't it a bit risky for you to be trying this at your age?"

"Nonsense Sergeant Meredith. I'm sure I can still do it. After all, you only live once."

After surviving an explosion in a potting shed, and nearly choking to death on her false teeth, PC Meredith felt that she'd experienced enough high-risk activity for one day.

However, before he could say another word, she had lifted the hot water bottle up to her lips, and was proceeding to try to inflate it.

He watched in disbelief as she spent the next few minutes gasping, groaning and wheezing into the opening. Miraculously, the bottle started to inflate. However shortly afterwards she started to turn blue again, before collapsing backwards towards the sink once more. PC Meredith managed to catch her just in time.

"I think you've had enough drama and excitement for one day," he said through gritted teeth as he lifted her onto a chair.

"I think you might be right," she replied, breathing deeply, and once more trying to regain her composure.

After a short while she was back to her cheerful self, seemingly oblivious to what had just happened.

"Will that magnifying glass do the job Sergeant Meredith?"

"Yes thanks. I have to ask though. How did he use this for fishing?"

"Floats. He used to make his own floats. As he got older, he needed it to see what he was doing."

"Oh, I see."

"What do you need the magnifying glass for, Sergeant?" shouted Norman from down the hallway, completely unaware that his wife had just nearly died - *twice*.

"We've found a diagram and some writing on the table. It's very small though."

As Florrie Beswick took her husband a nice cup of tea, PC Meredith made his way back out into the garden.

"You took your time," said PC Walton, now convinced something really bad was about to happen.

"Right, let's see what all this writing is." continued PC Meredith.

After several minutes of close scrutiny, he was none the wiser. In fact, he was even more confused.

"Looks like a foreign language, but then again it doesn't."

"Care to expand on that?"

"Well, some of the letters are definitely from the alphabet… but a lot of them definitely aren't. I can't make out whether they are symbols… like old hieroglyphic's… or something else,"

PC Walton had now had enough, and stepped back from the table. PC Meredith, however, was becoming more and more determined. He reached underneath it, and started pulling at the iron lever on the drawer. After several minutes of grunting and heaving, the lever still hadn't moved.

"Give us a hand with this, will you?"

"Should you be doing that?"

"Why not…? I mean, what could happen…? It's only a table!"

"Er… a table which seems to have appeared all by itself, destroying a rather substantial late Victorian potting shed in the process!"

PC Walton did not intend to have anything to do with his colleague's stupidity. However, this did not deter PC Meredith from continuing to pull and tug at the iron lever.

For the next five minutes, he grunted away trying to move it, but no matter how hard he tried, he could not move it.

Standing up, he kicked the iron lever in frustration.

The lever made a loud clicking sound and slowly slid forward, and then all by itself rotated clockwise and stopped.

The two officers watched in stunned silence, as accompanied by a dull whirring sound, the drawer slid open. Only it wasn't a drawer at all – it was a seat of some description, with the concave shape of what looked like three buttocks set into the surface. Then, as they watched open mouthed, and accompanied by the sound of turning cogs, two iron handles rose up from either side of the tabletop.

PC Meredith was the first to speak.

"Now that's not something you see everyday, is it?"

"Well I hope you're pleased with yourself. We're probably both about to be killed!"

PC Meredith moved over to the table to take a closer look.

"Do you really think you should be doing that?"

"Do you realise, that after three years on the force, the nearest I've got to some serious investigative police work is when we had to track down those two nutters who were going round mowing peoples lawns without permission in the early hours of the morning?"

"Oh yes, I remember, Two Mowers Harris, and Three Strimmers Sugden. Got fifty hours community service and all their gardening equipment confiscated, didn't they?"

"So if you think I'm going to just walk away from this without trying to solve the mystery, then you can think again."

PC Walton had had enough though and walked away, as PC Meredith moved back to the table.

Leaning over it, he carefully sat down on the strange looking seat. He shifted and wriggled about on it, as his two buttocks failed to find a comfortable position. He then studied the two pegs. He knew there must be a reason for them, but he was unable to draw a conclusion.

He tried pulling the gold peg out of the hole it was in, but it would not budge. Eventually after a great deal of pulling and twisting, he managed to wrench it out. It made a deep clicking sound. He examined it closely. He couldn't figure out what kind of metal it was - it looked like gold, but felt more like brass. It was very heavy for something so small, and it had a strange odour to it.

He started rolling it around the palm of his hand with his thumb as he tried to come up with a theory, which his brain was never going to be capable of. Then, in what even a reckless man would consider an act of recklessness, he pushed it into the red hole at the side of the map.

The humming noise suddenly stopped!

Overcome by a completely misplaced sense of his own intelligence, he pulled the gold peg out of the red hole.

The table started to make a humming noise again.

He repeated this a few more times, with the same result.

"I think I've discovered something!"

PC Walton popped his head out from behind the tree he was now hiding behind.

"You do realise you're about to die!"

PC Meredith just grinned.

He put the gold peg back in one of the holes, only this time he put it into one of the black holes within the map.

The table began to vibrate again, only this time more loudly, and now the gold peg, along with the identical silver one, started to glow and pulse brightly, accompanied by a deep humming sound.

31

Instead of doing what any other sensible person would do – jump off and run away - PC Meredith threw himself across the table and grabbed hold of the handles on either side.

PC Walton peered round the trunk of the tree long enough to see what was happening, and started to run to the aid of his colleague.

As the table continued to vibrate, PC Meredith clung on for grim death.

Just as PC Walton got to within a few yards of the table, the humming and vibration suddenly stopped.

They both had just enough time to look at each other with relief, before there was a loud bang. This was followed a few seconds later by an explosion.

The blast blew PC Walton backwards across the garden.

The air was filled with clouds of smoke, and the even stronger smell of rotten eggs, burnt fish and sulphur.

PC Walton picked himself up off the ground a few seconds later, covered in soil and bits of plant, and peered through the smoke.

The table was nowhere to be seen.

Neither was PC Meredith!

* * * * *

In the workshop of Johnson Pratt & Livingston, two mechanics were enjoying their bacon butties and a brew. A loud explosion, followed by the sudden appearance of an old table at the bottom of the inspection pit, blew them backwards off the two oil drums they were sitting on. Draped across the top of the table was what looked like a Policeman?

"What the…?!" they both shouted before passing out.

Chapter Four

A GROUP OF PEOPLE STOOD round Doreen Fudge as she started to regain consciousness down at Edgware Road tube station.

"Is she drunk?" said one of them.

"I don't think so," replied another.

"Bet she is, isn't she Poocums?" shouted a large woman at the back.

She was wearing a grey plastic Mac and carrying a small Yorkshire terrier, which yapped constantly.

"No, I don't think she is," said a small man wearing a check jacket. He was staring at the chocolate stains on Doreen's face and blouse, and the empty crisp packets and chocolate wrappers in her handbag. "It looks to me like she's eaten herself unconscious."

"Eaten her self unconscious?" shouted a tall bald man with glasses. "You can't eat yourself unconscious."

"Oh yes you can," replied the man in the check jacket. "I remember a woman at our office passing out after eating seventeen jam doughnuts in under five minutes."

At that moment, Doreen began to sit up. She stared at the people around her and clutched her handbag tightly to her chest. With a tremor in her voice she said quietly, "Did any of you see it?"

"See what?" said the tall man with glasses.

"See *it*?" repeated Doreen.

"What are you talking about, love?" asked the man in the check jacket.

"The creature," said Doreen quietly. "The little orange dragon-like creature. He was wearing a black T-shirt, and holding a plastic carrier bag."

"See, Poocums?" shouted the large woman at the back. "I told you she was drunk!"

"Little orange dragon in a black T shirt?" replied the tall bald man with glasses.

"Yes, yes!" shouted Doreen, "And he was wearing slippers. Old grey carpet slippers. He was whistling too, a Kylie Minogue song. You know, the one that goes *La la la, la la la la la,la la la…I just can't get you out of my…*"

"She's not drunk," shouted the tall bald man with the glasses, turning round to face the crowd, "She's completely plastered!"

"Told you so, Poocums," shouted the large woman at the back gleefully.

This was all too much for Doreen. As a train pulled into the station, she saw her chance to escape the humiliation. Pushing the man in the check jacket aside, she barged her way through the crowd and rushed across the platform onto the waiting train. Tears were streaming down her face. The doors closed and as the train pulled away, Doreen stared back at the platform sobbing and trembling.

The crowd of people on the platform shook their heads. The man in the check jacket picked himself up off the floor and straightened his crumpled clothing. The rest of the crowd, realising that the entertainment was over, made their way towards the escalators.

The large woman put her yapping dog down on the floor and began rummaging through her handbag. At the same time, a group of Japanese students came rushing round the corner dragging wheeled suitcases behind them. As they pushed past her, Poocums' lead got trapped around the wheels of one of them.

"Poocums!" she screamed, as the dog was dragged along the ground yapping and howling.

She started to run down the platform after them, shouting and waving her arms frantically. The Japanese students waved back at her smiling. Some of them even took photographs.

She watched in horror as the Japanese students, along with poor little Poocums, disappeared onto a train. As it started to pull out of the station, she could see part of Poocums lead, hanging out between the doors. She could also see the top of his head as he jumped up at the windows.

In an attempt to try to grab the lead, she dived towards the train. Unfortunately, she failed to notice a large pile of suitcases in the middle of the platform.

"Don't worry, Poocums, Mummy's here!" she cried, as she flew through the air like an elephant being fired out of a canon, and crashed into them.

Trying desperately to unravel herself from the pile of suitcases, she could only watch helplessly as the train, along with Poocums, disappeared out of sight into the tunnel.

"Poocums, my baby!" were her last words before she passed out.

Chapter Five

IN A DIMLY LIT ROOM somewhere in the Underground an odd-looking elderly creature, wearing a battered trilby and an old trench coat, surveyed the mess. He looked across at the corner where the stone table should have been.

"Where's my table?" screamed Wattage.

In a small dusty storeroom, further down the tunnel from Wattage's study, Spoogemige sat on the bottom of an old hospital bunk bed fiddling with the straps of his broken sandals. He pretended not to hear Wattage shouting.

The room was one of several situated along a dark complex of disused tunnels near to the old abandoned Brompton Road tube station. The walls of the tunnel were covered in flaking paint and cracked green tiles dating back to Victorian times. Faded signs, pointing to long abandoned platforms, were just about visible in the gloomy candlelight. Bits of old machinery covered in decades of dust lay scattered around the floor. At the far end of the tunnel, a metal door with a mesh grill blocked the entrance to the black void of an old lift shaft.

Brompton Road Tube Station on the Piccadilly Line, and the adjacent tunnels had been closed to the public since the 1930's. Since then it had stood, abandoned in the darkness.

That was until a strange group of subterranean creatures moved in.

The Stobes.

They had moved there for one simple reason. To get away from another group of equally strange creatures, that lived in the deeper, disused levels.

The Darkenbads.

The Darkenbads were a particularly frightening and psychotic gang of creatures, who carried out muggings and other acts of senseless violence on a regular basis. They were nearly always the ones responsible for starting the regular battles that took place.

The labyrinth of tunnels and ventilation shafts around Brompton Road weren't perfect though. To start with, they were worryingly close to the mainline stations on the Piccadilly Line, used by thousands of 'Topsiders' every day. In addition, they had been abandoned for nearly eighty years, and there was no electric power or lighting. This meant that it was very dark. However, despite this, it was still better than living with the constant threat of ambush down in the deeper levels.

It was now home to most of the Stobes, although some remained in hiding down in the lower levels.

Wattage was the elder of the group. He was small and dumpy, with narrow blue eyes and puffy cheeks. His oversized pumpkin-like head contained a few wisps of grey hair, over which he usually wore a dark brown trilby hat. His hands were broad and strong, with incredibly long wrinkly fingers. As well as the trilby, he also wore an old navy blue trench coat. It was about three sizes too big, and looked rather ridiculous.

This wasn't unusual.

The Stobes, like all the other creatures who lived in the underground, were scavengers. They wore whatever they could get their thieving little mitts on. Their main sources of clothing were items left lying around at station platforms. This meant that the average Stobe looked like they had run through a jumble sale covered in glue. Sometimes, they would also carry out daring midnight raids known as 'Sherlocks', on the Lost Property Office at Baker Street. These were very dangerous, and not for the faint-hearted.

Wattage, therefore, was not in the least bit worried about his appearance. What he was worried about though, was the disappearance of his table.

He had been studying the table in detail, since it was found half buried, in one of the disused sections of the Northern Line several weeks ago.

And despite not being exactly sure what it was, what it was used for, or where it came from, he had begun to develop a theory, and spent a considerable amount of time exploring it and in the process grown quite attached to it.

Wattage continued to stare at the empty space where his table should have been. The more he stared, the angrier he became.

Chapter Six

BY THE TIME DOREEN ARRIVED at the offices of
Clegg Platt & Shuttleworth, she was still sobbing and
shaking. She was also over two hours late. This did not
go down well with her immediate superior, Irene
Fontwell, who glowered at her through a pair of black
horn-rimmed spectacles.

Irene Fontwell was the longest serving employee of
Johnson Pratt & Livingston. She had joined the company
shortly after the war, though nobody was exactly sure
which one. It might have been the Second World War.
Then again, it could have just as easily been the Crimean.
She was in charge of the accounts department, which she
ran with the kind of ruthless and humourless efficiency
that would have made Stalin proud.

Her horn-rimmed spectacles framed a face that only a
mother with very poor eyesight could love. It had a
permanently fierce expression on it. An expression that
said, 'I hate life, and after ten minutes in my company so
will you'. Her black hair was just as fierce. Scraped back
tightly into a bun, it was held in place by two metal
needles.

She had never married, which was probably not through choice. There were rumours that she was once engaged, sometime back in the fifties, to a Doctor. However, the day before the wedding he died in tragic circumstances. Two bottles of whisky, thirty-six sleeping pills, a shotgun and a gas oven were found next to his body.

During all the years she had worked there, Irene Fontwell had only been late for work once. That was in 1967, when she was run over by a bread van. Even then she was only late by twelve minutes, after crawling the remaining three hundred yards covered in cuts, bruises, three muffins, and a small brown Hovis.

Doreen stood in the middle of the office sobbing and shaking. Irene Fontwell continued to glare at her. Her expression had changed from fierce, to that of a ravenous alligator.

"Young lady, do you realise you are over two hours late?"

"Yes, Miss Fontwell. I'm so sorry, but something really horrible happened in the underground."

"I am not interested in your excuses," snapped Irene. "You are supposed to be here on time. This is the second time you've been late this month."

"I'm so sorry," Doreen sniffled, trying to regain some composure. "I'll make sure it never happens again."

"It certainly will not, because this time I'm going to report you to Mr Johnson!" Miss Fontwell roared.

On hearing this, Doreen started to cry even more. It was not a pretty sight. Her nostrils flared, her ears and cheeks turned bright red, and her whole body started to shake. She began to make a loud wheezing sound as she sniffed, spluttered and sweated profusely, until she started to resemble a carthorse with terminal colic.

It wasn't long however, before Irene Fontwell decided to take charge of the situation. Standing up and angrily smoothing down a long black dress that wouldn't have looked out of place at Queen Victoria's funeral, she marched swiftly over to where Doreen was standing sobbing and trembling. Then, with the hand speed of Muhammad Ali in his prime, slapped her across the face with enough force to dislodge the teeth of a pit bull terrier.

It certainly did the trick. The crying immediately stopped. But only because Doreen was now lying unconscious on the floor.

The sound of Doreen's body hitting the floor woke up Malcolm Gimlick, who up to that point had been enjoying a nice morning nap in the next office. The intolerable boredom that is Johnson Pratt & Livingston had forced him to perfect certain unique skills in order to control an overwhelming urge to leap out of the window. One of these was his ability to go to sleep, sitting upright, with his eyes wide open, whilst holding a pencil.

He had worked there for over thirty years after being made redundant, on health grounds, from his previous job as a train driver on the London Underground. The reason he was made redundant was that he kept stopping at green lights and carrying straight on at red lights. This resulted in a number of minor collisions and major delays. Eventually, it was discovered that he was colour blind. His sister Joyce still worked there, at the Lost Property Office at Baker Street, and Malcolm would regularly visit her during lunchtimes.

Today was no exception. However, as he made his way out into the main office, he noticed a small group of people gathered around someone lying on the floor. Doreen, to be precise.

Irene Fontwell was leaning back against her desk, a look of horror on her face as the realisation of what she had just done began to sink in.

"You've gone too far this time, you bad-tempered old fossil!" shouted one of the women trying to wake Doreen up.

"I saw it all!" shouted the young man cradling Doreen's head in his hands.

"She's gone mad, belongs behind bars. Actually no, she belongs in a psychiatric ward!"

Malcolm Gimlick stared at Irene Fontwell with a look of disgust on his face. She seemed to be in some kind of frozen trance.

"Please tell me you didn't hit her?"

Irene Fontwell said nothing. She just stood there, her glasses hanging from one ear, her breath coming in short sharp gasps.

He walked over to where Doreen was lying and knelt down beside her, gently stroking one of her chubby puffed-out cheeks.

"Doreen, love?" he said in a low gentle voice. "Can you hear me, Doreen?"

Doreen's eyes slowly opened, and a loud sigh of relief spread around the room.

"Oh Malcolm, she hit me! Miss Fontwell hit me, Malcolm!"

He helped Doreen to her feet and looked round, but Irene Fontwell was no longer there. However, the sound of footsteps could be heard rushing down the stairs at the back of the office, leading down to the garage workshop.

"Watch where you're going, you daft old bat!" a voice shouted from somewhere down the same stairwell.

A few seconds later, two mechanics in overalls covered in bacon and eggs, burst into the room.

"You won't believe what's just happened to Darren and me!" said the older mechanic.

"Oh yeah," said Malcolm, "Well you won't believe what just happened up here either."

"Well let me put it like this," replied the older mechanic. "If you can beat a large explosion, followed by the sudden appearance of a table, with a policeman draped over it, then I'd love to hear it!" he continued sarcastically.

Down at the bottom of the inspection pit in the garage, a stunned and shaken PC Meredith tried to gather his composure.

The first thing he needed to do was find a way out of the inspection pit.

Standing up on the table, he reached up to try to grab the edge. However, as he did so, he kicked the gold peg out of the hole it was in. He watched as the peg bounced across the tabletop, and started to spin around another of the holes. He jumped up and down in panic, but this only made the peg jump up and down too. So he stopped jumping. But it was too late, and he watched in horror as the peg dropped perfectly into another of the holes.

As the table started to hum and vibrate loudly again, he made a desperate lunge and just managed to grab the edge of the pit with both hands.

As he hung from the edge, he looked down and watched, as with a bright flash and an explosion, the table disappeared.

Malcolm, Doreen and the other staff arrived down in the garage a couple of minutes later, to be greeted by the sight of a police officer lying gasping for breath at the side of the inspection pit. His uniform was in tatters, and covered in black engine oil. Plumes of smoke surrounded him.

"Are you alright, Officer?" asked Malcolm Gimlick in a worried voice.

PC Meredith slowly picked himself up off the floor.

"I'm not really sure…"

He stared down into the inspection pit. The table had gone.

"See? What do you make of that then?" shouted the older mechanic, pushing his way through to the inspection pit.

Peering through the smoke, he too noticed the table had gone.

"Where's it gone?"

"Where's what gone?" said Doreen.

"The table,"

"There's nothing there," replied Doreen.

"I can see that. But it was there five minutes ago, wasn't it Darren?"

Darren shook his head sheepishly, and began to wonder whether he had dreamt the whole thing.

"It was actually in a back garden in Knightsbridge five minutes ago," mumbled a still stunned and shaken PC Meredith.

"Knightsbridge? What was it doing in Knightsbridge?" replied Malcolm Gimlick.

"Apart from standing in the middle of the ruins of a potting shed, not a lot,"

"Oh, this is all too much!" sobbed Doreen.

The strains of the day's events were beginning to take their toll on poor old Doreen. Having a close encounter with a three-foot orange dragon whistling Kylie Minogue songs in the Underground, is a very unsettling way to start the day. However, to then be publicly ridiculed by a group of strangers and finally punched in the teeth because you're an hour late for work is really adding injury to insult.

Now she was staring down into a smoke filled garage inspection pit, with a police officer who had apparently taken to travelling from one place to another on an exploding table.

"Malcolm, will you take me home, please? I don't feel very well."

"Of course I will. I was on my way to see my sister, Joyce, at Baker Street anyway."

PC Meredith meanwhile, had recovered his composure sufficiently to call PC Walton on his radio.

"You'll never believe what's just happened to me!"

"Where are you?" crackled PC Walton's voice down the radio.

PC Meredith, not wanting to appear more stupid than he looked, turned round to the others.

"Where am I?" he asked, feeling decidedly dazed and confused.

"Johnson Pratt & Livingston in West Brompton," said Darren.

"I'm in Johnny Pratt's living room....in West Brompton."

"West Brompton...? That's miles away... are you alright?"

PC Meredith looked down at his ripped oil-covered tunic and shredded trousers.

"I think so. How are you?"

"Well, apart from being covered in soil and rose bushes, I'm fine. Though I haven't a clue where my helmet's gone."

"You think you've got problems?"

PC Meredith sighed and looked down at what was left of his shoes, which were still smoking.

"All I remember was a loud bang, lots of smoke, and then when I got up you and the table were gone."

"I know. That's all I remember until I found myself sprawled across the table at the bottom of a garage inspection pit."

"Is the table still there?"

"No, it's disappeared again."

"Where's it gone now?"

"How am I supposed to know? All I do know, is it's not here anymore,"

"Well there's one thing for certain. It doesn't like hanging around anywhere for long." said PC Walton sarcastically.

"Look, I'll meet you back at the police station," replied PC Meredith. "Perhaps then we can try and figure out how to explain all of this, without being thrown off the force on the grounds of insanity."

45

Chapter Seven

THE TOPSIDERS, WAITING ON PLATFORM four at Holborn station, were unaware they were being watched. However, behind the metal grill of an old door on the disused platform further down the tunnel, a dark crimson eye was observing their every move from the shadows. Rodolp was surveying his territory.

His breathing was heavy, slow and rasping. The menacing bulk of his large pale rodent body leaned forwards, straining for a closer view. Every now and then, the lights from the windows of passing trains would glint on his huge razor-sharp golden teeth.

Moving back from the grill, Rodolp made his way towards an old rusting spiral staircase which led down into the blackness of the deep and abandoned levels of the underground far below. Here, other strange creatures would be moving, hurriedly and uneasily, through the labyrinth of narrow tunnels, stairwells and disused lift shafts. Gathering, scavenging and surviving.

He moved slowly and deliberately, upright on his huge back legs, his long black tail slithering ghostly silent behind him. His long claws scraped on the dusty, dirty floor. At the top of the stairs, he stopped. Raising himself to his full height of over five feet, he lifted his nose high to smell the warm, sickly sweet, dusty air.

As Rodolp descended the staircase, echoes of sound drifted up out of the darkness below. Amongst them was a familiar one. It was the sound of a small dragon whistling.

A sinister smile spread across Rodolp's face. He looked down at his powerful chest, and the two deep brown diagonal scars running part way across it. The scars, burn marks, were a permanent reminder of his last encounter with the dragon. On that occasion, Scorchington had escaped. However, the next time they met, he would make sure Scorchington would be the one left with the scars.

"Soon my little orange foe... Soon!" snarled Rodolp, as he skulked off into the tunnels below.

Chapter Eight

HIGHER UP, IN A TUNNEL complex near the disused Brompton Road station, Wattage was busy rushing around summoning the Stobes together for an urgent meeting in his study.

As Spoogemige sat cross-legged on the floor in the corner, dejected and hurt, the other Stobes began to arrive. One by one, they made their way out from the numerous rooms, corridors and tunnels around the station. Some of them only just back from scavenging trips elsewhere in the underground.

First to arrive was Criblee, Spoogemige's best friend and roommate. Like Spoogemige, Criblee was one of the junior members of the gang. Although unlike Spoogemige, he was usually more sensible.

Shorter in height than Spoogemige, he had a mane of long golden white hair which he wore tied in a pony tail, revealing a narrow very pale face with piercing large yellow and orange eyes. He wore a long baggy blue checked shirt with holes in both elbows, over a dirty-yellow vest. On his legs, he wore a pair of pale green tights full of holes, and on his feet, a pair of battered brown brogue shoes with different coloured laces, one yellow, and one red.

He walked over to the corner where Spoogemige was sitting, and squeezing his shoulder gently, crouched on his haunches next to him.

It was only then that he noticed the rubble and debris in the corner of the room, where Wattage's table usually stood.

"Frobbling twazlets Spoogemige, what's happened?"

Spoogemige looked at him sheepishly, while fiddling with the remaining buttons of his cardigan. He said nothing.

Next to arrive was Fuddlerook, one of the Stobe elders. He was carrying an old black bin liner, filled with the spoils of the morning's scavenging.

His long, coarse black hair reached all the way down to the small of his back. A wild unkempt beard and huge battered ears framed his face. His massive legs and arms bulged through an old red diver's suit. It was full of rips and tears, and the right sleeve was missing. But despite his savage looking appearance, his warm, dark almond eyes reflected a calm and gentle temperament. And despite his increasing years, he was still the one person you would want by your side in a fight.

After another five minutes had passed, Fligboge arrived, muttering and cursing under his breath. He was decidedly odd-looking even by Stobe standards. He was short, thin and bald with a face with bore more than a passing resemblance to a beaver - a beaver with a moustache. A big, bushy, dirty brown moustache permanently covered in spit, from his constant muttering and cursing. He wore a dirty white shell suit, with blue stripes up each side. It was about four sizes too big, so he had to use strips of black electrical insulation tape to hold it in place. However, these were always coming undone, and he was always tripping over them. This would inevitably result in even more muttering and cursing.

Then, in complete contrast to Fligboge, Vember arrived.

As she glided into the room, both Spoogemige and Criblee caught their breath and gazed longingly at her. Though neither would admit it, they were both in love with her. Tall and slender with wild flowing locks of raven hair and the face of an angel. Her big round dark-grey eyes sloped downwards slightly and sparkled with mystery. As she walked across the room, the long ivory robe she was wearing made it look like she was floating across the floor. Spoogemige felt his heart beat faster. Criblee too, was watching breathlessly to see where she would sit. She smiled at them both, before moving across to where Fuddlerook was examining the contents of his bin liner.

She crouched down next to him, and kissed him gently on the long scar running down the left-hand side of his face. This scar was a constant reminder to her of how Fuddlerook had saved her life a year ago, during one infamous and terrifying battle down in the deeper levels. Fuddlerook occupied a very special place in her heart.

Spogworth arrived hurriedly and out of breath. He was carrying an old suitcase with the lid missing, under one arm, and a small yapping Yorkshire terrier under the other.

"Look at this twazlet I found wandering round one of the tunnels near St James Park" he shouted.

Spogworth was one of the Stobes keenest, yet, when it came to anything useful, least successful scavengers. Amongst the useless items he had bought back in the past were a broken pram wheel; a box of false teeth; a trumpet that had been crushed under the wheels of a train; and a child's doll with the head and one arm missing.

However, even by his standards, a yapping dog took some beating.

The rest of them watched in a mixture of disbelief and pity as he made his way over towards where Fligboge was sitting, muttering to himself.

"What do you make of this little twazlet?" he panted excitedly, "I wonder what it is!"

Fligboge looked up at Spogworth and grimaced. With his flattened rodent features and bloodshot eyes, he was a seriously ugly Stobe. His right ear was missing, bitten off in a fight, and he covered it up with a hideous brown bobble hat. A single bent and twisted whisker protruded from his nose. He fiddled with this constantly, with his grubby little claws.

"It's a dog," said Fligboge. "A small, irritating, annoying yapping little dog."

"Is it? Are you sure?" Spogworth replied.

"Well what do you think it is then? A tin of biscuits? Or maybe a pair of furry shoes?"

Spogworth looked at Fligboge, unsure as to whether he was being serious or not. He then looked at the dog, which had stopped yapping as if pondering the same thing.

He put the dog down on the floor and sat down beside it. He started to rummage around inside the suitcase, eventually pulling out an old grey duffle coat with all the toggles missing, and a frying pan covered in grease and dirt.

Spogworth smiled at the duffle coat. It was certainly going to be a big improvement on the badly stained green surgical gown and disgusting red and white striped children's pyjamas he was currently wearing.

The dog began yapping again and, after relieving itself all over Fligboge's leg, trotted off towards Wattage.

He looked at the dog, then across at Spogworth, and shook his head. "Right then! Who's missing?" He enquired.

He was suddenly pushed out of the way by a large set of antlers, with a pair of oven mitts hanging from them.

"Excuse me," said a shrill high-pitched voice. "Sorry I'm late, but I was just finishing baking some lovely rat and gravel pies for tea."

The voice belonged to Hetty, a short, fat creature bearing a very strong resemblance to a moose. She was dressed in a blue two-piece jacket and skirt combination, over a frilly white blouse.

Hetty was in charge of all the cooking and cleaning, and spent her days rushing round the station trying to keep things tidy and in order. Considering the disgusting personal habits of the other Stobes, this was an almost impossible task.

Eventually the remainder of the Stobes arrived and made their way into the room, squeezing in wherever they could find a space in the small, dimly lit room.

It would be difficult to imagine a more peculiar group of creatures. It was as if someone had taken the occupants of Noah's Ark and put them all in a huge cooking pot. Then, after stirring in a sprinkling of alien life forms from a different Galaxy, poured the mixture out into different shaped containers before planting them in a peat bog and leaving them for several years to see what happened.

To describe them as weird would be an understatement.

"Where's Scorchington?" said Wattage, looking round the room.

The other Stobes dropped their heads down and pretended they hadn't heard the question.

"Once again, where is that twazlet of a dragon?" he continued, his voice becoming agitated.

Eventually Fligboge lifted up his head. "I saw what looked like the troublesome little orange twazlet about an hour ago, but he seemed to be making his way back here."

"Are you sure it was him?"

"Well if it wasn't him, then there must be another short-arse dragon down there who whistles and farts at the same time!"

Wattage raised his arms above his head and clenched his fists. Then with a roar, he brought them down fiercely and started punching the tops of his knees, just as he usually did when he was annoyed. This time unfortunately, he punched them a little too hard, eliciting a loud and very painful crunching sound.

As the rest stared in horror, Spoogemige leapt to his feet and rushed over to where Wattage now lay in a heap on the floor whimpering.

"Are you all right?" he said nervously.

"Of course I'm not!"

Spoogemige tried to help him to his feet, but in the process managed to stand on his hand. As they stumbled sideways, Wattage's trench coat got tangled up in Hetty's antlers. With a loud crash, all three of them fell backwards.

"Aaaaarrrrrghhhhh!" screamed Wattage as Hetty landed on top of him.

The others rushed over and began trying to untangle them all, and help them back to their feet.

During the ensuing chaos, no one noticed a small white, sack-like creature fly into the room and onto the top of the metal bookcase, hanging on the far wall.

"Right!" shouted Wattage, finally struggling to his feet and limping across to the middle of the room. "If everyone has finished knocking people over..." He glared at Spoogemige. "I'll try and explain to you, why you've all been summoned here. Some of you may be aware, that a few weeks ago. I found an old stone table, down in one of the disused sections of the Northern Line."

"You mean that one that used to be here, and now isn't?" said Fligboge.

"Exactly," replied Wattage.

"Well, as you can see, it seems to have been blown to pieces!"

"Making a disgraceful mess of this room as well," said Hetty with a frown.

"We can worry about that later, Hetty." snapped Wattage.

"You mean *I* can worry about it later. If it's left to you lot to clean up, we'll still be hoof-deep in rubble this time next year!" replied Hetty indignantly.

"Yes alright, Hetty," shouted an increasingly frustrated Wattage. "We'll make sure you're not left to tidy it all up."

"Huh, and pigs might fly." mumbled Hetty.

"Enough!" screamed Wattage.

Hetty gave Wattage one of her disapproving looks, and started fiddling with the oven mitts on her antlers.

"As I was saying," he continued, "I want to know which of you did it, and why?"

"What makes you think it was one of us?" said a highly offended Fligboge.

"Well who else could it be?" replied Wattage angrily.

"And how do you know it was blown up if you weren't here?" continued Fligboge.

"Well look at all the damage and rubble in this room – and where's the table now?" snapped Wattage.

Spoogemige pressed his head deeper into his chest, and avoided all eye contact with anyone.

"And anyway, even if someone wanted to blow it up, how would they do it? It's not as if there's a ready supply of explosives lying about waiting to be nicked down here!" continued Fligboge sarcastically.

Not being the brightest of individuals, everyone had expected Spogworth to have already lost the plot. However, as he fiddled with his single bent whisker with one grubby claw, he raised the other one in the air.

"Can I ask a simple question?"

The other Stobes looked at him and frowned. Even though they hadn't heard the question yet, they knew it would be a stupid one. It always was. Whenever Spogworth opened his mouth, something stupid came out of it.

So they were utterly gob smacked when Spogworth finally spoke.

"If..," He paused, stopped fiddling with his whisker, and began to scratch the side of his bobble hat. "...If...it had exploded, then wouldn't there be lots of bits of it all over the room?"

He looked round the room.

"...and I can't see any bits of it anywhere."

The room fell silent, as everyone stared at Spogworth.

Was this yet another piece of Spogworth nonsense, or was it a brilliant theory?

They looked over at Wattage to try to gauge his reaction. Wattage was staring at Spogworth, completely mesmerised.

"Umm, well in fact... you do have a point," replied a stunned Wattage.

There then followed a long silence, during which time everyone looked around the room, and then back at Spogworth.

He spoke again.

"So as there doesn't seem to be any bits of it here, then it obviously isn't here anymore."

"You mean it just vanished by itself?" asked Criblee.

Well if it did, it certainly made a lot of mess before it went!" said an increasingly agitated Hetty.

"How can something just vanish all by itself you daft Stobe?" shouted Fligboge.

"Well, maybe it could be a magic table?" replied Criblee innocently.

"Of course, silly me. Maybe it once belonged to a magician. It must have been the table where he kept all his tricks. It'll be somewhere else right now, complete with rabbits, cards and a top hat!" said Fligboge, now starting to enjoy the arguments and bickering.

"Actually, that is not as daft as it may sound." Replied Wattage, with a frown on his face.

He started to pace around the room, fiddling with the brim of his Trilby.

Suddenly Spoogemige stood up and, slowly raising an enormous hand above his head, coughed politely.

Nobody heard him at first; they were all too busy bickering.

He coughed again louder, but still nobody took any notice of him so he decided to get their attention in a different way. He started running on the spot. The sound of his huge feet stamping on the dusty floor soon did the trick.

As everyone looked across at him, he nervously started to speak.

"I saw what happened to the table."

Almost immediately, everyone started tutting and raising their eyes to the ceiling in a knowing fashion.

"I knew it. I knew that accident prone twazlet would be behind it," jeered Fligboge.

"Let him near anything, and he'll knacker it," he continued.

Wattage raised his hand to quieten everyone.

"Go on Spoogemige?" said Wattage.

"Well I was a bit bored, and went for a wander into your study."

"Why?" replied a surprisingly composed Wattage, who usually got extremely irate if anyone went near his room when he wasn't there.

"And I started to look at the table," continued Spoogemige.

"You just know what's coming next, don't you?" said Fligboge with a grin.

"Let him finish!" shouted Wattage sternly.

"Well....I put one of those two pegs in one of the holes on the table top... and then it started to vibrate and make a humming sound." continued Spoogemige.

"Nice one, Disaster Boy!" jeered Fligboge once more. "This could be your best yet by the sounds of it," he continued.

"Will you put a sock in it!" shouted Wattage at Fligboge.

"Alright, keep your trilby on!" replied Fligboge.

"Get to the point Spoogemige, what happened next?" continued Wattage.

"Well, I tried to stop it making the noise,"

"And how did you do that?"

"Oh I'll bet this is going to be a classic," laughed Fligboge. "What did you do? Don't tell me... I'll bet you kicked it, or something like that?"

Spoogemige dropped his head down, and tried to look away.

"Ha ha! I knew it, he frobbling well kicked it, didn't he! The silly twazlet kicked it!" cried Fligboge, now laughing uncontrollably.

Wattage looked at Spoogemige with increasing frustration.

"Did you kick it?"

"Yes!"

"And what happened?"

"It...it started making more noises, and things started coming out of it,"

"What kind of things?"

"Well first there was a drawer, and then some handles,"

"And?"

"Well then I moved away, and it sort of went 'bang!' I don't remember much after that,"

Fligboge was by now rolling round the floor hysterically, clutching his sides with laughter. The rest of the Stobes were also struggling to keep a straight face, and one by one burst out laughing. Even the normally calm and sensible Fuddlerook's shoulders began to shake as he too began to giggle at both Fligboge and the hapless Spoogemige.

"Oh…this is better than the lighting generator…" shouted Fligboge.

At this, the whole room descended into mayhem, as everyone began howling with laughter.

"So is that it?" replied Wattage, struggling to be heard above the laughter.

"I can't remember. I think so, but I'm not sure," whimpered Spoogemige.

Wattage realised that continuing this conversation under the current circumstances was not going to achieve anything. He would need to get Spoogemige somewhere quiet and alone if he stood any chance of getting any more details.

Kicking Fligboge in the back to try to stop him laughing, he raised his arms in the air.

"If we can all calm down and stop behaving like silly…" he shouted. He had to repeat himself several more times, until eventually the laughter died down to the odd giggle and splutter, and after Fuddlerook had put his hand over Fligboge's mouth and put him in a head lock, eventually silence. "If what Spoogemige has told us is true…" he continued. "Then I am afraid we could be in great danger."

"Why?" said Fuddlerook.

"Well I can't be certain, but the more I've been studying this table, the more I have come to the conclusion that it might be some kind of ancient, possibly even alien, transportation device. A sort of Teleporter."

"What the furtling heck is a Teleporter?" said Fligboge.

"Well it's something which doesn't actually exist, apart from in theory." replied Wattage.

"A bit like Spoogemige's brain you mean?" said Fligboge sarcastically.

Once again, there was the start of the sound of giggling.

"If you haven't got anything positive to say, shut up!" said Wattage sternly.

Fligboge shrugged his shoulders, raised his eyes to the ceiling, and muttered to himself.

"I don't understand what you mean?" said Fuddlerook.

"Well according to several books I have read, which have been written by a group of Topsider's called Physicists, a Teleporter is a kind of machine which can move instantly, from one place to another – it's called Teleportation, and involves dematerializing an object at one point, and sending the details of that object's precise atomic configuration to another location, where it will be reconstructed. What this means is that time and space are eliminated from travel –it could be transported to any location instantly, without actually crossing a physical distance," replied Wattage.

Everyone looked at Wattage with a mixture of confusion, and utter boredom.

The average Stobe is not the brightest of creatures, and the odds of any of them understanding anything requiring an IQ of more than twelve are worse than winning the lottery without buying a ticket. Therefore, there was about as much chance of them understanding a word Wattage had just said as a sheep understanding how an internal combustion engine works.

"So you've seen it do this then?" shouted Fligboge from the corner of the room.

"No, as I've said, it's just a theory which I happen to agree with." replied Wattage.

"Of course, if it hadn't disappeared…" he continued, "…I would have had more time to find out what exactly it is and does!"

"So now it's no longer here, you'll never know?" said Fuddlerook.

"Well I did make some notes, and also made some drawings of it, so maybe I might be able to think of something."

"So what do you want us to do?" enquired Fuddlerook, trying desperately hard not to laugh again, as Fligboge wriggled and squirmed in his arms.

"We must try and find it?"

"Find it! Find it where, for twazlets sake? It could be anywhere," said Fligboge, as he broke free from Fuddlerook's grip, and began to compose himself.

"It's impossible," said Vember. "There must be a hundred miles of tunnels down here."

"What if it's not down here?" said Spoogemige suddenly. "What if it's disappeared up there?"

Spoogemige lifted his arm and pointed up at the ceiling.

"What if it's gone up there? What if it's gone outside, where the Topsiders live?"

The room fell silent, and everyone looked nervously up at the ceiling.

"Well, we've got to somehow find it. If I'm right about its powers, then in the wrong hands, this table could mean serious trouble for everyone who lives down here."

"How?" said Fligboge.

"Have you been listening to a word I've said?" barked Wattage.

"Yes," replied Fligboge. "But I still don't see how a table that disappears all by itself is a problem."

"It's that very power that makes it a problem." said Wattage.

"Why?" continued Fligboge.

"Because it does!"

"Why?"

"Because, if it gets into the wrong hands, then it could be used in a dangerous way!"

"Such as?"

Wattage pointed up to the ceiling. "It could be used to travel out there!"

"So what?"

Fligboge shrugged his shoulders to emphasise the point.

"If it's used to travel out there, out into the Topsiders world, then it's a problem."

"Why?"

"Because, you stubborn frobbling twazlet, if someone from down here, travels on the table to somewhere up there..."

Wattage jabbed his arm angrily in the air repeatedly, pointing his fingers at the ceiling, and raised his voice so that he was now shouting.

"...then the Topsiders up there will find out about the existence of us down here, and that is a *huge* problem! Now what part of that don't you frobbling well understand?"

"But you don't need a magic table to travel out there."

Fligboge shook his head and held his arms out.

"You can just walk out there, if you really wanted to, but nobody does. So what makes this furtling table so dangerous?"

"Because, it's a lot easier, and a lot quicker, to get out there if you've got something which can make the journey in a fraction of a second. That's what makes it so dangerous. Now do you understand?"

"No!"

"Look, if any of the Darkenbads manage to get hold of this, you know they will use it! They will use it to cause havoc and mayhem!"

Fligboge didn't answer. Instead, he lowered his head, and started muttering and dribbling to himself. The rest of the Stobes began to mutter to each other too.

Wattage began to calm down and regain his composure.

"So now you see why we have to find it. Find it before someone, or…" Wattage paused and took a deep breath "…*something* else does!"

The room fell silent again. This time it was tense, black silence. Everyone knew what the 'something else' referred to. It was a 'something else' that no one ever spoke about. A 'something else' that struck fear into all the creatures that inhabited the underground. A 'something else' that was dark and sinister.

And that 'something else' had a name.

Darl!

"He's dead!" boomed Fuddlerook, reaching up and touching the scar on his cheek.

"I saw him go under the wheels of the train. I know I did. I saw it with my own eyes. You were there too, Vember, you saw it."

Vember reached across and put an arm gently around his shoulder.

"He is. No one, not even he, could have survived that." she replied, trying to reassure Fuddlerook. However, deep down inside, she knew she couldn't be sure, and a shiver ran down her spine.

"He might be dead, but what about that rat? That evil twazlet of a rat isn't." said Spogworth.

"And what about the rest of the Darkenbads?" said Criblee. "They're still around aren't they?"

"Rodolp and the rest of the Darkenbads rarely stray too far from the deep levels now," said Wattage. "And we all know not to go down there anymore. Well, apart from Scorchington."

"Talking of our little orange friend," said Hetty: "Shouldn't we be trying to find him before the daft little twazlet gets himself into even more trouble?"

"Yes," replied Wattage. "Before we do anything regarding the table, we must find Scorchington."

Fuddlerook raised his hand.

"I'll go. If he's gone walkabout he could be anywhere, including the deeper levels."

"I'll come with you." said Vember.

Immediately both Spoogemige and Criblee jumped up. "I'll go too," they both shouted at the same time.

"No you won't." said Wattage abruptly.

"You…" he said, pointing to Spoogemige, "…will come and tell me exactly what happened to the table in detail!"

"And you…" he said, pointing to Criblee, "…can help Hetty tidy this room."

Wattage walked over to Fuddlerook and Vember, and whispered quietly to them so none of the others could hear.

"If that idiotic dragon has gone off into the lower levels, then it could take forever to find him. Look for him in the most obvious places, but, if he's not there, you might have to try a different approach. You might have to seek out some information from another source,"

Wattage held his arms to his side and discreetly made small flapping motions with them, whilst looking seriously into Fuddlerook's eyes.

"I know it's not a pleasant thought, but you might have to go down that route as a last resort," he whispered.

Fuddlerook understood what Wattage meant, and began to feel uncomfortable at the thought. However, he also knew that if it meant finding Scorchington, then however unpleasant and dangerous, he had to try it.

"You know, I'm fine going on my own," he said to Vember. Fuddlerook knew he would feel a whole lot happier if he could persuade her not to go with him. The expression on Vember's face, however, made it perfectly clear that she was going with him.

As Fuddlerook and Vember made their way out of the room, Fuddlerook patted Wattage on the shoulder.

"Don't worry, we'll find the troublesome little Stobe."

Wattage smiled at his old and dear friend, with whom he had shared so many adventures.

"I know you will, but take care of yourself. And take care of Vember too."

"As if it were my own life." replied Fuddlerook with a smile.

Chapter Nine

AS CRIBLEE AND HETTY PREPARED to clear up the mess in Wattage's study, the others made their way out into the tunnel. None of them noticed a small, white, sack-like creature fly out of the room at the same time, and down the tunnel in the opposite direction.

Hetty began clearing up the mess in Wattage's study in her usual thorough and organised way.

Firstly, she brought in a large white sheet from the kitchen. She then laid it out on an area of floor away from the rubble. After making sure her blouse was neatly tucked in, she removed the oven mitts from her antlers and placed them slowly and precisely over her hoof like hands, like a surgeon preparing for an operation. Then, using an old piece of cardboard as a shovel, she began to scoop up and carry the rubble across to the sheet, and drop it in a neat pile in the centre of it.

Criblee on the other hand, was going about it in his somewhat less thorough manner.

After kicking some bits of rubble a few feet to the left, he began picking up some larger pieces and moving them a few feet to the right. He then bent down and started to push some of the smaller pieces of rubble between his legs, to create yet another pile a few feet behind him. Now, instead of a big pile of rubble, he had three smaller piles of rubble. Standing up, he proceeded to carry small handfuls of rubble over to the side of the room where there wasn't any mess, and put them on the floor. He wasn't exactly cleaning up, more like redistributing.

Meanwhile, Spoogemige followed Wattage sheepishly down the tunnel, towards the room they used as the kitchen. Sitting down at the old steel door balanced on four piles of bricks, which they used as a table in the middle of the room, Spoogemige tried to explain exactly what had happened.

Wattage listened carefully. The expression on his face though made it obvious he was not convinced.

Spoogemige started to panic. His shoulders hunched up, and his feet began to twitch involuntarily under the table. His could feel his legs vibrating. He could feel a runner coming on.

Wattage sat down again at the table, and pulled out a piece of paper. He began scribbling furiously on it.

"Is that all? Can I go now?" whimpered Spoogemige.

Wattage ignored him. He was too busy scribbling on the paper and muttering to himself. Every now and then, he would stop, and scratch the brow of his trilby, frantically.

Spoogemige got up from the table and made his way out of the kitchen and down the tunnel to his room, a dejected stoop in his shoulders. Picking up an old battered guitar with two of the strings missing, he lay down on his bunk and stared up at the ceiling. Wrapping his enormous hands around it, he started to play a soft delicate tune, and began thinking of Vember.

Closing his eyes, he imagined the two of them together, up there on the outside where the Topsiders lived. Under a cloudless blue sky, he heard their laughter blown along on the gentle breeze as they ran through the streets.

He pictured them both lying next to each other on the grass in a park. He knew such places existed. He had seen pictures of them in magazines. Up there where the Topsiders lived, there was light and sunshine. Not the dark claustrophobic world he lived in. Up there was space. Space and open ground where someone could run and run. He would show her just how fast he could really run by chasing cars, and she would laugh until she cried, before falling into his arms.

Spoogemige closed his eyes. Small green teardrops of happiness ran down from them, leaving a trail on his pale cheeks, as he drifted deeper and deeper into his daydream.

Back in Wattage's study, Criblee had been distracted from his idea of tidying up. He was now amusing himself by charging up and down the corridor using an old lawnmower as a scooter. However, the clattering and banging of the rotating blades on the old concrete floor made so much noise that there was soon a large group of less than pleased Stobes heading in his direction. They bore more than a passing resemblance to a lynch mob.

Criblee quickly abandoned the lawnmower, and ran back into Wattage's study. He was followed seconds later by the angry mob led by Fligboge, who was muttering and cursing even more than usual.

Criblee rushed to hide behind Hetty. She was in the process of picking up some old papers she had found underneath the rubble, and not in the least bit amused as he pushed behind her.

"I'll shove that dammed contraption somewhere really unpleasant, you daft little twazlet!" shouted Fligboge, as he barged into the room.

He was met by a very angry Hetty staring at him fiercely, hooves on hips.

Fligboge and the rest of the group immediately dropped their heads and skulked back out again. Hetty was not to be messed with when she was angry.

"Criblee! Stop fooling about, and take these to Wattage." said Hetty sternly, handing him the pile of papers she had found.

Criblee sheepishly took the papers and walked back down the tunnel, towards the kitchen. He glanced nervously from side to side, unsure whether or not someone was about to leap out of the shadows and give him a slap. In the kitchen, Wattage was still scribbling furiously. He had taken his trilby off, and was chewing the brim as if he had not eaten for a week.

"Hetty found these. She thought you might want them." whispered Criblee.

Wattage lifted his head momentarily, grunted, and nodded in the direction of the table. Criblee put the papers down and tiptoed out down the corridor towards the room, he shared with Spoogemige.

Walking into the room he looked down at Spoogemige lying on his bunk, eyes closed, holding his battered old guitar tightly.

"Are you ok?"

Spoogemige opened his eyes and looked up.

"No. Not really."

Chapter Ten

DEEP IN THE LOWER LEVELS, Fuddlerook and Vember made their way cautiously through the dark tunnels in search of Scorchington. Having failed to locate him at any of the usual places, they now had no alternative but to try the different and more dangerous 'last resort' approach suggested by Wattage.

The air was damp and thick with dust. The old paraffin lantern Fuddlerook was carrying struggled to light up more than a few yards in front of them. This part of the underground had a particularly unpleasant atmosphere. It was somewhere that few of the Stobes ever ventured. These were the tunnels inhabited by an especially unpleasant and mysterious group of rarely seen creatures.

The Cribbit Snocklers!

These strange inhabitants of the deep levels kept to themselves. They did not take kindly to visitors. Neither Fuddlerook nor Vember had ever encountered them before, but they had both heard the stories. They had heard all about these tiny bat-like albinos, with their piercing blood red eyes and white, luminous bodies that glowed in the dark but were almost invisible in the light.

It was this strange characteristic, which made them so dangerous. It enabled them to sneak around the underground, and listen into everything that went on. In the dark and secret world of the underground, knowledge was power, and the Cribbit Snocklers had more knowledge than anyone else did.

They were obsessed with information and gossip. Or, to put it another way, they were the most incredibly nosey creatures on the planet.

You want to know something? Ask a Cribbit Snockler. You want to know what's happening in other parts of the underground? Ask a Cribbit Snockler. In fact, if there is something going on that a Cribbit Snockler doesn't know about, then it probably isn't going on.

There is only one thing more important to a Cribbit Snockler than gossip and information, and that's trading gossip and information. In addition, there is only one thing a Cribbit Snockler will trade it for. More gossip and information!

However, Cribbit Snocklers will only trade their information and gossip for information and gossip, which is of greater importance than the information and gossip you want from them. This means having to tell them everything you know, on the slim chance that you know something they don't, and, that it's also something they actually want to know.

Nothing upsets a Cribbit Snockler more than someone trying to fob them off with minor gossip.

Being in possession of all this knowledge has given the Cribbit Snocklers a ridiculous and completely misplaced sense of their own importance. Despite being less than a foot tall and useless in a fight, they display an amazing level of sneering arrogance. They are, without exception, the rudest and most annoying creatures you could ever be unfortunate enough to meet.

However, meeting them is harder than trying to find a needle in a haystack, at night, wearing a blindfold, whilst suffering from concussion.

Unfortunately, for Fuddlerook and Vember, the Cribbit Snocklers were now their best chance of finding out where Scorchington was. Therefore, they continued to make their way further down into the lower levels.

As they followed the tunnel round a corner, they suddenly heard a low rumbling noise, getting louder and louder. The whole tunnel began to vibrate, accompanied by flashes of light. Fuddlerook stopped, reached behind and pulled Vember tightly against his back, whilst at the same time delving inside his battered old diver's suit and pulling out a long screwdriver.

Looking to the left, he could see they were standing next to a metal door with a grill overlooking one of the train lines. They both stayed still and silent until the train had passed. They then continued down the tunnel, Vember's hand holding on to Fuddlerook's waist.

As they approached another corner, Fuddlerook stopped and turned round to check that she was all right. Vember smiled and placed her hands on his broad powerful shoulders. Of course, she was all right. She was with Fuddlerook, her indestructible and fearless protector.

As they carried on, the tunnel started to become a little lighter, until in the distance they could see what looked like about half a dozen magazines hanging from the tunnel roof. There was also a horrible smell in the air.

Fuddlerook held his hand up to Vember to tell her to stay where she was. Then he slowly made his way towards them, his right hand clutching his screwdriver and his left hand leaning against the side of the tunnel wall.

Vember watched as Fuddlerook moved closer, holding her nose to try to stop the stench, when suddenly something dropped down from the roof of the tunnel directly in front of her. She jumped backwards in surprise.

It was a newspaper, or, to be more precise, the London Evening Standard.

She watched as it swung backwards and forwards in front of her, and then stopped.

Slowly, one of the pages started to turn itself over, and out from behind it appeared a small, pale and luminous sack-like body hanging upside down from the tunnel roof on the end of a pair of stumpy, claw like hands.

Vember gasped as a small ugly head with long, pointed ears slowly peered round the newspaper until she was looking directly into a pair of bloodshot, red eyes, separated by a very long dirty pink nose with three black scabby nostrils. It also smelt atrocious.

It looked at Vember with a condescending sneer on its face, and then with complete indifference it disappeared back behind the newspaper. She watched as the claw-like hands on the end of wings that resembled used fish-and-chip paper turned the pages one after the other, occasionally shaking the paper up and down to straighten it.

Further down the tunnel, still unaware of Vember's encounter, Fuddlerook was just about to prod one the magazines hanging from the ceiling when a voice suddenly spoke.

"Oi! Yes you in the stupid diver's suit, and the 1970's hairstyle! I'd think very carefully about prodding Stubb with that stick. He's been up all night with the trots."

Fuddlerook fell backwards in shock onto the floor of the tunnel. His hands sank into something very sticky, and very smelly.

"See what I mean?" continued the voice. "That floor was clean until last night. Now look at it! It's enough to put a dung beetle off his food, and as for the noise... I've never heard anything like it. I feel like I've been held hostage at an all-night farting contest."

Fuddlerook looked up at the tunnel roof and covered his ears. He grimaced as the voice carried on. It was a horrible high-pitched vibrating shriek of a voice. It sounded like a Dalek who'd just found a balloon filled with helium.

"Oh yes. You cover your ears!" It sneered. "We'd all like to cover our ears, but if you're a Cribbit Snockler it doesn't do any good. Oh no, no good at all. Because being a Cribbit Snockler, we're all blessed - or cursed depending on your point of view - with incredible hearing. Oh yes, we can hear a pin drop at Baker Street during rush hour. So you can't possibly imagine how bad someone with a terminal farting problem sounds through the ears of a Cribbit Snockler."

The voice carried on ranting, as Fuddlerook pulled himself to his feet and tried to work out exactly where it was coming from.

It seemed to be coming from what looked like Hello Magazine, which was hanging next to the magazine he'd been about to prod. He now recognised this as a copy of the Radio Times.

Just as Hello Magazine finished ranting, one of the other magazines on the far left started to speak.

"Did you know that it takes the biggest oil tanker in the world twelve miles and over two hours to stop?" said Commercial Shipping Monthly.

"That's nothing," interrupted May's edition of Top Gear Magazine. "Apparently, there's a car that can reach over two hundred miles an hour, powered by nothing more than fertiliser."

"There you go, Stubb," laughed Hello Magazine. "You could power a whole fleet of them."

Fuddlerook stood frozen to the spot, and tried to figure out what in God's name was going on. At that moment, the Radio Times let out a long wet dribbling fart.

"Oh not again!" shouted the Christmas Edition of Gardner's World. "Will you just clear off to the other end of the tunnel? And don't come back until you've sorted your bowels out,"

Fuddlerook watched as a small pale luminous sack-like body, appeared from behind the Radio Times. Its tiny bloodshot eyes stared at him. They didn't look like they'd had much sleep. It then folded up the Radio Times and tucked it under one of its wings. Muttering to itself, it trundled off across the tunnel roof on short stumpy claw-like hands.

"There's a really good documentary about sharks on later tonight, if any of you are interested!" it shouted back as it disappeared out of sight.

"We haven't got a television, you idiot!" yelled Hello Magazine.

Fuddlerook shook his head in disbelief, then looked back towards where Vember was standing motionless in front of the other creature.

Squelching his way out of the hideous smelling gunge, he started running over towards her, waving his screwdriver in the air. The creature in front of Vember turned round just as Fuddlerook arrived and disappeared back up into the blackness of the tunnel roof.

"Are you alright?"

"I don't know. What the hell are they?"

"Cribbit Snocklers. Unpleasant little twazlets aren't they?"

Suddenly a voice echoed down from the hole in the tunnel roof above their heads.

"I see they're putting up the congestion charge again."

"*What?*" barked Fuddlerook, now beginning to lose patience with the whole situation.

"And it looks like there's going to be a possible tube strike on Thursday." continued the voice.

There was a rustle of paper, and then the small, pale and luminous sack-like creature swung down from the ceiling again. It hung in front of them, the newspaper now neatly folded under one of its wings.

"You know if you spent more time reading and less time running around tunnels shaking a screwdriver at everyone, you might get to know what's going on," Said the creature nastily. "And anyway, what exactly are you going to do with that screwdriver... put some shelves up?"

Fuddlerook stared at it angrily and contemplated whether to stab it.

"I see you've already met the others," it said, looking at Fuddlerook. "But allow me to formally introduce myself, and the rest of my little band of creatures, whom you have so rightly identified as Cribbit Snocklers."

The voice still sounded like a Dalek on helium, and whilst not as shrieking as the others, it was actually even more unpleasant.

"My name is Neb," it continued. "I am what you would term the boss, top dog, head honcho, governor." His chest puffed up with pride as he extolled his own virtues. "And behind you, is the rest of my clever little band."

Vember and Fuddlerook turned round to find the six creatures from the other end of the tunnel were now hanging directly above their heads. They all had their magazines neatly folded underneath their wings.

"From left to right we have Dranoel, my number two, Bodge, Rollo, Lug, Pratt, whom one of you has already met, and last but not least, Stubb, whose current bowel problems are causing considerable tensions at the moment."

Fuddlerook and Vember looked up at the six ugly creatures and shuddered. *All this for a little orange dragon*, they thought.

"So, as I presume this isn't a social call," sneered Neb, "Exactly what information do you want from us?"

He moved his head forwards until it was only inches away from Vember's face.

"And, more importantly, what information have you got for me in return, my very pretty Stobe?"

Vember winced as she smelt his foul smelling breath and pulled back as his bloodshot eyes stared into hers, his long nose twitching.

"What information do you want?" Cut in Fuddlerook protectively.

"How about a cure for Stubb's bowel problem?" shouted Bodge sarcastically.

Neb turned round and grinned at Bodge, then turned back again to look at Vember.

"Ah! The beautiful Vember, and the brave mighty Fuddlerook. We are indeed honoured."

"How do you know who we are?" replied Vember defensively.

Neb threw back his ugly little head and laughed. It was a horrible, high-pitched shrieking laugh. The others all joined in; until the tunnel echoed with the most appalling sound either Vember or Fuddlerook had ever heard.

"How do we know who you are? Oh my precious little Vember, that's so funny. We are the Cribbit Snocklers." He shouted at the top of his voice, still laughing manically. "We know everyone, and everything. We know where everyone is, and what everyone is doing." Neb smiled, and moved closer to Vember's face again. "And you are here, because you want to know where a certain little orange dragon is." He paused and moved even closer so that he was less than an inch from Vember's face. "And as we both know that it is a foregone conclusion that I do know, then the question becomes, what are you going to give me in return?"

Vember didn't have time for this. She moved forward, staring Neb straight in the eyes, and forced him to move slowly backwards along the roof of the tunnel on his grubby little claws.

"Let me tell you what I'm going to give you, you putrid little sack of puke." She hissed.

Fuddlerook looked across in alarm. The other Cribbit Snocklers stared in shock, and shifted uneasily on the tunnel roof. No one had ever spoken to Neb like this before. Not even the elusive and terrifying Darl, or his equally frightening right hand rat, Rodolp. Vember continued to force Neb back along the tunnel roof.

"You're going to tell me exactly where I can find my friend Scorchington. Because if you don't, I'm going to take that newspaper..." she pointed her finger so it was almost touching him, "...and shove it somewhere even darker than this tunnel."

Neb stopped moving backwards, and smiled at Vember.

"Quite a little temper, haven't we?" he grinned. "In fact it just so happens, that I was reading an article on anger management only last week in the Daily Mail. I can lend it to you if you want?"

Vember lunged forward to grab hold of Neb but he was too fast, and quickly disappeared up into another hole in the tunnel roof.

"I'm afraid you won't get anything out of me with this kind of attitude." Shouted Neb from inside his hole. "Oh no, my pretty strong-headed Stobe. If you want to know where your little orange friend is, I suggest you start being nice to me, and tell me something of interest. Something I can use...something IMPORTANT!" His voice echoed loudly and sneeringly to emphasise the last word.

"And if I don't?"

"Well, let me see…" Neb dropped back down out of his hole clutching what looked like a cockroach, and proceeded to bite its head off. He looked down at Fuddlerook, who was watching his every move, the screwdriver ready in his hand. He then looked across at Dranoel, who was moving slowly away from the other Cribbit Snocklers. "If I'm not mistaken, there is a certain large rat, goes by the name of Rodolp I believe, who would be most grateful to know the whereabouts of your little orange friend." He continued to eat the cockroach, which was still wriggling about in his claw. "Apparently, he has something of a score to settle with him. He is a most unpleasant character. Likes to kill things just for the fun of it."

Suddenly, Dranoel dropped down from the ceiling and flew away. Fuddlerook leapt across to try to catch him but he was too late, Dranoel was gone. The dull flap of his wings reverberated around the darkness of tunnel as he disappeared out of sight.

Neb looked down at Fuddlerook and back at Vember, a sinister smile spreading across his face.

"I suppose we now have what could be described as a Mexican Standoff."

The other Cribbit Snocklers chuckled to each other and looked across at Fuddlerook in a superior manner.

"Your screwdriver isn't going to do you any good now, is it?" taunted Pratt.

Stubb, who was nearest to Fuddlerook, wasn't too sure. He promptly let out a loud fart. Neb turned round and gave him a scornful look, before turning back to Vember.

"As I was saying, before I was so rudely interrupted by my disgusting colleague. The situation is quite straightforward. Tell me all you know about Wattage's recent experiments, in particular the one's regarding a certain stone table, which has recently…" He paused for dramatic effect, "…*disappeared*, and I might decide to tell you where your little orange dragon friend is."

"And if we don't?" replied Fuddlerook, moving angrily over to Vember's side.

"Well, my large, hairy friend. If you don't, then I'm afraid my rather impatient colleague Dranoel, will inform a certain large, violent rat of your friend's whereabouts instead."

Neb threw his head back and laughed. It was a loud, evil, mocking laugh. He turned round and bowed theatrically to the others, who immediately started whooping and applauding their leader.

"Wicked!" said Bodge.

"Respect!" shouted Lug.

"Nasty!" grinned Rollo.

"You're the man. Whoop Whoop!" shouted Pratt, as if he was applauding Tiger Woods at a golf tournament.

The others looked at him sneeringly and started muttering, all except Stubb, who had skulked over to the other side of the tunnel in order to try to regain some control over his bowels. He failed. Once more, the air filled with hideous gassy vapours and more foul-smelling sticky gunge covered the tunnel floor.

"Can I borrow your screwdriver for a moment?" said Neb sarcastically to Fuddlerook, looking over in the direction of Stubb. "I have an urgent need to use it on someone."

Chapter Eleven

DOREEN AND MALCOLM GIMLICK MADE their way down the escalators at West Brompton station. Doreen held tightly onto Malcolm's arm, still trembling slightly.

"I tell you what Doreen, when we get to Baker Street, how do you fancy a nice big bar of chocolate from the vending machine?"

Doreen's chubby little face lit up with a big smile.

By the time the train had pulled into Baker Street station, Doreen was beginning to feel much better, and was looking forward to that nice big bar of chocolate.

Walking down the platform towards the escalators, they noticed a large woman wearing a grey mac that was torn in a number of places. She was sitting on a bench sobbing gently. She had a large bruise on her forehead, and her tights were ripped at the knees, revealing more bruises.

As they walked past, Doreen thought she recognised her, and turned to look more closely. Sure enough, it was the same loud-mouthed woman, who had taken so much pleasure from Doreen's unfortunate situation earlier that morning.

Malcolm, being such a kindly soul, was just about to offer her assistance, when Doreen grabbed hold of his arm fiercely, and pulled him away towards the escalator.

"What's the matter you fat old cow? Someone nicked your stupid, yapping dog or something?"' snarled Doreen as she stepped onto the escalator.

"Doreen!" gasped a shocked Malcolm.

"That..." Doreen pointed angrily at the woman, "...is one of the group of people who took great pleasure laughing at me this morning, when I was still trying to recover from a close encounter with an orange dragon wearing carpet slippers and whistling Kylie Minogue songs."

Malcolm looked at Doreen with an expression of horror and disbelief. He was beginning to think the poor girl was cracking up, or, even worse, that she was on drugs.

"What are you talking about, love?"

"I'll tell you all about it when I've had some chocolate," Doreen rushed off up the escalator, muttering loudly to herself. "I need chocolate... chocolate... Now! I must have chocolate now!"

At the top of the escalator, Doreen sprinted off in the direction of the vending machine, while Malcolm stopped to catch his breath.

When she finally reached the vending machine, there were a group of people standing in front of it. She barged her way through them like a rugby prop forward, scattering them across the floor. It was only then that she realised she didn't have any change in her purse.

"Malcolm!" she screamed. "I need money, and I need it now!"

The group of people, who had been in front of the vending machine, were still picking themselves up off the floor when Doreen started to bang on the sides of it.

"Give me chocolate. Give me chocolate now, you miserable piece of junk!" she screamed at the machine.

Malcolm arrived breathlessly at the vending machine, just at the moment Doreen was preparing to head-butt the glass panel at the front of it.

"Doreen! For God's sake, calm down. You'll get arrested if you carry on like this!"

Doreen however, had been too long without chocolate to be reasoned with. She was suffering from acute withdrawal symptoms. She needed chocolate. And if that meant going head first through a piece of toughened safety glass, then so be it.

Malcolm tried to restrain her, but failed. Several members of the group of people Doreen had knocked over earlier joined in to help him, but also failed. It was like trying to subdue a rabid hippopotamus who had just spent thirty-six hours at an acid house rave party.

Pushing them all onto the floor, she grabbed both sides of the vending machine and, with a blood-curdling roar, was just about to smash her head through the front of it when she was suddenly stopped by the sound of whistling coming from the back of the machine.

She recognised the tune instantly. Bending down, she watched, as the rear panel was pulled slowly to one side. A pair of small orange claws then reached in, and began to take the bars of chocolate from their metal shelves, and put them into a plastic carrier bag.

A small, orange dragon's head, with a screwdriver hanging from one side of its mouth, and a piece of burnt toast hanging from the other, leant inside and looked round to check there were no more left. Then, with a puff of green smoke, it disappeared back out, and began replacing the rear panel.

Doreen stared in horror at the inside of the vending machine. All that was left was a small piece of burnt toast lying on the bottom,

Gripping the sides of the vending machine even tighter, her whole body started to shake and wobble, as the full implication of what had just happened sank in.

The group of people, having picked themselves off the floor once more, had no intention of hanging around to be knocked over for a third time and ran away in fear.

"Give me back my chocolate, you thieving little orange sod!" she screamed, violently shaking the vending machine.

Malcolm, by this time, had managed to pick himself up off the floor, and was staring at Doreen as she continued her assault.

Eventually Doreen ran out of energy, and slumped to her knees staring into the empty vending machine. Malcolm walked over and knelt down next to her.

"Look Malcolm," she blubbered. "They've all gone. That orange dragon has broken into the back of it, and stolen them all."

Malcolm looked inside the vending machine. Apart from being empty it was still intact, which considering it had just been ram-raided by Doreen was quite miraculous.

"Are you sure it wasn't already empty when you got here?"

"No Malcolm, it was full. Full of chocolate bars, *my* chocolate bars. Now that dragon has them all. Well not for long!"

Doreen got up and rushed round the side of the vending machine. There was a small gap at the back. It was only about a foot wide, but wide enough for something small to squeeze behind - something small and orange.

On the floor were some crumbs of burnt toast and a solitary bar of chocolate. Doreen noticed that there was in fact a trail of bits of burnt toast leading down the corridor on the right. She started to follow it. The trail eventually led to a door on the right hand side of the corridor. Here the trail stopped. Doreen tried the door, but it was locked. There was a small metal grill near the top of the door. Standing on tiptoe, she tried to look through it, but whatever was on the other side was hidden in darkness.

"There's nothing through there apart from an old disused stairwell, missus." said a voice behind her.

Doreen turned round to see an elderly man in a uniform pushing a trolley full of boxes.

"Are you sure?"

"Well I've been working here for over thirty years, and I've never seen it opened. Why do you ask?"

Doreen was about to tell him about the orange dragon breaking into the vending machine, but then decided not to. She'd had enough humiliation for one day. With a weary sigh, she made her way back along the corridor to where a very concerned looking Malcolm was waiting next to the vending machine.

"Let's go and see Joyce at the Lost Property Office. I don't like the idea of you being on your own. Besides, I'm sure Joyce will have some funny stories about some of the things people have left on the underground. Go on, it'll take your mind off things for a while."

Doreen looked at Malcolm and smiled. He really was a very sweet and kind man. "Alright Malcolm, why not?"

As Doreen picked up her bag from the floor, Malcolm handed her a bar of chocolate. It was the bar of chocolate from behind the vending machine.

"Here you go. Will this do? I'm sure Joyce will have more too."

Doreen smiled once more and took the bar from him. However, as they walked past the vending machine, Malcolm looked down at the piece of burnt toast lying in the bottom of it. He had to admit, there were certainly some very strange things going on today.

Chapter Twelve

EXTREMELY PLEASED WITH HIS SUCCESS at the vending machine, Scorchington decided to break the rules even further. And what better way to break the rules than with a single-handed 'Sherlock'?

No one had ever done a solo 'Sherlock' before. Not even Fuddlerook.

He had heard rumours that Spogworth had once attempted it. However, at Moorgate, instead of 'whizzing' one of the trains on the Metropolitan Line that goes to Baker Street, he ended up 'whizzing' one of the trains on the Northern Line that does not. He eventually finished up at Finchley Central, where several members of the Pussycat Brolls attacked him and took him hostage.

The Pussycat Brolls are a roaming pack of female feral cats, which use sharpened umbrellas as weapons. They are extremely vicious. When Spogworth eventually escaped two days later, it was minus an ear and five of his six whiskers.

* * * * *

Stobes often have to travel to many different parts of the underground during their scavenging trips. Usually these trips are made late at night, when the underground is closed. Late at night, there are no 'Topsiders' to worry about. There are also no trains, which mean they can use the mainline routes and stations. This is much quicker, as well as better lit, offering safer passage.

However, occasionally, Stobes have to make these journeys during the daytime. In order to get from one station to the next as quickly as possible, Stobes use a technique known as 'whizzing'.

This involves hitching a ride underneath the rear compartment of a train. This way Topsiders can't see them. It is very dangerous, of course. However, Stobes have been doing it for so many years that they have developed special skills, which enable them to do it relatively safely. That is of course providing they 'whizz' the right train.

* * * * *

Scorchington made his way down the disused stairwell. It was narrow, dark and dusty. He blew a large jet of fire to light his way. At the bottom of the stairwell was a metal door that opened out onto the Circle line in the main tunnel, just down from the station platform. He waited until he could hear the familiar rumbling of a train. Just as the rumbling stopped, he opened the door, stepped out onto the rails and quickly ran towards the back of the now stationary train. Climbing underneath, he wedged himself across the chassis. Being only three feet tall meant it was a stretch. He was glad Baker Street was only one stop down. Once he was secure, he carefully balanced his plastic carrier bag on his chest so it didn't dangle down and hit the middle rail carrying the electric current.

As the train pulled out of the station, the passengers were blissfully unaware that clinging to the underside of the train was a three-foot orange dragon.

Scorchington, though, was also blissfully unaware that something else was hitching a ride on the back of the same train. Something small white and sack-like.

The train accelerated through the winding tunnels, the vibration of the wheels on the lines echoing on the walls. Scorchington, though, was too busy listening to his iPod to notice. His feet tapped rhythmically against the chassis and his head rocked back and forth, a huge smile on his face as the lights shone and bounced on the tracks as the train hurtled through the tunnels. Scorchington loved 'whizzing' trains. He loved the speed and the danger.

The train pulled into Baker Street, and Scorchington waited for the passengers to get off before dropping down from the underside of it and making his way a few yards back down the tracks into the darkness of the tunnel. He was careful not to step on the middle rail carrying the electric current. He knew all too well what happened if you touched the middle rail. He had witnessed it first-hand a few years ago when Spoogemige stood on it.

Along with Fuddlerook and Fligboge, they were making their way to Blackfriars Station on the District Line in the early hours of the morning. Spoogemige had decided to stretch his legs with a run. As he disappeared off down the tunnel, there was suddenly a massive flash of blue light accompanied by a blood-curdling scream. When they got round the corner, they were met by the sight of Spoogemige, standing in the middle of the tunnel shaking and screaming with clouds of smoke coming off his body. They eventually managed to pull him off the rails, but the voltage had done permanent damage. His hair was now permanently stuck up in the air, and his hands and feet were twice the size they used to be.

Scorchington waited in the shadows of the tunnel, his body pressed tight against the wall. He pulled out an old watch from his carrier bag and looked at the time. It was 8.35pm.

It wasn't really, it was in fact 5.35pm, but Scorchington's watch was three hours fast. It hadn't always been three hours fast. It was actually only one hour fast when he found it on the platform at Regent Street three years ago. However, since then, it had gained an hour each year. Next year it would be four hours fast, but Scorchington couldn't be bothered changing it. Instead, he simply deducted three hours in his head.

This was still far from accurate, as he never factored in the change to and from British Summertime, but it was close enough for Scorchington.

The Lost Property Office at Baker Street closes at 6.00pm. Whilst Topsiders can only get into it via the main road entrance on Baker Street, staff who work there can get in via a door and stairwell directly from the underground station. The door is fitted with a 'J' Lock, which requires a four-digit code to open. This code however, was common knowledge to the Stobes. Fligboge had overheard a member of staff, telling another member of staff a few years back. The code was 1096A.

As Scorchington waited, he turned his iPod on again. He loved music and had a wide and diverse taste. This was because all the music he listened to was on pilfered iPods and mp3 players. As Stobes don't exactly have the technology to charge batteries, he would simply discard them when the battery went flat, and pilfer another one. His current iPod had obviously belonged to a young girl. It was filled with boybands, girlbands and a lot of Kylie Minogue. He didn't really like any of the music, apart from one Kylie Minogue track – 'Can't Get You Out of my Head'. However, he had now been listening to just this track for over a week and was beginning to get a bit sick of it. So he wasn't too disappointed when it suddenly went silent mid-song. The battery was finally dead. He took the earphones out, unclipped it from his t-shirt and threw it down the tunnel into the darkness.

He looked at his watch again - it was 9.05pm. Well, 6.05pm. The Lost Property Office would now be closed.

However, it was also now rush hour. The platform at Baker Street was filled with Topsiders on their way home.

Any other Stobe would have waited a few more hours, until the platform was deserted. Then again, any other Stobe would not be attempting a solo Sherlock in the first place. But Scorchington was no ordinary Stobe, and he had a plan. It wasn't really a plan, because he hadn't planned it or thought it through. It was simply a thought, which had just entered his head in the last three seconds.

Reaching down into his carrier bag, he pulled out his grey carpet slippers and put them on. He then pulled out a blue hoodie that he had found earlier that day, and put it on, pulling the hood tightly around his face. He smiled to himself. To complete his disguise, he rubbed some black soot and dirt from the tunnel walls onto his legs and tail. To Scorchington, it was a brilliant disguise. To anyone else he looked like a three-foot orange dragon that had just fallen down a chimney.

Composing himself, he puffed out his chest and tensed his short stubby arms like a bodybuilder. He was just about to make his move when he remembered he had forgotten a crucial element in his preparation. Reaching once more into his carrier bag, he pulled out a loaf of bread. Three short bursts of fire later, and he was happily munching on burnt toast.

Toast eaten, it was time for action. He knew he was going to have to move fast, and wished Spoogemige was with him. If Spoogemige had been there, it would be easy. He would just climb onto his back and they'd be off in a barely visible blur.

However, he was not, so he would just have to run as fast as he could. It was at times like this he also wished he had proper-sized wings, and could actually fly. However, he didn't, and he couldn't. All he had were a couple of flimsy, tiny flaps. They were useless, and did nothing but make his t-shirt feel uncomfortable.

A train pulled into the station and, as all the Topsiders started to cram themselves onto it, Scorchington squeezed down the side of it and jumped onto the platform. Then, with all the speed a three-foot tall, stumpy orange dragon wearing carpet slippers and carrying a fully laden plastic carrier bag can muster, ran across the platform towards the stairwell on the far side.

Miraculously, none of the topsiders spotted him. Actually, that is not strictly true. A small girl of about five years of age spotted him.

"Look Mummy! Look at that little dragon running across the platform!" she panted excitedly.

"What have I told you about making up stories about strange creatures living down here?" replied her mother sternly. "This is the last time you have Smarties. All those E numbers!"

"But Mummy, I did... look... there he is!"

The mother had looked. However, by then, Scorchington was hiding out of sight round the corner.

He made his way up the stairwell to the door of the Lost Property Office, but when he reached the door, he discovered another problem. The 'J' Lock was too high for him to reach. After several minutes of jumping up and down, he realised he needed a plan B. Considering he'd never really had a plan A, a plan B was not something he'd given much thought.

He looked round for something to stand on, but there was nothing. He looked inside his carrier bag to see if there was anything in there. Unsurprisingly, there wasn't. Then he had a brainwave. He took off the hoodie and started swinging it around his head, then flicked it up to try and lasso the handle of the 'J' Lock. It didn't work straight away. In fact, after half an hour it still hadn't worked. He walked away from the door, and in frustration threw the Hoody backwards over his head.

It landed perfectly on the top of the handle. Climbing up it, he got near enough to reach the lock. He entered the code '1096A' then started to pendulum back and forth across the door, until eventually there was a clicking sound and the door swung open.

Picking up his carrier bag, he made his way up the stairs towards the main part of the Lost Property Office. It was a wonderful place. To a Topsider, all it contained was junk, but to a Stobe it was an Aladdin's Cave. The first thing he did was make his way to where all the iPods and mp3 players were. There were dozens and dozens of them, in all shapes and sizes.

It wasn't long before one of them caught his eye. It was inside its own protective leather case. On the front was the picture of a creature that looked very much like a dragon - a huge, fierce grey dragon - with enormous wings. He picked it up, put the earphones in his ear and turned it on. He looked at the menu screen as he scrolled down it. Oh yes, he had never heard any of these songs before. These were definitely not boybands. He continued to scroll down – Metallica, Black Sabbath, Linkin' Park, The Killers, Nickleback. He selected one of the bands – Red Hot Chilli Peppers – and turned up the volume.

For the next ten minutes Scorchington stood there, hips thrusting from side to side and arms punching the air. He then started to play air guitar. He'd seen both Spoogemige and Criblee do this sometimes when they were listening to their iPods. After playing air guitar and air drums to another two tracks, he turned it off. He then picked up another three iPods and, stuffing them in his carrier bag, made his way up a flight of stairs to the next room.

He was just about to walk in when he heard voices. He stopped in his tracks and listened carefully. They were Topsiders' voices.

"Have you seen anything strange down here recently, Joyce?"

"No not really, Malcolm. Although I have noticed that there seems to be a lot of lost property going missing on a regular basis."

"Like what?"

"Well all sorts of things, but mainly clothing and iPods. Mind you, the paperwork down here is not exactly kept up-to-date, so they could have been claimed by their owners."

"I don't suppose there's also an epidemic of break-ins on vending machines, by any chance?" said Doreen.

"Well it's funny you should say that, but over the last couple of months, the one here has been stripped bare three times. Probably kids playing a prank."

"A dragon, more like! A thieving little orange dragon!"

"I beg your pardon Doreen. Did you just say 'dragon'?" replied Joyce.

"Oh trust me; it's a dragon alright - about three feet tall, and orange. It wears a black T-shirt and carries a plastic carrier bag. It whistles too - Kylie Minogue songs. And it also farts a lot!"

Joyce and Malcolm stared at Doreen in stunned silence.

As Scorchington listened, his head straining forwards so he caught every word, he suddenly heard footsteps coming up the stairs. He quickly moved back, and looked for a hiding place behind some tall shelving units that were piled high with items of lost property. He finally managed to wedge himself between a group of headless mannequins and a basket filled with umbrellas.

Moments later, two police officers walked past and into the room where the other Topsiders were.

"Hello PC Meredith, nice to see you again. We met earlier today. I'm glad to see you managed to get cleaned up." said Malcolm.

"Oh, uh, yes, hello." replied PC Meredith.

"So, what brings you down to Baker Street? Not looking to see if anyone's found an old table by any chance, are you?"

Scorchington's ears quickly pricked up.

"Don't talk to me about that table. Thanks to that table, PC Walton and I have been sent down here to investigate the recent thefts."

"He's right. The Super didn't believe a word of our story. Accused us of making the whole thing up," said PC Walton. "Mind you, thinking about it, it does all seem a bit farfetched."

"Could someone please explain what's going on?" asked Joyce.

PC Meredith proceeded to tell her all about the sudden appearance of the table in a potting shed in Knightsbridge. Then how it had suddenly disappeared again with him on it, and reappeared where Malcolm and Doreen worked at West Brompton.

All the time, Scorchington was listening in silence in the other room.

"Well what's all this nonsense Doreen's been saying about an orange dragon?" said Joyce.

Everyone turned to look at Doreen.

"Orange dragon?" Gasped PC Meredith.

It was then Doreen's turn to explain the events of her day. Everyone stared with various expressions of disbelief as she described her encounter earlier that morning.

When she had finished, a stunned silence descended on the room.

Scorchington realised he needed to get back to the others as quickly as possible, and tell Wattage what he had overheard. He was filled with excitement. Not only had he become the first Stobe to carry out a successful solo Sherlock, he now had crucial information that might help to track down Wattage's table.

He waited for the Topsiders to stop talking and leave, but half an hour later they were still talking. Scorchington felt his eyelids growing heavy. He was by now a very tired little Stobe, and decided to have a power nap while he waited.

By the time he had woken up with a jolt, the Lost Property offices were in silence and darkness. He looked down at his watch and waited for his eyes to adapt.

Like all the creatures that lived in the underground, Scorchington had amazing night vision. His eyes quickly adjusted, and took on an almost fluorescent glow. He looked at the time. It was 3.05am the following morning.

"Frobbling twazlets!" he said to himself.

He had been asleep for over five hours. Even though it was only 12.05am by standard time, it was still very late. The underground was now closed, so there were no trains to whiz. He would have to make the long journey back to Brompton Road on foot, and alone. The underground was a dangerous place for a Stobe to be alone at this time of night. At this time of night, Stobes always travelled in groups for protection. At this time of night, the Darkenbads would be roaming around looking for victims.

Scorchington made his way down the stairwell and out onto the deserted platform of Baker Street. The air was stale, and strange muffled echoes occasionally drifted out from the blackness of the tunnels on either side. He suddenly felt very vulnerable.

He stepped down onto the tracks and made his way into the tunnel, his small body dwarfed by the arch. Slowly and nervously, he disappeared into the darkness.

Chapter Thirteen

FUDDLEROOK AND VEMBER WERE NOT prepared to tell Neb anything about Wattage's table. They knew that a Cribbit Snockler armed with that kind of information would be far too dangerous. Fuddlerook had even resorted to threatening violence, but that too had failed. The Cribbit Snocklers had just sniggered and gone back to reading their magazines before finally retreating into their holes to shout abuse at them.

Fuddlerook and Vember were left with no alternative but to try to find Scorchington by a process of elimination. This was not an easy task. He was not exactly the most predictable of Stobes.

They had now been searching for several hours, slowly and methodically working their way through the maze of tunnels and abandoned lift shafts.

It was very late, and becoming increasingly dangerous for them. However, they knew that it was nothing compared to the danger Scorchington would now be facing if he were still down there, alone.

They made their way along a disused tunnel, before eventually finding themselves on the main Victoria Line.

Rounding a bend, they arrived at platform two of Warren Street.

Climbing onto the platform, Fuddlerook turned to Vember.

"Are you alright?"

Vember smiled. She was tired and hungry, but aside from that she was fine. She looked at Fuddlerook and the determination etched on his face. She knew that he would not rest until they had found Scorchington. His loyalty to the group was unwavering, and he would face any adversity with selfless strength and courage.

"I'm fine."

They made their way towards the escalators and began the long climb up towards the upper levels of the station. As they climbed, Vember suddenly heard a noise from down below. She stopped and turned round. Looking down into the darkness, she could hear what sounded like the flapping of wings. She should have alerted Fuddlerook, but she didn't. As Fuddlerook continued to climb upwards, Vember began to make her way back down the escalators to the platform below.

Fuddlerook reached the top of the escalators and turned round to wait for Vember, but she was nowhere to be seen. A sickening feeling came over him. He leapt back down the escalators, his huge legs powering him down them three steps at a time. Reaching the bottom, he ran across towards the platform, when, suddenly, an arm reached out from the shadows and grabbed him around the neck. Pulling him sideways, another hand clamped tightly over his mouth. He grabbed the arm holding his neck, pulled it away fiercely, twisted round, and pushed his attacker up against the wall. He was just about to bring his fist down into his attacker's face when he realised it was Vember.

They looked at each other, and Vember bought a finger up to her lips.

"Shush."

Turning round, he looked across towards the far side of the platform. He could make out two shadows at the tunnel entrance. One of them was very small, and hung upside down from the roof. Its body glowed and pulsed in the half-light.

It was a Cribbit Snockler.

The other, much larger shadow stood on the edge of the platform, its rodent-shaped body silhouetted against the tiling on the walls.

They couldn't make out exactly what was being said, but whatever it was, it seemed to please the larger shadow. Its head rolled back and as it did, its mouth opened wide, revealing a set of huge jagged teeth.

"Oh no!" exclaimed Vember in a whispered gasp. "It's Rodolp!"

"And the other one must be Dranoel." replied Fuddlerook.

As they watched from the darkness, Rodolp turned round and stared down the platform in their direction. Fuddlerook reached inside his diver's suit and pulled out his screwdriver in readiness. They pressed themselves back against the wall as Rodolp sniffed the air. It was a rasping, exaggerated sniff, filled with threat and menace. He continued to stare down the platform, his crimson eyes penetrating the darkness.

Fuddlerook and Vember remained motionless in their hiding place, until eventually Rodolp turned back to face Dranoel.

This time they could hear his voice clearly. It was deep and slow, devoid of any emotion, and chillingly threatening.

"So you are sure that is where he is?"

"Of course I am," replied Dranoel. "I've been following his every move. He is at this very moment making his way back via the Metropolitan Line. I would imagine he'll be somewhere around Euston Square by now."

"Excellent." replied Rodolp.

"So come on, what have you got for me in return?" said Dranoel.

Rodolp looked at him, then rolled his tongue around his teeth and spat out a lump of something horrible.

"You'll have to wait."

"We don't work like that."

"You do today!"

Rodolp looked up at him while scraping a large piece of snot out of his nose. "Of course if that's a problem, then maybe you should do something about it?"

Dranoel thought through his options.

a) Start a fight with a five-foot killer rat whilst armed with nothing.

b) Start a fight with a five-foot killer rat whilst armed with a rolled up copy of Gardener's World.

c) Start a fight with a five-foot killer rat whilst armed with a rolled up copy of Gardener's World and some heavy sarcasm.

d) Don't start a fight with a five-foot killer rat.

After a few moments of deliberation, Dranoel chose option d).

Hidden in the shadows, Fuddlerook and Vember realised they were going to have to move quickly if they were going to get to Scorchington before Rodolp.

They turned to each other, and Fuddlerook pointed towards the escalators. If they could get to the top without being spotted, they could reach the Victoria Line, and then use one of the abandoned lift shafts to drop down onto the Metropolitan Line, just before Euston Square.

Looking back down the platform again, however, Fuddlerook noticed that Rodolp and Dranoel were no longer there.

Chapter Fourteen

IN THE DARKNESS OF THE tunnels of the Metropolitan Line, Scorchington made his way wearily towards Euston Square. The battery on his latest iPod had died, and he had toasted his last slice of bread.

He was now beginning to regret his solo Sherlock. He was tired, hungry and feeling very lonely. His feet were aching and his carpet slippers were in tatters. In addition, the handles on his carrier bag had snapped and he now had to carry it tucked under one arm, which was very uncomfortable. He was also starting to feel very cold. Stopping to take the hoodie out of his carrier bag and put it on, he sighed and looked around. Was there no end to this tunnel?

He looked down at his watch. It was 3.05am. He shook the watch violently and looked again. It was still 3.05am. He banged it against the side of his head angrily, and looked once more. No, it was still 3.05am. In a wonderfully childish temper tantrum, he threw it up in the air and breathed a huge jet of fire at it. He looked down at the remains of the watch lying smouldering on the tracks and smiled. *That'll teach it*, he thought.

Scorchington continued to make his way down the tunnel. He rounded a bend in the track and gazed at a deserted platform. When he finally reached it, he stopped and looked around for a moment before slowly pulling himself up onto the platform, dragging his plastic carrier bag behind him.

He sat his weary body down on the platform edge and, with his legs swinging gently backwards and forwards, stared down at his carrier bag. He picked up the empty loaf wrapper and stared longingly at it. At that precise moment, he could think of nothing better than a nice piece of toast.

He reached down and pulled the battered carpet slippers off his feet and gawked at them. He'd grown quite attached to them over the months and felt sad they were now worn out. *Maybe Hetty could fix them for me*, he thought. He was in the process of putting them into his carrier bag when a strange feeling came over him. He stopped swinging his feet and stopped breathing. Sitting motionless on the platform edge he leaned forward and looked into the tunnel on the left, and then into the tunnel on the right. He couldn't see anything, but he sensed something wasn't right.

He suddenly felt a huge stabbing pain in his back. He reeled round to see Rodolp looming out of the darkness above him, his claws about to slash down on him again. He threw himself down onto the tracks just as Rodolp's claw came scything across, missing his face by millimetres. As he lay on his back on the tracks, Rodolp's powerful body arched over him, his long black tail swishing from side to side, his enormous gold teeth bared and dripping with saliva. Scorchington leapt to his feet and, breathing a large jet of fire in Rodolp's direction, started to run into the tunnel. The jet of fire missed, and Rodolp jumped down onto the tracks and darted after him.

"Time to die!" he roared, as he closed in on him.

Suddenly Scorchington stopped and looked down at the battered carpet slipper, which he was still gripping tightly. Holding it high in the air, he breathed fire onto it and then swung round. Then, with all the strength he could summon, he hurled the burning slipper in the direction of Rodolp.

Fuddlerook and Vember arrived just in time to see Rodolp running towards them with a burning slipper wedged in his mouth. They watched in disbelief, as Rodolp continued running past them, and disappeared into the tunnel on the opposite side of the platform screaming.

Moments later, Scorchington limped onto the platform and slumped to the ground.

"Scorchington!" cried Vember, running towards him.

As Vember grabbed hold of Scorchington and held him tightly, Fuddlerook jumped down onto the tracks and began to make his way into the darkness of the tunnel after Rodolp.

"No!" shouted Vember. "Leave him be. Scorchington is hurt!"

Scorchington sat upright and smiled at her. As Vember moved her arms from around him, she noticed blood on her hands.

"Oh, Scorchington, you're wounded."

She turned him round. The back of his hoodie was slashed open, and covered in blood. She gently pulled it over his head. His t-shirt underneath was also slashed and stained with blood.

As Fuddlerook rushed over to them, Vember looked up at him. Her dark grey eyes filled with tears.

"Don't worry Scorch," he said calmly. "We'll soon have you back home, and then Hetty can patch you up."

Scorchington smiled and slowly got to his feet. He limped slowly over to the platform edge, got down on his knees and reached down onto the tracks to retrieve his carrier bag.

"I think you could do with a bit of help getting back, my friend." Said Fuddlerook, smiling.

He reached down, and swung Scorchington up onto his back.

"Vember," asked Scorchington, "Will you carry my bag for me?"

Vember smiled and took it from his hand, and then the three of them began their journey back to Brompton Road. As they made their way slowly into the tunnel, Scorchington rested his head against Fuddlerook's broad shoulders and sighed.

"I did a solo Sherlock today, you know." Were his last words before he fell asleep.

Chapter Fifteen

BY THE TIME FUDDLEROOK, VEMBER and Scorchington arrived back at Brompton Road, the rest of the Stobes were asleep. Wattage and Hetty however had stayed up waiting.

They made their weary way into the kitchen to be greeted by a very relieved Wattage and a pastry-covered Hetty.

Hetty always baked whenever she was nervous. The table and shelves were now groaning under the weight of thirty-seven rat and gravel pies.

* * * * *

Rat and gravel pie, is the staple diet of the Stobes. Of course, they do eat other things they can pilfer, such as chocolate and crisps, but pies are their main preference. In the underground, there is no shortage of rats and gravel. Hetty makes it to her own special recipe, using diesel oil to give it a nice thick syrupy taste. However, the most important ingredient is the pastry. This is made from a combination of cement and plaster from the tunnel walls, mixed with copious quantities of saliva.

* * * * *

Hetty looked like she had been attacked by a gigantic bag of cement. Her blue two-piece suit was covered in grey powder and there were various bits of pastry hanging from her antlers.

Wattage however, seemed more than pleased with the safe return of his friends. He pulled Fuddlerook to one side and led him out of the kitchen and down the tunnel to on old storeroom. Fuddlerook didn't really want to hear. He was tired and hungry. He wanted food, followed by a long undisturbed sleep. However, at this moment in time it didn't look like he was going to get it.

At the door, Wattage turned round.

"Come on my friend, quickly. Hurry up!"

Fuddlerook plodded down the tunnel and into the storeroom. Meanwhile, Hetty and Vember were tending to Scorchington's wounds.

"Oh deary, deary me," muttered Hetty, as she pulled Scorchington's t-shirt off and studied the slash marks across his back.

"Well, all this blood makes it look a lot worse than it is."

As Vember held one of his claws gently, Hetty began to wipe the blood off his wounds.

"I need to speak to Wattage." said Scorchington.

"That may be," replied Hetty "But not until I've tidied and dressed these wounds."

"No, it's really important, Hetty."

"Well, if you want to apologise for going missing yet again, I suggest you wait. Anyway, he's been so pre-occupied for most of this evening that I doubt he'll take any notice of you. Honestly, I don't know what he's been up to, but he's been messing about in one of the store rooms like a big kid all night."

Scorchington started wriggling about on the table and making long deliberate sighing noises.

"Look Hetty, I need to see Wattage right now. I overheard something at the Lost Property Office at Baker Street, something he's going to want to hear."

"Have you been attempting a Sherlock on your own, Scorchington?"

"Not attempting Hetty...*doing*! You're playing nurse to the first Stobe to ever carry out a successful solo Sherlock!" He turned round and grinned proudly at Hetty. She, in return, frowned at him and smacked him on the nose.

"Your mischief-making and walkabouts are starting to cause no end of trouble round here, Scorchington. It's about time you grew up, and stopped being so irresponsible."

Scorchington was suddenly not a happy dragon. He had expected to be welcomed back like a conquering hero. In one night, he had achieved a solo Sherlock *and* got information about Wattage's table. To top it all, he had seen off Rodolp in a fight. What does a Stobe have to do round here to get some respect?

Of course, he had completely ignored the fact that Fuddlerook and Vember had spent all night risking their lives to find him. Or that his solo Sherlock could have been a disaster, and revealed the existence of the Stobes to the Topsiders.

Scorchington went into a sulk. For a moment, he considered setting fire to the bits of pastry hanging from Hetty's antlers, but thought better of it. Those antlers could be lethal weapons when Hetty had a strop on. So instead, he decided to just sulk. Of course, just in case no one had noticed he was sulking, he started sighing loudly, and tutting too. For good measure, he also folded his arms petulantly across his chest, and started to bang his foot against the table leg.

Vember looked sternly at Scorchington.

"I think you've caused enough disruption for one night, Scorch."

Scorchington started to climb off the table.

"I'm not finished with you yet." said Hetty. Scorchington jumped off anyway. "I said I wasn't finished with you, young Stobe!"

As Scorchington walked away, he turned around and stuck his arm out.

"Talk to the claw! This dragon ain't listening."

He then trounced off out of the room. Hetty and Vember looked at each other, and then burst out laughing.

Down in the storeroom, Fuddlerook was struggling to stay awake as Wattage rambled on. All he wanted to do was sleep. As he sat on the floor, his head fell slowly down onto his chest and he drifted into a deep sleep.

Wattage looked across at his friend and smiled. If anyone deserved to sleep right now, it was Fuddlerook. He walked out of the room and came back a few moments later with a blanket and pillow. Lifting Fuddlerook's head gently forward, he placed the pillow onto his shoulder and then slowly lowered his head onto it. He then opened up the blanket, and covered him over with it.

Fuddlerook had looked over so many of the Stobes in the past. Now Wattage would look over him, and make sure he got his much-needed sleep.

Back in the kitchen, Vember had herself fallen into a deep sleep, cuddled up against Hetty, and Brompton Road was now silent apart from the sound of contented snoring and a little orange dragon sighing and tutting.

Bored with his sulking, Scorchington made his way into the storeroom where Wattage and Fuddlerook were.

"Want to know what a garden in Knightsbridge and a garage in West Brompton have got in common?" he shouted across at Wattage.

"Shhhhhh." whispered Wattage, pointing to Fuddlerook asleep on the floor.

"Well, do you?"

"What are you talking about?"

"Your table!"

Scorchington proceeded to explain what he had overheard at Baker Street regarding the table. Wattage's eyes were as wide as saucers as he listened.

When Scorchington had finished, Wattage went back to his papers and started writing things down again.

Scorchington wasn't sure whether he was pleased or disappointed that Wattage hadn't reprimanded him over his solo Sherlock. Under normal circumstances, he would have received a serious dressing down. *Maybe Wattage doesn't know yet,* he thought as he walked off down the tunnel to his room.

He opened the door to the small cupboard where he slept. Inside were two shelves running across the width. On the top shelf were some blankets and a pillow. The lower shelf was full of various items of clothing – mainly t-shirts, as well as a large collection of iPods and mp3 players, all with dead batteries. There were also several loaves of sliced bread piled neatly on one side. Some were white, some brown, and some wholegrain. On the right hand wall was a coat hook. As Scorchington looked at this, he realised something was missing.

Walking quickly back to the kitchen, he saw Hetty and Vember cuddled up, fast asleep on a chair. Underneath the chair was what he was looking for, his plastic carrier bag. He picked it up, taking care not to disturb Hetty and Vember, and then made his way back to his cupboard.

The handles were, of course, broken, so he punched a hole in one side with his sharp claws and then hung the bag in its rightful place on the coat hook. Climbing onto the top shelf, he reached behind him to check out Hetty's handiwork. There was a thick, yet soft bandage wrapped around the middle of his back.

Pulling the blanket over his head, he stuck a foot out and pulled the door shut, before letting out a loud fart, and falling asleep.

Chapter Sixteen

THE FOLLOWING MORNING STARTED NOISILY. Scorchington had woken up in no better frame of mind, and was wandering around sighing heavily, tutting, and generally banging about in a huff. He was determined to prove that when it came to long drawn-out sulking, no one could beat a small orange dragon.

Criblee, on the other hand, was busy tearing up and down the tunnel on his lawnmower, proving that when it came to creating the most noise using something with only three moving parts, no one could beat a young Stobe.

As he charged once more down the tunnel, a huge arm reached out from behind the door of a storeroom and, grabbing him by the throat, lifted him off the lawnmower and held him in the air, legs dangling.

Fuddlerook frowned sternly at him, before lowering him back down onto the floor. Criblee swallowed nervously and hung his head sheepishly.

"Put it away now!"

Criblee started to push the lawnmower back down the tunnel.

"Carry it!" boomed Fuddlerook's voice.

"Just give him a furtling good hiding, will you?" shouted Fligboge from somewhere further down the tunnel.

Thankfully, Fuddlerook did not carry out Fligboge's request. Instead, he gave him another stern frown, then turned around and walked down the tunnel towards the kitchen.

Criblee struggled to try to lift the lawnmower up. He received no help whatsoever from anyone else. After much straining and grunting, he managed to pick it up and staggered off down the tunnel, swaying from side to side and banging into the walls under the weight of it.

In the kitchen, Hetty was scurrying around preparing breakfast. A large number of rat pies were laid out on the table, the result of last night's nervous cooking frenzy.

She had spent the last hour cleaning her suit, but there were still grey powder marks here and there, as well as a single piece of pastry hung from the end of one of her antlers.

Hetty stood at the end of the table, her hooves folded across her chest. She looked like a school matron waiting for the children to arrive quietly and sit down in an orderly fashion to eat their breakfasts in well-behaved silence.

However, it was the Stobes who were about to arrive for breakfast. Instead of well-behaved silence, it would be carnage and mayhem.

One minute the kitchen was quiet and orderly, the next it was filled with shouting and screaming, accompanied by much barging and pushing. This eventually degenerated into large amounts of gratuitous kicking, punching and biting, as everyone jostled for the biggest piece of pie or the best place to sit.

Even the normally calm and graceful Vember demonstrated just how vicious she could be in a food scrum. As Spogworth pushed in front of her, she grabbed hold of him in a headlock and rammed his face repeatedly into one of the pies, before hurling him to the floor and stamping on him.

Spoogemige, meanwhile, used his great height to good advantage by reaching for one of the pies on top of the shelves. However, just as he lifted it down, Fligboge climbed up his legs and bit him in the stomach, forcing him to drop the pie.

For the next ten minutes, the kitchen resembled a scene from a disaster movie. Then, as quickly as it had started, it ended, and the room was quiet once more.

Hetty stood in the middle of the floor and surveyed the wreckage. It looked like a plague of locusts with ASBOs had just visited. She looked down at her suit.

"So much for wasting my time cleaning this." she said to the empty room whilst staring down at her suit, which was once again covered in pastry.

* * * * *

Down in the very deepest levels of the underground, Rodolp was having an equally bad start to the day.

He stared at his reflection in an old mirror hanging from the bare walls of a dark and dirty room. The mirror was cracked in several places, and covered in stains.

He looked at his teeth, which normally shone bright gold. However, they were now tarnished black. His gums were also covered in blisters, and the end of his nose was dripping septic puss from a weeping burn wound.

His distorted reflection in the cracked mirror only served to make him appear even more menacing.

Picking up a wire brush from the floor, he started to scrub his teeth to try to remove the tarnishing. It didn't, but what it did do was burst the blisters on his gums, so that blood started streaming from them.

"*Aaaarrrgggghhhh*!" he screamed. "The next time I see that dragon I'm going to skin him alive. I'm going to tear the flesh from his bones, and eat his vital organs. And then when I've finished, I'm going to KILL HIM!"

He skulked out into a dark narrow tunnel, and made his way towards a flight of steps, which led to another tunnel. As he climbed the steps, he noticed a shadow move slowly and deliberately across the wall at the top of the steps.

The hairs on Rodolp's back stood on end, and a shiver ran down his spine. A shiver of anticipation. He thought he recognised the shape and the way it moved. He lowered his head slightly in deference.

Then, his voice barely above a whisper, he spoke.

"Is that you, Dark One?"

The shadow stopped moving. It remained motionless for several moments, before moving back across the wall until it was directly in front of the top of the steps.

Rodolp raised his head and looked at the black shape. He still couldn't make out any detail. It was as if it was hidden behind another cloak of darkness.

He began to move up the steps towards it. The air was filled with an ominous tension. Rodolp did not scare easily, yet at this moment his heart pounded anxiously.

As he approached the top of the stairs, the shadow began to move backwards, further into the blackness surrounding it.

Rodolp watched its every move, his crimson eyes trying to penetrate the black shadow, which seemed to follow the shape wherever it moved to.

Slowly it started to make its way towards a corridor leading off to the right. Rodolp followed it from a distance. As he did so, he noticed that it seemed to be limping.

At the far end of the corridor, an old fluorescent strip light flickered. Yet even as the shape got nearer, the light failed to penetrate the cloak of darkness that enveloped it.

Rodolp watched the shadow turn a corner and disappear out of sight. He ran after it, but as he turned the corner, all he could see was the blackness of another unlit corridor. He turned round and began to walk away.

Then as he reached the flickering fluorescent strip, he heard a deep, chilling voice echo out of the darkness behind him.

"I will be with you again soon Rodolp. Very soon."

Rodolp looked back over his shoulder and smiled. He then walked back down the corridor to the top of the steps, and made his way down into the darkness below.

Chapter Seventeen

A LOUD SHRIEK REVERBERATED AROUND the walls of Wattage's study. Moments later, Wattage ran out waving his hands in the air and grinning like a maniac.

"I've done it!" he exclaimed loudly.

"Done what?" shouted a voice sounding very similar to Fligboge from further down the tunnel.

"I've worked out how the table disappeared!"

He then proceeded to run up and down the tunnel, shaking his fists in the air and jumping up and down like a hyperactive rabbit that had just been let out of its hutch for the first time in six years.

A number of Stobes rushed out into the tunnel to see what all the fuss was about. Most, however, just peered out from their rooms and watched nervously from a distance.

"Quick, hurry up. Now, straight away!" shouted Wattage to no one in particular, before running back into his study.

The tunnel fell silent, as everyone looked around to see who was going to make the first move. There was an embarrassingly long pause, as everyone simultaneously tried to think of the most plausible excuse for not going.

Stobes are, amongst other things, highly competitive creatures. They will turn even the simplest of situations into a competition in a split second. They are also natural anarchists when it comes to any kind of authority.

Wattage may well have been the elder statesman of the group - indeed, everyone accepted that he was in fact the leader – but that didn't stop them ignoring his authority if they felt like it.

Wattage's demand for everyone to go to his study is a perfect example. If he had just invited everyone to come to his study, then everyone would have happily trotted off to see what he wanted.

However, the fact that he had not only 'told' them to go to his study but told them to 'be quick' and 'hurry up' meant that the gauntlet of authority had been thrown down. No self-respecting Stobe could ignore this challenge. It was now a competition to see who would be the first to chicken out, and follow the order.

Wattage's head poked out of the doorway of his study.

"Come on, come on, I haven't got all day." he said with a glare.

It was Spoogemige and Criblee who cracked first, and started to make their way to the study. Competition over, the rest of the Stobes were now quite happy to follow.

As they all pushed and barged their way into Wattage's study, no one noticed Dranoel fly into the room ahead of them and onto the shelves in the far corner.

The Cribbit Snocklers were about to find themselves in possession of the most important information they had ever had.

"Right, I want you to all listen very carefully."

Everyone did as they were told, with the exception of Fligboge who, as usual, decided to be stubborn.

As everyone tried to pretend to be interested, Wattage began to tell them his theory regarding the table.

Thanks to Scorchington's foolish solo Sherlock, he knew that the table had travelled first to a garden in Knightsbridge, and then to a garage in West Brompton.

In one hand, he held up a large piece of paper with six big dots drawn on it, and in the other hand he held a book on Astronomy.

He looked around the room to make sure everyone was listening.

"This piece of paper with the dots on is a drawing I made of the holes on the top of the table. I thought it might be some sort of diagram, but couldn't work out what. Then I was looking through this book here…" Then he waved it in the air, like a teacher about to set his pupils some homework. "…And realised there was a diagram of a star constellation almost identical."

Everyone in the room looked at him with an expression of boredom.

"What's a star constellation?" asked Spoogemige, trying to show some interest.

"They are groups of stars which have been given names by Topsiders in order to make maps of the stars and distant galaxies," replied Wattage.

"You mean like the tube map of the underground?" Asked Criblee.

"Yes, exactly."

Most of the Stobes were struggling to understand all of this. Wattage could see this, but he carried on anyway.

"If you look at this star constellation called Ursa Major…" He held up a picture in the book. "…You can see that the stars that make it up are in almost exactly the same position as the dots on this piece of paper."

"I can see it does look similar, but what does it mean?" asked Vember.

"Well, that's a good point. I didn't know for sure, but then I looked at a tube map of the underground, and it hit me…the stars in the star constellation, the holes in the diagram off the table, and six stations on the tube map, are all in exactly the same position!"

Even the most sceptical of the Stobes slowly began to realise that maybe Wattage was on to something here.

"Could it just be a coincidence?" said Fuddlerook.

"Well I thought that too," replied Wattage. "But I remembered that under each of the six holes on the diagram on the table were what looked like words. I couldn't make out what they said, because although they had letters, there were also symbols in them too. But I do remember that they all started with a letter. And those letters were A, M, A, P, M & D. Now if you look closely at the names under each of the six big stars in the constellation Ursa Major – they all begin with same letters."

One by one, the Stobes leaned across to look closer.

"Furtling Twazlets!" exclaimed Fligboge. "He's right!"

Sure enough, the names of the stars making up this star constellation all began with the same letters as those from the table – Alkaid, Mizar, Alioth, Phelda, Merak and Dubhe.

Wattage let out a sigh of relief, then proceeded to show them a tube map.

When he put the dots from the diagram on the table next to them, they were in the same position as West Brompton, Earls Court, Gloucester Road, South Kensington, Brompton Road and Knightsbridge tube stations.

The room fell silent, as even the most stupid Stobe realised what Wattage had discovered.

"And, thanks to Scorchington's solo Sherlock, we know that the table has already been to a garden in Knightsbridge and a garage in West Brompton," said Wattage.

"And, as it started off from here at Brompton Road, we can work out the three places it's probably going to go near next." He continued.

"Somewhere near Earls Court, Gloucester Road or South Kensington?" said Vember.

"Exactly."

"But the table didn't actually go to the tube stations, it went near them, so how do you know where in those areas it's going to go?" asked Fuddlerook.

"Well, if Scorchington is right about what he overheard at Baker Street, the two places the table has already been to were both north of the tube stations, and seem to be a distance of about three hundred metres from them. So I looked at a map, and I have worked out the three possible places where the table might turn up next. They're all about three hundred metres north of the tube stations. It's only a guess, but at least it's a starting point."

Spoogemige raised a hand in the air.

"But how do you know the table is moving to them in order? It could be moving to them randomly."

"I don't. That's why we're going to have to do it by a process of elimination."

Fligboge was the next to speak. "This means we're going to have to go up there, where the Topsiders live, doesn't it?"

Wattage sighed and dropped his head down. The rest of the Stobes began to shift uneasily. A nervous silence descended on the room.

"I'm afraid it does," he replied.

"But we can't," said Hetty. "We can never go up there. You know we can't. If the Topsiders find out about our existence, we're finished."

"Why can't we just forget about the table altogether?" said Fligboge.

"I wish we could," replied Wattage. "But if it gets into the wrong hands, then we could be finished anyway."

In the corner of the room, Dranoel was listening to every word. If the Cribbit Snocklers had anything to do with it, the wrong hands were exactly where it would end up.

Wattage slowly explained his plan of action.

They would split up into three groups, with each group given one location to search. If it wasn't at any of those, then they would all make their way to the next.

"Without wishing to be awkward..." said Scorchington. "We don't know how big the Topsiders world is."

"Exactly," said Fligboge, unwittingly agreeing with Scorchington. "It's not going to be like 'whizzing' a train down to Oxford Circus to nick some food and clothing."

"I agree," said Vember. "We could be out there for ages."

Hetty was next to speak.

"We'll have to make some sort of disguises."

"*Disguises?*" laughed Fligboge. "How are you going disguise us as Topsiders? Will you look at us?"

He did have a point. Whilst some of the Stobes did have certain characteristics similar to Topsiders, the vast majority didn't. In fact, most of them would struggle to pass without notice in a zoo.

Even the mighty Fuddlerook was looking anxious.

"I just don't think we can do this," he said. "Even if we could find out where the table was, and even if it wasn't too far away, there's no way we could go up to the Topsiders world without being seen. It's just not possible."

Wattage lowered his head and sighed deeply.

"You're right, my friend. But unfortunately, we have no choice."

"Well I don't know about anybody else," interrupted Hetty. "But all of this has made me feel hungry again. Does anybody want some pie?"

The rest of the Stobes, glad for some light relief from the seriousness of what they were about to undertake, nodded in agreement.

In the ensuing stampede to get to the kitchen, Fligboge stood on Vember's robe, resulting in it tearing right the way up her legs.

Spoogemige and Criblee thought that all their dreams had come true at once as they stared at the bare flesh of her long shapely legs, leading up to the bits a young Stobe shouldn't know about.

Fligboge didn't get chance to apologise, as a vicious right hander to the face, followed by a crunching knee to the groin, sent him sprawling across the floor into the mop and bucket.

The rest of the Stobes trampled over the top of him. All that is, except Scorchington.

He stopped, looked down at him and smiled. The dirty water from the bucket had spilled all over his clothing. Scorchington smiled as he stepped over him, and let out a loud fart.

In the kitchen, it was once more feeding time at the zoo. The minute Hetty put the pie down on the table it was pounced on and devoured immediately. It was the equivalent of putting a side of beef into a tank full of Piranhas.

Wattage however, had stayed behind to go over the details of his plan once more. He knew that if his plan stood any chance of success, it needed planning with military precision.

He also knew that even the best plans often go wrong. It was therefore important to a have a contingency plan just in case.

However, having enough contingency plans to allow for all the mistakes likely to be made by a group of Stobes would take forever. It would also take every single tree in the Amazon rainforest to provide enough paper to write it all down.

So he'd just have to hope that for once, they'd do as they were told and get things right. This was like hoping that the Inland Revenue would announce they were abolishing income tax and were going to give everyone their money back.

Over in the corner of the room, Dranoel was in dire need of a poo. Whilst Cribbit Snocklers are brilliant at sneaking about unnoticed, they are useless with door handles.

Wattage had closed his study door so that he wouldn't be disturbed, which meant that until someone opened it, Dranoel was trapped, unlike the poo, which was trying to work its way out of his bottom.

He contemplated having one there and then, but he realised that it would give the game away. Flying around in silence is easy for a Cribbit Snockler. Having a poo in silence isn't. Cribbit Snocklers are genetically programmed to poo noisily.

All Dranoel could do was try not to think about it, while clenching his bottom tightly.

Eventually, Wattage stood up, and stretching his arms in the air, made his way over to the door and opened it. He'd done it. He'd worked out his plan.

Dranoel too had nearly done it. Three times, he had nearly done it. He flew out of the room like a bat out of hell. Which was, of course, exactly what he was.

Unfortunately, he was in such a hurry to get out, that he forgot to take his usual stealth flight path to avoid being seen, and instead, in a blind panic, flew straight into the top of Wattage's trilby.

The impact knocked Wattage to the floor. The impact also resulted in a sudden evacuation of Dranoel's bowels. A jet of rancid poo sprayed out all over Wattage's trousers. As Wattage picked himself up from the floor, Dranoel headed once more for the doorway. This time, he made it, and with a steady stream of poo squirting out of his bottom, flapped and farted his way down the tunnel.

Wattage staggered to his feet, and in stunned silence, made his way out into the tunnel. As he peered through the half-light, he could make out the white shape of Dranoel disappear into the blackness at the end of it.

His worst fears had now been realised. It would only be a short time before the Darkenbads knew everything. There was no longer any question about whether they should go and look for the table. Now, they had no choice.

Chapter Eighteen

THE STOBES WERE IN A SOMBRE mood as they filed in to Wattage's study.

They had all hoped that he wouldn't be able to work it all out. That even he would realise that it was too dangerous. But as they made their way in, the expression on Wattage's face told everyone that they were about to do the unthinkable.

They were about to venture into the world of the Topsiders.

Once again, none of the Stobes noticed Dranoel - this time accompanied by Neb - fly into the room.

Wattage stood in the middle of the room, holding pieces of paper.

"Right - unfortunately, one of the Cribbit Snocklers was hiding in the room when I was telling you all about the table, and heard everything. So it won't be long before this information is passed to the Darkenbads. Therefore, it is now imperative that we find the table first."

He shuffled uneasily on the spot, fully aware of how nervous everyone was. Even Fuddlerook looked anxious.

"We're going to split into three groups."

"Do we get to choose which group we're in?" shouted Fligboge.

"No. I've already worked them out," replied Wattage.

"On what basis?" said Fligboge.

"On the basis of what I think will be best," snapped Wattage tersely.

"Frobbling typical." mumbled a less than happy Fligboge.

"Right. Group one, will be led by Fuddlerook, with Fligboge, Scorchington, the Gerbil Brothers and Plankton. Group two, will be led by Vember, with Spoogemige, Criblee, the Battenberg Twins and Germ." Spoogemige and Criblee grinned and shook with joy. "And the third group, will be led by me, with Spogworth, Hetty, and the Mole in the Wall Gang."

Fligboge was far from happy with his group. Then again, he was such an awkward twazlet that he wouldn't have been happy whichever group he was in.

"Now I've worked out which group will going where," continued Wattage. "Fuddlerook, you'll be taking your group to a place called The Natural History Museum. It's not far from South Kensington on the District Line. Vember, your group will be going to a place called St Stephens Church. It's just round the corner from Gloucester Road on the Piccadilly Line. I will be taking my group to somewhere called Cromwell Hospital, which is just down the road from Earls Court, also on the Piccadilly Line."

He walked over and handed a piece of paper to both Fuddlerook and Vember. On it were written the name and address of exactly where they were going.

"So we'll wait until midnight when the Underground closes, and make our way out then."

"What if it's not at any of these places?" asked Fuddlerook.

The Battenberg Twins spotted a slight problem with Wattage's plan. However, the Battenberg Twins were very quiet Stobes. In fact, they were so quiet no one could recall actually ever hearing them speak.

Two little stumpy claws reached up and they both coughed politely at the same time, in order to attract attention.

"Excuse me, but how will we let the other groups know if we find the table?" They both said, at exactly the same time.

They spoke so quietly and timidly that no one heard them. So they repeated the question. Still no one could hear them. They looked at each other, shrugged their tiny shoulders, and asked again, only this time a little louder.

"EXCUSE ME, BUT HOW WILL WE LET THE OTHER GROUPS KNOW IF WE FIND THE TABLE?" they both shouted at the same time.

Everyone in the room pressed their hands, claws, hoofs and paws over their ears, as the deafening high-pitched shriek of the Battenberg Twins voices reverberated around the room. The shrieking was so loud and high-pitched, that it was highly likely at that moment hundreds of dogs all around London were looking down at the ground trying to figure out where it was coming from.

"WE'RE SO SORRY. BUT WE DON'T KNOW HOW TO SPEAK AT A NORMAL VOLUME. WE CAN ONLY SHOUT...or whisper quietly," they continued, at the same time of course.

No one heard the last bit. They were all still trying to shake the deafening ringing noises out of their heads.

"Why do you always both speak at the same time?" said Hetty eventually.

"We just do. We always have,"

"Pardon?" said Hetty.

"WE JUST DO. WE ALWAYS HAVE!"

Everyone held their ears once again. After a few moments, Spogworth spoke.

"It was a good question though."

"What was?" said Fligboge.

"The question the Battenberg Twins just asked."

"All I heard was a deafening, high-pitched shriek." continued Fligboge.

Spogworth was beginning to gain confidence in his public speaking. In the last few days, he had opened his mouth on at least three occasions and not been laughed at. Indeed, he was starting to think that he maybe wasn't as thick as everyone said he was.

"They asked how we let the other groups know if we find the table." He continued.

One by one, they looked over at Wattage. He'd know the answer to this. After all, it was his plan, and he was thorough if nothing else. Wattage however, was staring down at the floor, and fiddling with the brim of his Trilby.

"Well?" shouted Fligboge. "How do we?"

Wattage clasped his hands together and looked sheepishly around the room.

"He's not thought of that, has he?" laughed Fligboge. "Biggest brain in the underground, and he's not thought of that!"

It was Scorchington who surprisingly came to his rescue.

"Simple. We use apples."

"What do you mean 'apples'?" said Hetty.

"Apples," replied Scorchington. "I've seen Topsiders use them to talk to each other."

"Apples," said Spogworth.

"Yes apples, and blueberries." Continued Scorchington.

"*Apples*?" said Hetty. "Oh, I don't like the idea of that. I'm not walking round talking to a piece of fruit,"

"No, they're 'Apples', not apples. They're mobile phones." said Scorchington.

"Well, I'm certainly not walking round talking to a piece of fruit whether it's mobile or not." continued Hetty.

"They're what the Topsiders call mobile phones, you stupid, cloth-eared moose!" replied Scorchington.

"Don't you call me cloth-eared, you nasty little dragon freak!" snapped Hetty.

"Alright, enough is enough!" shouted Wattage.

"Don't you shout at me, Turnip Head!" snapped back Hetty. "If you'd grow up and stop messing about with these daft experiments, none of this would have happened in the first place!"

When Hetty got annoyed, she *really* got annoyed. The emotionally erratic side of her character would come out, and nothing anyone said would calm her down.

Hanging from the ceiling in the corner of the room, Neb and Dranoel were finding it desperately hard not to join in. This was exactly the kind of conversation they loved - nasty, bitter, insulting and rude. It was Cribbit Snockler heaven.

However, despite the temptation, they remained silent.

Instead, they would settle for some good old blood-soaked carnage. The kind of blood-soaked carnage that would follow once they'd passed all this information on to a certain group of creatures.

"So how do we go about getting these Apples?" Asked Wattage.

"I've got five." said Spogworth, continuing to surprise everyone.

"And I've got one, too." said Scorchington.

"So why haven't you told us about them before?" said Fligboge.

"No one talks to me much when I'm stood next to them," replied Spogworth, "So I didn't think for one minute anyone would be interested in phoning me. Anyway, they don't work down here."

"What do you mean they don't work?" said Fligboge.

"They don't work underground. Can't get a signal." Said Spogworth.

"Can't get a signal? So what use are they to someone who lives underground, you stupid twazlet?" screamed Fligboge. A big vein in right side of his forehead started throbbing.

"He's going to do himself an injury if he carries on like this," said Hetty in a matter of fact way. "Just look at that vein on his forehead. It's got a life of its own. It'll just explode if he's not careful. I've tried telling him but he won't listen."

"And what about you?" Continued Fligboge, pointing to Scorchington. "Why don't you use yours?"

"I've only got one, you stupid twazlet. Who am I going to talk to?"

"Spogworth, for instance, you idiot!"

"We can't get a signal down here, you thick twazlet." screamed both Spogworth and Scorchington at the same time.

"Well, will they all still work out there?" asked Fuddlerook pointing to the ceiling.

"Mine will," said Spogworth.

"Mine doesn't," replied Scorchington. "Flat battery."

"Well, go and get yours then." said Wattage, to Spogworth.

While Spogworth went off to get his Apples and Blueberrys, Wattage decided to go over the plan once more.

"We will wait until after midnight. The electric current will be switched off on the mainline tracks then, so we'll be able to travel to the stations a lot quicker. Also, at that time of night, there hopefully won't be many Topsiders about. If the table isn't at your location, then use one of Spogworth's phone contraptions and let me know. Then make your way back to Earls Court station, which is above ground so you'll be able to get a signal so I can let you know if we find the table."

Chapter Nineteen

NEB AND DRANOEL, NOW IN possession of the information they needed, made their way out of Wattage's study and glided through the dark labyrinth of tunnels, until they reached an old abandoned lift shaft.

Hanging above it was an old rusting pipe. They landed on the underside of it, using their stumpy-clawed feet to grip the rust covered surface tightly.

Hanging above the void, they looked down into the blackness, their bloodshot red eyes trying to penetrate the darkness.

"I hate this bit," said Neb.

"Horrible, isn't it?" replied Dranoel. "You never know who or what is going to be waiting at the bottom."

"Ah well," said Neb. "We'd better get on with it."

They both let go of the pipe at the same time, and with their wings pointing backwards like the tail fins of a plane, plummeted down the shaft.

It took only a few seconds for them to reach the bottom. As the floor of the lift shaft came hurtling towards them, they opened their wings fully and came to a surprisingly graceful halt a few inches above a set of razor-sharp stained golden teeth.

"How impressive," said Rodolp. "Especially as I've not eaten yet."

He skulked off down a dark tunnel towards a flight of steps. Neb and Dranoel followed behind, upside down on the tunnel roof.

Rodolp stopped and looked up at them. Neb and Dranoel stopped and looked down at him.

"What exactly does a Cribbit Snockler taste like? Chicken, I suppose."

He carried on walking.

"Yes, chicken. Because everything tastes like chicken, doesn't it?" he continued.

Neb and Dranoel decided to hang back, and follow at a distance.

"I remember eating a cat. Just like chicken - a chicken with fur, claws and whiskers. And an umbrella if I remember right." he reached the top of the steps, and turned round.

"Never eat an umbrella. It only causes problems the following morning. An umbrella is a difficult thing to pass, if you know what I mean? Especially if it's got a curved handle."

Neb and Dranoel made their way nervously over to Rodolp. He was standing at the top of a flight of steps leading down to another tunnel. To the left was a narrow corridor. It was partially lit by an old fluorescent strip light that flickered on and off continuously.

Rodolp walked off down the corridor and Neb and Dranoel followed him, still keeping a safe distance. It was obvious that Rodolp was in a strange mood, even by his standards.

As Rodolp reached the light, he turned round. It was then that Neb and Dranoel noticed the blisters all around his mouth.

"Have you taken up fire-eating as a hobby?" said Neb.

"He needs a bit more practice if he has." chuckled Dranoel.

Rodolp snarled at them, bearing his huge teeth, and clenching his claws.

"Who hasn't cleaned their teeth today?" said Neb. "Dental hygiene is so important, you know. You'll never get a date with teeth like that."

"He's right," said Dranoel. "He knows all about teeth. He's becoming somewhat of an expert, in fact. He found thirteen issues of 'Dentistry Today' down at Embankment Station. He's hardly had his head out of them ever since."

"Certainly haven't," replied Neb. "Fascinating subject. You know what they say – 'Healthy gums attract healthy chums.'"

"I'll show you exactly what teeth were designed for," snarled Rodolp, as he leapt across towards Neb and Dranoel.

"Hold it, hold it, big fella," shouted Neb, as he saw the huge rodent bulk heading straight for him, teeth snapping, tail swishing from side to side.

"You don't want to eat me," he continued.

"Oh, yes I do!" snarled Rodolp.

"No you don't! Because if you do, you won't find out what I've got to tell you." Neb was beginning to think he might have pushed his luck too far this time. "And I'm sure you'd sooner be chomping your way through a nice piece of freshly slaughtered dragon."

Rodolp stopped just short of where Neb was hanging from the ceiling of the corridor.

"You've got thirty seconds to persuade me otherwise," said Rodolp menacingly.

Neb swallowed nervously. He checked out the distance between his head and Rodolp's teeth. It was about six feet. *Could Rodolp jump six feet?* he wondered. He pondered this for a few seconds, but still wasn't sure.

"Twenty seconds," said Rodolp, casually flicking a piece of something horrible from between his teeth with a long razor sharp claw.

"Ten," he continued, opening his mouth nice and wide to emphasise the point.

"OK. You win!" said Neb finally.

"That's usually the case," replied Rodolp condescendingly.

Neb began to tell Rodolp of the Stobes plans. As he told him everything he had overheard, an increasingly broad smile spread across Rodolp's face.

When Neb had finished, Rodolp turned round, and began to walk back down the corridor. As he reached a corner, he turned round.

"I presume you want some information in return? Or did you tell me all that simply because I'm a nice guy and you feel we're really starting to bond?"

Neb was speechless. Rodolp was now using both sarcasm *and* irony.

"So what have you got for me?" said Neb, as he inched his way along the tunnel roof.

"Well, let me put it like this," said Rodolp, now leaning casually against the side of the tunnel wall. "It will certainly take your breath away."

"Now come with me," he continued. "I want you to tell the others what you heard."

This wasn't part of the plan. Neb had just wanted to tell Rodolp, and that was that. He would have then gone back with some useful information in return, with the added bonus of knowing that a number of Stobes were about to be pointlessly slaughtered.

Neb hurriedly started to try and invent a plausible reason for why there wasn't any point in them going, when Rodolp interrupted his chain of thought.

"I won't ask again."

Neb was good at turning things to his advantage. It was something that came naturally to him. He was far more intelligent than most of the other creatures who lived in the underground. However, there was an uncompromising finality in the tone of Rodolp's voice, which worried him.

"If you want that information from me, then follow me. Now!"

Neb and Dranoel made their way reluctantly across the ceiling of the corridor and followed Rodolp to an old, battered door, covered in dirty, flaking red paint. Rodolp opened it, revealing a rusting metal ladder leading vertically down into a pitch-black void.

As Rodolp began to climb down the ladder, it creaked and vibrated. The sound echoed off the walls. Normally Neb and Dranoel would have just flown down something like this. However, there was something unnerving about the whole place. They watched Rodolp disappear down into the darkness, listening to his claws scraping on the metal rungs. Anxiously, they both made their way onto the ladder and began climbing down.

It took an age to reach the bottom. When they finally did, Rodolp was waiting for them, holding open another dirty battered door.

"After you," he said.

His voice seemed to have dropped an octave. It was sounding more and more threatening. The simple phrase 'After you' seemed to be loaded with violent innuendo.

Neb and Dranoel walked tentatively through the door, to find themselves in another narrow corridor. There were some rotting electricity cables running along the ceiling. A loud muffled bang reverberated down the corridor as Rodolp closed the door behind them.

At the far end, the corridor opened out into a large well-lit tunnel. It was divided in two, by a long wall of old dusty plasterboards that ran down the entire length of a long deserted platform. The wall didn't reach all the way to the roof of the tunnel, but stopped about a foot short. A cool sickly draft blew continually through this gap. The tiled curved wall of the tunnel was covered in old faded posters and direction signs. On the platform floor laid piles of bricks, and abandoned tools.

Half way down the platform, stood the remains of an old ticket office. With the exception of one solitary broken pane, all the windows were missing.

Standing next to it, leaning on the counter, was a tall, striking looking creature dressed in a skin-tight leather biker's suit. It clung to the curves of a shapely and athletic female body. Heavy black boots, covered in metal studs, tapped on the broken tiles of the platform floor.

As the long black fingernails of one of its hands scratched against the surface of the counter, the other caressed the serrated blade of a large dagger. Coal-black dead eyes, stared fiercely out from an angular, yet powerfully attractive face. The skin was pure white. Across one cheek ran a deep blue scar. It wasn't blood that ran through those veins. A wild tangle of unkempt long black hair was tied back roughly with a piece of electric cable, revealing long triangular shaped ears, curving around the back of her head.

She stared down the tunnel directly into Neb's eyes as he hung from an old light fitting on the roof. Dranoel shuffled over nervously and tried to hide behind him.

"You've not met Ripperton have you?" said Rodolp.

Neb and Dranoel wished they still hadn't. There was something even more menacing about her than Rodolp. They shifted uneasily on the light fitting, causing it to creak on its flimsy ancient screws.

Ripperton continued to stare at them like a cold, emotionless killer. Which was exactly what she was.

Neb and Dranoel were so busy staring into Ripperton's eyes that they didn't notice the other members of the Darkenbads appear silently on the platform.

The Cribbit Snocklers had been trading, or as was often the case considering their violent nature, giving information to the Darkenbads for many years. Yet this was the first time they had ever actually been to where the Darkenbads lived.

They usually met somewhere else, somewhere neutral. As it was Rodolp whom they nearly always passed the information to, they would meet down in the part of the underground where he lived, alone and reclusive.

It suddenly dawned on both Neb and Dranoel, that they had in fact met very few of the Darkenbads.

They had assumed Rodolp was the most dangerous member of the gang. However, as they continued to watch Ripperton, they began to realise they could be wrong. There was something very dark and unnerving about her.

The last time Neb had felt this on edge, was during his previous encounters with the terrifying Darl.

Darl. The mention of his name was enough to strike terror, into every creature in the underground. Neb was no exception. Yet this one called Ripperton had a similar effect.

A worrying theory began to take shape inside Neb's head. Fortunately, before he could reach a potentially horrific conclusion, he was distracted by the sound of an ugly little thing hurling insults at him.

"Oi, Bat Breath!"

It was about four feet tall and wearing a bin liner and a battered grey balaclava. Its body was painfully thin. The bin liner hung off its non-existent shoulders in the same way a tent would hang off a lamppost. Its waist was far too long. Its whole body seemed to consist of one long waist with a pair of feet on the bottom. Sticking out from the middle of the balaclava were the facial features of a Ferret. A Ferret which had at some point, been hit in the face with a hammer.

"Yes, you - Fart Gob!" continued Skerrett.

Considering Skerrett had the most appallingly bad breath in the underground, there was a wonderful touch of irony to his insult.

Neb looked down. The pungent stench of Skerrett's foul smelling breath drifted into their nostrils. It made both Neb and Dranoel feel like throwing up. For something to smell so bad it made even a Cribbit Snockler want to throw up was testimony to just how bad Skerrett's breath was.

A fat blob wobbled its way down the platform to where Skerrett was still hurling insults up at the roof of the tunnel.

Dressed in the remains of an old postbag, and wearing a gas mask, Wobblett had a vague similarity to a Wombat. He made his way over to the plasterboard dividing wall, and proceeded to start punching it. His big fat blobby fists smashed repeatedly into the wall. Bits of plaster flew in all directions as he continued to pummel the wall for no apparent reason.

"He's in training," said Rodolp, looking on in a mixture of pride and pity. "We really ought to get him some flesh to practise on."

Neb and Dranoel watched him slowly destroy part of the wall. They really did need to get out more.

The sound of something trying to cough up snot and vomit at the same time was the next thing to attract Neb and Dranoel's attention.

They turned round to see a small creature jumping down the platform. It was wearing a tattered, yellow, woollen jumper, a pair of chef's trousers and Doc Martins.

As it leapt up and down the platform, it continued to cough up large amounts of snot and spit. Its head resembled that of a very thin toad. A very thin toad with green hair shaped like a bush. Sticking out of the middle of its hair was a large barbed fin, covered in what looked like dried blood.

It stopped directly underneath Neb and Dranoel, and looked up at them.

"Flem by name, Flem by nature!" it announced. A large stream of projectile snot and saliva splashed onto the tunnel roof narrowly missing them.

"Vloody good shhott!" said an obviously drunken voice.

It belonged to what appeared to resemble a mutant Badger. It was slumped against the wall. Long, fearsome looking claws clutched the half-empty bottle of gin resting on its large, fat stomach. A dirty red Puffer jacket, slashed and ripped in several places, hung open revealing a filthy string vest. It stood up slowly, then began to stagger down the platform in the direction of Wobblett, who was still punching the living daylights out of the wall.

Whilst one claw gripped the bottle of gin tightly, the other tried to hold up a pair of baggy underpants covered in food stains.

"No Vloody helashtic," it said, as it fell into then slumped over an old pile of bricks.

"Hallow me to hintroducsh myshelf," It stood up and attempted to make a theatrical gesture, but this only resulted in its underpants falling down. As it tried to grab them, it fell back down onto the pile of bricks.

"My name is Gobbit," it continued. "Thish lot sheem to think I have a drinking problem. Thish is in fact true. Only yeshterday for instance, I couldn't find anything to drink. It wash a problem."

Placing the now empty bottle of Gin on the floor, Gobbit staggered to his feet, only to fall backwards and slide down the wall into a drunken heap.

"However, I never ever mix my drinksh," he said before passing out.

This wasn't strictly true. On a number of occasions, Gobbit had indeed mixed his drinks. Whilst gin was his preferred tipple, he was no stranger to meths, paraffin and diesel oil.

A bald-headed, baby-faced giant of a creature suddenly barged into the tunnel from the doorway behind Rodolp. His whole body was covered in nothing apart from hundreds of tattoos. A pair of woollen swimming trunks protected his modesty.

He looked up at Neb and Dranoel and smiled. He then bent down, picked up a large brick and, laughing like a maniac, threw it at them.

"Ha ha. Kill the bats. Kill the bats, ha ha. Kill the bats!" screamed Woogums, revealing a mouth filled with broken teeth.

Neb and Dranoel managed to move out of the way just in time as the brick demolished the light fitting and most of the ceiling around it.

He then sat down on the floor and started chewing on a piece of broken tiling. Neb and Dranoel watched from the relative safety of another light fitting further down the platform.

After the creature had finished eating the tile, he picked up a brick and began to eat that.

"Explains the teeth," whispered Neb to Dranoel.

Rodolp walked down the platform to the ticket office.

"Right, you bunch of psychopathic freaks!" The tone of his voice was complimentary. Warm even. Well, warm in the same way that the inside of a fridge is warm compared to an Arctic blizzard.

A muffled voice interrupted him from behind a welder's mask.

"What's with the bats?"

A large ungainly shape lumbered up next to him. Dressed in an old dark grey boiler suit, its huge scarred hands gripped a large sledgehammer. The bright orange tufts of a beard stuck out from underneath the welding mask.

"I'm not going to ask what you've been doing with that," said Rodolp to Grizthrop.

Rodolp motioned for everyone to gather round.

"Our friendly neighbourhood Cribbit Snocklers have some rather interesting news," He looked up at Neb. "Go on then. We haven't got all night."

Neb nervously delivered the entire story regarding the Stobes, the table, and their plan to get it back. He gave them all the information, right down to the last detail.

When he had finished, the platform remained silent for a few minutes.

Rodolp was the first to speak.

"Three locations - three groups. I'm not interested who goes with who. Sort it out amongst yourselves."

He turned and walked off down the platform.

"Just remember. The dragon is mine."

"I work alone." said Ripperton.

"Not this time." replied Rodolp, smiling.

Ripperton glared at him, and stabbed her dagger into the top of the counter.

"Save your anger for later. You'll have plenty of opportunities to use that in a few hours time."

As he reached the doorway, he turned around and looked across at Gobbit.

"One of you had better sober HIM up."

"The tank, the tank, the tank," shouted Woogums excitedly.

"I would have thought so," Rodolp sneered over his shoulder, as he slammed the door shut behind him.

"The tank, the tank," continued Woogums, as he rushed over to where Gobbit laid slumped unconscious against the wall.

Picking him up and throwing him across his shoulder, he charged off down to the far end of a platform, and through an archway leading to a dimly lit flight of stairs. At the top of them, he turned the handle of a heavy metal door. It creaked and groaned as it grinded open, revealing an old ventilation shaft.

A metal ladder hung precariously from one of the walls. Cold damp air rose up from the darkness below.

Woogums stepped out onto the top rungs of the ladder. It shifted and vibrated. Bits of rotten mortar broke away from the brickwork under the weight.

Holding on with one hand, he lowered Gobbit off his shoulder, paused for a moment, grinned, and then dropped him into the darkness.

There was silence for about three seconds, followed by a large splash.

"Tank, tank!" screamed Woogums in excitement.

"Aaaaaargggggh!" screamed Gobbit in shock, as the freezing water in the oil tank at the bottom of the shaft violently sobered him up.

Meanwhile, Rodolp made his way along the dark tunnel leading back to his room. As he approached his room, a shiver ran down his spine, and once again, the hairs on his back stood on end.

He could sense he was being watched. He turned round quickly and walked back out into the tunnel. His eyes probed the darkness. He could see nothing.

Walking back into his room, he lit the wick of an old paraffin lamp. The lamp barely lit half of the small room. He stood in front of the cracked mirror, and examined the blisters on his gums in the dim light.

He reached down and lifted a small towel from a hook in the wall. Bringing the towel up to his mouth, he moved his face closer to the mirror.

Suddenly he froze.

Standing behind him was a dark shadow. Its reflection stared at him through the mirror. Then, from out of the shadow stepped a black shape. It moved slowly towards him until the mirror filled with blackness.

Rodolp was unable to move. He wanted to move. He wanted to run away, but his feet seemed to be held by some invisible force to the concrete floor.

Piercing white, fluorescent eyes now stared out from the black shape. A long arm reached out of the blackness and strong fingers gripped Rodolp's shoulder tightly.

"I told you I would return soon."

The voice was chillingly cold and threatening.

Rodolp lowered his head. The towel slipped from his claw and dropped to the floor.

"You've picked a good night to return, dark one."

"I know, my evil friend. I know."

Chapter Twenty

AT MIDNIGHT, THE UNDERGROUND BECOMES a strange yet wonderful place. The bright lights and hustle and bustle give way to dimly lit stations and platforms. Apart from the Topsiders on the night shift, they are deserted.

The train tunnels are exactly the opposite. When the Underground is open, the tunnels are dark. Miles and miles of brooding black labyrinths. The only lights they see are the trains rushing thousands of Topsiders from one station to the next.

After midnight, they turn into a different world. The curved ceilings of the tunnels transform into brightly lit vaults, as powerful arc lights flood them with dazzling brightness. The nightly ritual of repair and maintenance begins.

Topsiders in overalls and bright yellow helmets take over. They mill about like ants, scurrying through the tunnels. The rumble of huge mechanical machines echo around the walls.

If the Topsiders working on the section of the Circle Line just down from Sloane Square had taken the time to look up at the tunnel roof, they would have seen seven

Cribbit Snocklers marching along it. However, they did not.

At the same time, their colleagues on the District, Northern and Piccadilly Lines also failed to spot several groups of Stobes making their way along the tracks.

Further down in the lower levels, three groups of Darkenbads were heading for exactly the same places. And deep in the darkest part of the underground, Rodolp, accompanied by a sinister shadow, began his journey towards the world of the Topsiders.

Chapter Twenty One

AT SAINT STEPHENS CHURCH ON Gloucester Road, PC's Meredith and Walton knocked on the huge wooden door of the vestibule. It was very dark. The nearest streetlight was no longer working, thanks to a pointless act of vandalism involving a drunken teenager and a bottle of alcopop.

The brooding, Gothic mass of the church appeared very unnerving in the darkness. As they waited for someone to answer the door, the sound of a squeaking wheel attracted their attention. They turned round just as a shopping trolley filled with traffic cones rolled slowly down the road. It came to halt on the kerb a few yards further on.

The heavy wooden door of the church swung open, and Reverend Peter Watgod greeted them with a weary smile.

The front of his cassock was covered in porridge.

"Evenin', all." he said.

"Never heard that one before, Reverend." replied PC Meredith, staring at the front of his cassock.

They followed him through into the main part of the church.

"It's a lot bigger than it looks from the outside." whispered PC Walton as he stared up at the enormous vaulted ceiling suspended high above them.

Reverend Watgod walked over towards a large wooden pulpit. Perched on the top, was a gold eagle holding the open pages of a very large bible.

"We're not going to have to sit through a sermon are we?" said PC Meredith.

Reverend Watgod then pointed to an ornate alter table. Lying on top of it, and on the floor next to it, were the broken pieces of a very old stained glass window.

"I just heard a loud explosion, and rushed in to find all this damage."

Immediately behind the alter table stood another table.

An old stone table!

The familiar stench of sulphur, burnt fish and rotten eggs hung in the air.

"Oh God! Not again!" shouted PC Walton.

"Officers! Please, this is the house of the Lord!"

"Sorry, Reverend." said PC Walton.

"There must have been a few of them," said Reverend Watgod. "And strong too."

He walked over to the big empty hole where the stained glass window used to be.

"Fourteenth century."

He stared up at the stars twinkling in the night sky, then down at the porridge stains on his cassock. He picked up the hem of it and began to rub the front furiously.

"If they had used porridge instead of cement," he grunted. "It would probably still be up there."

He walked back to where PC Meredith and PC Walton were, for the third time in the space of twenty-four hours, examining the smoking table.

"It must have taken a few attempts."

"What do you mean?" replied PC Walton.

"To throw that through the window," he said, pointing to the table. "Mind you, when youngsters have a bit too much to drink, I suppose anything can happen."

PC Walton looked across at Reverend Watgod, and then up at the now empty window frame. It was at least twenty feet up the wall. Even a stupid person would have worked out that a team of Olympic shot putters would have found it challenging.

"Still, God does work in mysterious ways, you know?"

"Not half as mysterious as this table." muttered PC Meredith.

"If you don't mind, Officers, I'll leave you to it. If it's as hard to get porridge off a kitchen wall as it is off a cassock, then it looks like I'm going to be up all night!"

"That's alright," replied a puzzled PC Meredith.

He didn't have a clue what the Reverend was talking about, but to be fair, it was perfectly understandable that the poor man was still in a state of shock.

Under the circumstances, he did not try to explain to Reverend Watgod what had really happened. After all, how do you explain to a man of faith that his beloved church had just been vandalised by a mundane secular table, which travels instantly from one place to another, all by itself?

No, it would be better to let him believe it was a gang of very strong drunks.

As Reverend Watgod walked off, there was a low rumbling sound, followed by a large explosion.

At the same time that PC Meredith and PC Walton were hurled backwards across the alter table, another large stained glass window was blown out of the wall.

Reverend Watgod managed to throw himself to ground between two rows of pews just as the window crashed on top of him.

After the sounds of the explosion had died down, there was a moment of silence in the church, before a coughing mumbled voice spoke from underneath the rubble.

"I don't know how I'm going to explain this to the Bishop."

A few moments later, PC Meredith staggered to his feet. PC Walton was lying over the back of a pew with his feet in the air. Reverend Watgod was lying face down between two pews, his back covered in shards of broken, stained-glass window. The smell of sulphur, burnt fish and rotten eggs hung in the air.

The stone table was needless to say, no longer there.

After helping PC Walton to his feet, PC Meredith headed over to Reverend Watgod and began to help him up.

All three of them stood silently surveying the scene. The ornate alter table immediately in front of where the table had stood, was miraculously still in one piece. Most of the pews in front of it however, had been blown onto their backs. The floor was littered with red hymnbooks.

"Where's the table that was thrown through the window gone?" asked Reverend Watgod eventually. "Don't tell me they came and took it back while we weren't looking?"

PC Meredith looked at him pitifully.

"No they didn't, Reverend."

He realised that he would have to try to explain as best he could exactly what was going on regarding the table.

"The fact of the matter is this, Reverend," he continued. "The table actually appeared all by itself."

"Oh I hardly believe that, Constable." he replied with a faint snigger.

"I know it seems a bit far-fetched," continued PC Meredith. "But I'm afraid it's true."

Reverend Watgod looked at him with an expression on his face that was both quizzical and critical.

"So you're trying to tell me that this table has some sort of magic powers?"

"I don't know about that? But what I do know is that in the space of about twenty four hours, it has, all by itself, appeared then disappeared from a potting shed in Knightsbridge, to a garage inspection pit in West Brompton, and now your church!"

The expression on Reverend Watgod's face changed from quizzical to disbelief.

"How do you know this?"

"Because Reverend, we've seen it with our own eyes. In fact, I was sitting on it when it went from Knightsbridge to West Brompton. Dammed unpleasant episode it was as well, if you'll pardon my French, Reverend."

"Why, what happened?"

"I don't exactly know. But if the state of my uniform afterwards was anything to go by, I shudder to think."

"You mean you don't remember anything?"

"Nothing! One minute I was in the ruins of a potting shed in Knightsbridge, the next I was in the bottom of a garage inspection pit in West Brompton, surrounded by smoke, and covered in engine oil."

"Goodness me, PC Meredith! It sounds like you had a lucky escape."

Reverend Watgod looked up to the ceiling of the church, clasped his hands together in prayer and started muttering under his breath. The muttering went on for several minutes, until he turned round, faced the alter and started muttering again.

After several more minutes of muttering, he walked back over to PC Meredith and, leaning forward, whispered in his ear.

"It sounds like the work of Lucifer to me," He pulled back, and clasped his hands together in prayer once more. "I've said prayers to the Lord, but it might be an idea for you and PC Walton to do so also. If this is some dark power from Hades, then we are going to need all the prayer we can muster."

PC Meredith was not a particularly religious man, but so as not to offend the Reverend, he put his hands together and tried to remember the Lords prayer.

"Our Father…who…art in…"

"Heaven, PC Meredith, Heaven," cut in Reverend Watgod, rather sternly.

"Oh yes… Heaven… Hallowed be thy… oohhh… it's on the tip of my tongue… that's it… name…Thy…"

For the next few minutes, PC Meredith, with continual prompting by Reverend Watgod, worked his way uneasily through the Lords Prayer. When he finally finished, Reverend Watgod looked at him, and smiled.

"I think some regular attendance at church could be the order of the day for you, Constable."

PC Meredith looked back at PC Walton, who had been pretending to be engaged in some forensic activity during all of this, and smiled embarrassingly.

"Now that we've taken care of that," said Reverend Watgod. "Is there anything else I can help you with?"

PC Meredith sat down on one of the few pews that hadn't been blown over, and tried to think of something.

"Well, I suppose you could go and make us all a nice cup of tea if it's not too much trouble, whilst PC Walton and I try and figure all this out."

Reverend Watgod looked around the church and sighed.

"First the porridge, and now all this!" he said wearily. "I don't know where I'm going to begin."

As Reverend Watgod trudged off towards the vestry, PC Meredith and PC Walton looked at each other. PC Walton began to get his notebook out of the pocket of his tunic.

"What are you doing?" said PC Meredith.

"I'm writing everything down that's happened for the report."

"Have you forgotten what happened to us last time we did that?"

"No. But we've still got to write a report."

"No, we haven't."

"What do you mean?"

"If you think I'm spending another two hours trying to explain this lot, and risk losing my job on the grounds of insanity again, you've got another think coming!"

"We'll lose our jobs if we don't. The Reverend is hardly going to keep quiet about it. Anyway, it'll probably be front-page news once it gets out. I'll bet those stained glass windows were priceless."

"So, have you figured out what happened to that table yet?" enquired Reverend Watgod as he appeared a few minutes later, carrying a tray with three mugs of tea and a plate of digestive biscuits.

"I imagine this is going to be a difficult one to explain when you hand your report in." he continued.

"Well, it's certainly been a strange day." said PC Walton.

The three of them sat down on a pew and stared up at the big hole in the wall behind the alter table. Stars twinkled and glittered, and small dark clouds scurried across the night sky. The trees outside swayed gently in the cool breeze. Considering the events of the previous hour, the night suddenly seemed incredibly peaceful and silent.

"It's like the calm before the storm," said Reverend Watgod, as he dunked a digestive biscuit into his tea.

For the next five minutes, the three of them sat there in silence, apart from the occasional sound of slurping.

"Well I suppose we'd better get our report written up." said PC Meredith reluctantly.

"Should I start and tidy up the mess?" said Reverend Watgod.

"No. You'd better leave it as it is," said PC Meredith. "The crime scene boys will want to examine it first."

"In that case, I'll go and see if I can get the porridge off the kitchen walls."

"We'll let ourselves out when we've finished." said PC Walton.

"No, give me a shout when you're done. I'll need to lock the door after you."

As Reverend Watgod picked up the mugs and tray and headed off in the direction of the vestry, PC Meredith picked up his radio.

"I suppose we'd better get this over with and call it in."

Chapter Twenty Two

IN THE MAIN HALL OF the Natural History Museum in South Kensington, the fragile skeleton of a four million year old Oviraptor, suddenly exploded. A stone table now stood in its place.

Lubmila Stanisalv heard the explosion. She ran down the hallway as fast as she could, throwing her mop to one side in the process. It went straight through the front of a glass cabinet containing priceless artefacts. However, she was in such a hurry that she never noticed. When she arrived at the top of the stairs overlooking the main hall, she screamed. The part of the hall where the Oviraptor should have been was covered in broken bones and bits of wire.

At first, she failed to notice the stone table standing in the middle of the debris. She also failed to notice the large mop bucket on the second step.

As her left foot wedged in the bucket, she screamed once more and plunged down the stairs to land in a crumpled heap at the bottom. Five minutes later, she still couldn't get the mop bucket off her foot.

Despite being soaking wet, and with her foot jammed in a metal mop bucket, she clanked bravely across the

151

main hall towards a doorway. She went inside, and came out a few seconds later carrying a brush and dustpan.

"Minimum vage my bottom," she mumbled as she clanked over to the wreckage of the Oviraptor. She looked down at her dustpan and brush, and then at the three tons of dinosaur bones scattered across the floor. "There's never a big shovel ven you need one."

Chapter Twenty Three

IN A PUB OFF THE Earls Court Road, Topsiders were packed to the rafters. A live band was playing, and the music was loud and raw. It thundered out from a small stage in an endless wave of noise.

The crowd of Topsiders jostled with each other to get closer to the stage, or try to order drinks from the bar.

Rod, Charlie and Wedge stood at the side of the stage and waited for their turn to perform. They had recruited a new bass player for the night in the shape of Mags. Mags was small and blonde. She worked part-time at the same Pizza parlour as Charlie, and was studying art at St Martins College.

The Damnations finished their set and a fat bald man wearing a collarless shirt, red trousers and braces climbed onto the stage.

"Ladies and Gents – Let's hear it for The Damnations!"

The pub erupted in deafening applause and whistles as the band made their way from the stage. It was now Rod, Charlie, Wedge and Mags turn to entertain the crowds.

The Damnations had agreed to let Wedge use their drum kit. He sat down at the stool, and pulled a pair of drumsticks out of the pocket of his shirt.

"I'd now like to introduce the next band," continued the fat man. "Ladies and Gentlemen, I give you... The Rent Dodgers!"

The pub once more filled with noisy applause and whistles as they began to play.

As they opened up with 'Anarchy in the UK', by the Sex Pistols, three rather large female Topsiders pushed their way through the packed pub and attempted to reach the bar. Polite 'excuse mes' soon turned into pushing and barging as they forced their way through the crowd.

"Two Southern Comforts with Coke, and one Vodka with OJ." shouted Doreen Fudge, as she finally reached the bar, and slammed a truck-sized handbag on top of it.

She had decided to try to put the traumatic events of the day to one side, and go out with her friends. Of course, she hadn't told her friends what had happened earlier. After all, she wasn't even sure that Malcolm believed her story regarding her encounter with a small orange dragon - and he had witnessed what had happened in the garage inspection pit. Therefore she did not intend to open herself up to ridicule yet again.

After another three drinks, Doreen was well on her way to forgetting the events of the day and was ready for some dancing. She and her friends pushed their way through to a small gap near the front of the stage and bounced up and down to the music. The floor winced and groaned as the three of them crashed up and down.

The Rent Dodgers played another three songs before leaving the stage and heading for the bar. As they struggled through the crowd, Wedge was grabbed round the arm roughly. Turning round, he found himself staring at Doreen.

"Can I have your autograph?" she shouted above the noise.

Wedge thought she was trying to be funny, and tried to get past her, but she moved in front to stop him.

"I want your autograph...*please*," she shouted once more, before thrusting a pen and a beer mat into his hand.

Wedge took the pen and beer mat and started to write.

"My name is Doreen."

"I'm Wedge, and you're my first autograph." he laughed as he handed the signed beer mat back to her.

Meanwhile, Charlie, Rod and Mags had managed to squeeze their way to the bar. Wedge spotted them, and began to make his way over to them, but was pulled back by Doreen.

"Can you get me the autographs of the rest of the band?"

"I *suppose* so," replied Wedge.

Doreen looked round for her two friends but they had disappeared somewhere in the crowd, so she followed Wedge through the crowds to the bar to where Charlie Rod and Mags were.

Doreen got the rest of her autographs, and then spent the next half hour chatting and laughing with the band.

"Time please, ladies and gents!" Shouted one of the barmen.

Charlie had already arranged with the manager of the pub to leave all their instruments there until the following day, so along with the crowd of Topsiders they all made their way out into the crisp night air.

"Well, we've missed the last tube back," said Rod.

"No problem, we'll get one of the all night busses from the top of Earls Court Road." replied Charlie.

Doreen waited for her two friends to come out, but after a few minutes, she realised that they'd obviously gone without her.

"Charming." She mumbled to herself, before throwing her oversized handbag over her shoulder and running off down the road after Wedge, Charlie, Rod and Mags.

"Mind if I walk there with you?" she panted when she finally caught them up.

"Not at all." replied Wedge.

As they all walked down the street together, Doreen took a look at them and smiled. *These are a really nice group of people,* she thought to herself.

Chapter Twenty Four

VEMBER, SPOOGEMIGE AND CRIBLEE STOOD on the deserted platform at Gloucester Road station. Shadows danced across the tiled walls. A warm, gentle breeze blew down through the tunnels.

Eventually the Battenberg Twins and Germ joined them. With Vember in the lead, they moved cautiously down the corridors until they reached the escalators.

Here they paused. They stared at the long line of stationary metal steps leading up to ground level.

They began to climb, each locked in their own private fears.

At the top, a long line of barriers stretched across a brightly lit open space. On the other side of the barriers, a long corridor led to a large mesh grill. On the other side of this lay the unknown world of the Topsiders.

To Spoogemige and Criblee, it was all a tremendous adventure. They didn't have the experience of Vember. They didn't appreciate the dangers that lay ahead.

Spoogemige started running on the spot, and then, with a sudden and breathtaking explosion of speed, he vanished towards the barriers in a blur. Three seconds later he was leaning on the metal grill at the far end of the corridor and waving at them.

If he was hoping to impress Vember, it didn't work. She just glared at him.

When she and the rest of them reached the metal grill, she reached up and grabbed hold of one of his shoulders.

"Run off like that again, and I'll send you back to Brompton Road."

Her voice was uncompromising in its tone. Spoogemige looked down at her and suddenly felt even younger than he was.

The Battenberg Twins were already addressing the problem of the metal grill. A large brass padlock locked it. However, a few seconds later, it lay on the floor. The Battenberg Twins were master locksmiths. There wasn't a lock anywhere they could not break.

The six of them made their way out into the world of the Topsiders. The first thing they noticed was the cold. Down in the underground the temperature was always the same. Even the drafts that blew through the train tunnels were the same.

Vember led the way as they crept through the shadows. Spoogemige looked up at the vast emptiness above him. Small specs of brilliant white light sparkled through the darkness. Then he saw something that made his heart race. A huge white disk appeared slowly out from behind something else. A beautiful soft light danced across the buildings on either side of the road.

As Spoogemige stared up at the white disk, he was filled with wonder. The world in which the Topsiders lived was so different from his own.

Vember's hand reached up to his shoulder, startling him.

"Will you stop daydreaming?"

She led him firmly by the arm to where the others were standing opposite a large old building, with a big circular window in one of the walls.

"This must be the place," whispered Vember. "St. Stephens Church."

"What's a church?" asked Spoogemige.

Vember shrugged her shoulders.

They reached a large wooden door. Vember tried the handle. It was locked. However, that wasn't anything to worry about - the Battenberg Twins had it open in less than three seconds.

The cavernous main part of the church appeared deserted.

Unfortunately for the Stobes, it wasn't.

Vember walked over to where the remains of a stained glass window lay in pieces on the alter table. While Spoogemige stared in wonder at the ceiling, Criblee and the Battenberg Twins sat down in one of the pews just in front of the pulpit. Germ made his way silently up and down the rows of pews behind them, nicking the hymnbooks.

Vember turned round to watch him.

"Don't you dare nick anything."

Germ pointed his fingers at his chest.

"Me?" he protested. "As if!"

The minute Vember turned away, he slipped a large gold candlestick inside his overcoat and continued to pace around furtively.

Vember turned round again, to see him loitering next to a small table. On the wall behind it was a sign reading 'Collection Box. Please Give Generously'.

"Open your coat!"

"I'll catch cold."

"Open your coat NOW!"

Germ opened his coat, and nine hymnbooks and a gold candlestick fell on the floor.

"Hat!" she continued.

Germ took off his Bowler Hat. There, perched on top of his head, was the collection box.

"Can't you go anywhere without thieving stuff?"

"Of course I can't." He held his arms out to the side. "I'm a thief, what can I say?"

He screwed up his face. His eyes, which were very small to start with, disappeared under the folds of his baggy cheeks. He stroked his very long pointed chin, and tried to figure out how he could nick more stuff without Vember spotting it.

During all of this, Spoogemige continued to stare up at the ceiling. It was covered in ornate carvings and plasterwork. Usually when he looked up in the underground, all he saw were bricks. Bricks and tiles, and then more bricks and tiles.

He leaned back in wonder at how beautiful it was. It was only then that he noticed three white luminous sacks hanging from one of the carvings in the middle of the ceiling. They were all holding tiny red books.

"If you'll all turn to page one hundred and thirty four, we'll begin." shouted Neb.

The vaulted ceiling amplified the terrible sound of his voice. It bounced off the walls violently. Spoogemige, Criblee and Vember cupped their ears and grimaced. Germ threw himself to the ground, and pulled his overcoat over his head.

The Battenberg Twins, however, just sat there smiling and swinging their legs from side to side. They reached forward, picked up a red hymnbook, and turned to page one hundred and thirty four.

"*All things bright and beautiful, all creatures great and small. All things bright...*" sang Neb.

Dranoel, Stubb and the Battenberg Twins joined in.

Never before had such a gruesome and horrific noise been made in a church. Even God must have been holding his ears in despair.

Reverend Watgod came rushing out of the Vestry.

"What in all that is holy is going on?" he shouted, as he ran across to the alter table.

The sight that met his eyes was beyond the comprehension of even a man who believed in the devil.

"Oi mate! Did you know you've got bats in your belfry?" shouted Neb.

The rest of the Cribbit Snocklers burst out laughing.

Reverend Watgod looked up at them, then across to Spoogemige. His glazed eyes looked around the church, unable to comprehend the strange alien creatures who had invaded it.

He dropped to his knees, stared up in the air and cried out in desperation.

"Is this a test, Oh Lord?" He clasped his hands together and waited for an answer. He didn't get one. Well not the one he wanted.

"What's twelve multiplied by fifteen divided by nine?" said Neb.

"*What?*" screamed the Reverend.

"Well, you said you wanted a test," replied Neb.

"I'm talking to the Lord, you evil creature of Satan!"

Neb looked round at Dranoel and Stubb and nodded approvingly.

"Not bad. Not bad at all. He's definitely got potential," He looked back at the Reverend. "Now, try it with a bit more venom in your voice."

"Oh Lord, what have I done to anger you so?" cried Reverend Watgod. "Is it the porridge?" He bowed his head. "I've tried, Oh Lord. I've really tried, but it just will not come out. I've even had it on a boil wash."

Vember walked slowly over to him. With one eye watching the Cribbit Snocklers every move, she crouched down next to him, and put an arm round his shoulders. He looked up into her eyes.

She may have been a creature the likes of which he had never seen before, not even in books, but there was no denying her beauty.

He looked deep into her large, dark grey eyes. There was something hypnotic about them. For some inexplicable reason, he suddenly felt calm.

Which was a lot more than Spoogemige, Criblee and Germ did. They could see what Vember could not. Standing in the doorway at the far end of the church were Flem, Wobblett and Skerrett.

"Showtime." said Neb gleefully.

Wobblett charged down the isle in the direction of Spoogemige, punching his big fat blobby fists back and forth. Flem jumped over the pews in front of him and headed in the direction of Criblee and the Battenberg Twins. Meanwhile, Skerrett began to sneak towards Vember.

She didn't see him, but she smelt his rancid breath. As he reached underneath his bin liner and pulled out a long piece of lead piping, Vember turned round. With her hands still resting on Reverend Watgod's shoulders, she kicked a long slender leg towards this throat.

Skerrett reeled, as the force of the kick sent him flying backwards into a row of pews. Before he could get up again, Vember leapt across and wrenched the lead piping from his claw. Looking up at the ceiling, she hurled it at the Cribbit Snocklers, whilst at the same time delivering a ferocious blow to the side of Skerrett's head with her knee.

The Cribbit Snocklers dived just in time, as the lead piping smashed into the roof where they had been hanging.

"Cowardice is the better part of valour," shouted Neb as they flew across the church, and out of the large hole where the stained glass window used to be.

There was no way that Wobblett could catch Spoogemige. By the time he reached where Spoogemige had been standing, Spoogemige was on the other side of the church.

Criblee and the Battenberg Twins were not so lucky. As Criblee dived under a pew, Flem lashed out with a knife and caught Nuggley Battenberg on the back. It tore through his leather tunic right down to the bone. As blood gushed from the wound, Flem went in for the kill.

Despite being terrified, Criblee dived across and grabbed Flem's arm just as he was about to deliver the fatal blow. They both fell to the floor. Criblee banged his head on the side of a pew as they landed, which knocked him out.

Flem picked himself up, and stared down at Criblee. He raised the knife in the air, spat a stream of snot and saliva onto him and smiled. However, just as he was about to thrust the knife into Criblee's prone body, Doodee Battenberg leapt across and bit his arm. Flem shook the tiny body off, and threw it across the floor. Bending down, he pushed the blade to Criblee's throat.

Suddenly, his head was wrenched backwards as Vember grabbed him in a fierce headlock. She rammed her left knee into the side of his head repeatedly until he fell to the floor.

On the other side of the church, Wobblett collapsed from exhaustion as he tried in vain to catch Spoogemige.

Spoogemige ran over to Criblee. Kneeling down he cradled his head in his enormous hands. Vember tried to tend to Nuggley Battenberg's wound as best she could. She tore a strip of material from her robe and wrapped it tightly round the upper part of his back. Doodee Battenberg pulled a small biscuit out of her pocket.

"Eat. It will help,"

During all of this, Reverend Watgod had just watched in stunned silence.

Vember walked over to him. Striding over the unconscious body of Skerrett, she knelt beside him once more. She turned round to the other Stobes.

"Drag the Darkenbads outside. Make sure you hide them. I'll be out in a minute."

"I've got a bad back," said Germ, climbing out of from the back of the pulpit where he'd been hiding.

Vember looked at him with contempt. "Just do it!" she snapped.

As the rest of them began to drag the Darkenbads out, Vember reached out and put her hands on Reverend Watgod's shoulders.

"This Lord, this God that you shout for. Does he exist?" she whispered.

His hands were still clasped together, and he was trembling.

"He does in my heart."

"Yes, but does he actually exist? Have you ever seen him?"

"No. It is a thing we call faith. It means believing in something even though you can't prove of its existence."

Vember smiled at him. "Are all Topsiders like you?"

"Topsiders?"

"It's what we call the creatures in your world."

"My world? Where is your world?"

"Closer than you think." she smiled.

Vember looked round towards the entrance to the church. Spoogemige was standing in the doorway looking anxious.

"Close the door," said Vember.

She didn't want any of the others to see what she was about to do. Only Wattage knew about her special power. Even Fuddlerook, her greatest friend, and the one with whom she trusted her life didn't know.

It was a power handed down within her breed. A power she could only be use to protect the identity of the Stobes.

Vember looked into Reverend Watgod's eyes. She reached up and put her hands on the side of his head. He started to say something. It was a prayer. He was sure he was about to die.

Vember's eyes began to glow. They changed colour to a bright luminescent blue. The brightness was dazzling.

The light from her eyes became increasingly intense. It then changed from blue to green, and an almost blinding flashing of colour began to swirl round and round his head, lighting up the area all around with its supernatural glow.

Reverend Watgod was hypnotised. The blue and green light from her eyes seemed to penetrate into his mind. He felt dizzy, yet numb. It was as if her eyes were emptying his mind. With a shudder, he slumped forward into her arms, unconscious.

Vember gently picked him up, and carried him through into the Vestry, and into a small room next to it. There was a desk with a small mirror above it, and a narrow single bed. Next to the bed was a small table, on which lay a small pile of books and a glass of water. Above the bed was a cross. Vember stared at it. A shiver ran down her spine.

She laid him down gently on the bed, and pulled a blanket over him. Walking over to the desk, she looked in the mirror. Turning her head to one side, she reached up and pulled her long raven hair to one side, and stared at the small tattoo in the nape of her neck. It was a tattoo of a cross. She'd always had it. She didn't know where it came from, or what it meant.

She turned away from the mirror and walked back out of the room.

"Sleep well, Topsider. Sleep well," she whispered as she closed the door.

Spoogemige stood anxiously outside the church door. They had hidden Wobblett, Flem and Skerrett behind some bushes down the side.

As Vember came out, he smiled with relief. He noticed that her eyes weren't their normal, dark grey colour.

"Your eyes. They're a different colour." He said.

Vember smiled at him, lowered her head and placed the palms of her hands over her eyes. When she removed them moments later, her eyes were once more their usual dark grey.

"What was wrong with your eyes?"

"Nothing. It must just be the cold night air."

Spoogemige stared at her with a questioning look on his face.

"Where did you put the Darkenbads?" continued Vember.

"They're down the side here," said Criblee pointing to the bushes. "Are they dead?"

"No." said Vember, examining their unconscious bodies.

"We need to move them quickly. Back down to the underground." she continued.

"Leave the twazlets there. Let 'em rot!" spat Germ.

"We can't," replied Vember. "If the Topsiders discover them, they'll discover us too."

She grabbed hold of Wobblett's leg and dragged him out from underneath the bushes.

"Quickly, get the other two and pull them round to the front." she continued.

Spoogemige and Criblee took hold of Flem and Skerrett, and followed Vember to the front of the church.

"Will this be any use?" Said the Battenberg Twins. They were pushing an old supermarket trolley filled with traffic cones.

Vember smiled affectionately at Nuggley Battenberg.

"How are you feeling?"

"It's painful, but I'll be alright." he replied bravely.

After removing the traffic cones, they loaded the three Darkenbads into the trolley. Germ came out from behind a tree where he had been skiving as usual, and proceeded to place a traffic cone on each of the Darkenbads heads.

"What's the point of that?" snapped Vember.

"Nothing whatsoever, apart from giving me a laugh,"

"Spoogemige," said Vember. "Do you think you can get the Darkenbads and the trolley back to the underground very quickly without being seen?"

Spoogemige smiled. "Of course I can. Where shall I put them?"

"Push them into one of the tunnels and leave them there. With a bit of luck one of the trains will finish the job."

"What if they wake up before then?"

"I'll make sure the twazlets don't," shouted Germ, picking up an old piece of rusty railing lying on the ground. He was just about to begin battering the Darkenbads round the head with it, when Vember turned round and grabbed hold of it.

"You're very brave when it comes to fighting unconscious Darkenbads, aren't you?" she said scathingly. "If only you showed that much courage when they're standing up."

She threw the railing to the ground and sneered at Germ as he skulked off towards the bushes. She then turned to Spoogemige.

"Don't worry, those three will be out for hours."

She reached across and patted him on the shoulder.

"Go on. Off you go!" she smiled. "We'll meet you at Earls Court."

Spoogemige smiled back at her, and his heart gave a jump. He grabbed hold of the trolley. Hunching his shoulders up, his skinny legs began to move up and down. His enormous feet banged down on the ground. Then, with an explosion of speed, he, the trolley, and the Darkenbads disappeared down the road.

Vember pulled one of Spogworth's phones out from under her robe.

Outside Gloucester Road tube station, a small orange dragon rummaged around inside a plastic carrier bag, trying to find what was ringing.

"Yo," he answered.

As he listened, he munched on a piece of freshly burnt toast

Putting the phone back in his bag, he turned to the others.

"The table isn't at the church,"

Chapter Twenty Five

FUDDLEROOK, FLIGBOGE AND SCORCHINGTON
stared at the gigantic building in front of them.

Two enormous towers soared up into the darkness. A
huge curved arch connected them. On either side of the
towers, the building continued for what seemed like miles
in both directions, dominating the landscape.

They stood speechless. They had never seen anything
so big.

As they walked towards the steps leading up to the
entrance, each one of them felt incredibly small and
insignificant.

None of them noticed that Plankton was missing.

Even Plankton didn't notice he was missing. He was
too pre-occupied by the contents of a bin filled with
rubbish. It was only when he'd finished eating something
stale and disgusting that he looked around and realised he
was alone.

He wiped his grubby battered hands on his grubby
battered tunic, and stared up at the night sky. His facial
features were hidden behind ragged, knotted brown hair,
which was so long that it almost completely covered the
top half of his body.

Feeling depressed, he tried to remember where he should have been. He paced up and down the pavement, unsure of where to go or what to do. He didn't like this world of the Topsiders. It was big, cold and depressing.

As Plankton wandered up and down, he got more and more depressed as he began to realise he was stranded.

Hidden in the shadows of the entrance to Gloucester Road station, a dark sinister figure watched him and grinned.

Opposite the large building with the two enormous towers, Plankton suddenly spotted the others, making their way slowly up a long line of steps leading up to the huge doors at the entrance to the building. His heart pounded in his tiny chest. For a moment, he no longer felt depressed. Safety was only a few steps away.

He thought about shouting across to them, to tell them to wait. However, he couldn't be bothered. After all, he was only yards away from them. No, he'd catch them up at the top of the steps.

He didn't.

Just as he stepped off the pavement, he felt something grab hold of his hair from behind, and pull him violently to the floor. A tall dark figure dressed in black dragged him into the shadows and crouched down over his tiny defenceless body. Plankton found himself staring up into a pair of coal black eyes.

The last thing he saw was the serrated metal blade of a dagger glinting in the moonlight, as it plunged into his chest, and ended his life.

Ripperton stood up, and wiped Plankton's blood from the dagger with her fingers. She stared across the road and watched the other Stobes reach the entrance to the building. She smiled.

At the door, Scorchington turned round and stared across the road at the shadows on the other side.

"Where's Plankton?"

Fuddlerook turned round. He too looked across to the opposite side of the road.

"You know what he's like. He'll have got lost!" said Fligboge in his usual caring and concerned manner.

Fuddlerook lifted up the flap of the old leather shoulder bag he was carrying. The Gerbil Brothers popped their heads out and looked around. They were dressed in toy Action Man outfits.

"Need some advance scouting, Sir?" said Colin Gerbil. He was dressed as Arctic Warfare Action Man, and his voice was far too deep to come from such a small creature.

"Ready to lock and load. Sir!" said Frank Gerbil. He was holding a miniature plastic rifle, and dressed as Jungle Action Man. His voice was even deeper.

"Packed and ready to roll. Sir!" said Seb Gerbil, from behind a scuba diving mask with a snorkel hanging off it. He was dressed as Action Man Frogman.

They climbed out of the shoulder bag, jumped to the ground, and stood to attention next to Fuddlerook's feet.

"We've lost Plankton," said Fuddlerook. "Sneak back towards the station, and see if you can find him."

"Commence covert operation Plankton, Sir!" said Colin Gerbil to the other two.

The Gerbil brothers began to make their way down the steps. Every few moments, they would dive to the ground, roll over, and adopt sniper positions for no reason whatsoever.

"Furtling Twazlets!" exclaimed Fligboge. "It'll take them all night just to get to the bottom of the steps at this rate."

The Gerbil brothers ignored his comments, and eventually disappeared out of sight.

"Scorch! Locks!" said Fuddlerook.

Scorchington looked up at the huge wooden doors. The door handles containing the locks were too high for him to reach. Fuddlerook smiled. He bent down and cupped his huge hands together.

"Need a lift?"

Scorchington stepped onto his hands and Fuddlerook swung him up so he was level with the door handles. A large powerful jet of fire shot out of his mouth. Soon the locks were glowing bright red.

"Screwdriver." said Scorchington.

Fuddlerook held him with one hand, reached inside his diver's suit and pulled out a long screwdriver. He passed it up to Scorchington, who pushed it carefully into one of the locks at a slight angle. He tapped it up and then down, and then to one side. He moved closer to make sure it was in the correct position.

"Hammer or big hard fist." he continued.

Fuddlerook smiled and lowered him to the ground. He then stepped back from the doors, pulled one of his huge powerful arms back, and slammed his massive fist into the end of the screwdriver. It shot straight through the lock. As one of the door handles fell to the ground, the doors swung gently open.

"The Battenberg Twins would have had that opened in half the time." muttered Fligboge, as he walked passed Fuddlerook and Scorchington and entered the building.

Down on the road, the Gerbil brothers were busy diving to the ground, rolling over and adopting sniper positions. They didn't notice the three dark shadows crossing the road in the opposite direction, heading for where they'd just come from.

Moving into the shadows, they found the body of Plankton.

"It looks like Plankton's dead. Sir!" said Frank Gerbil.

"What now. Sir!" said Colin Gerbil.

Seb Gerbil prodded Plankton's body with one of his scuba diving flippers.

"Time to stop being dead. Sir!" he said.

For the next few minutes, Plankton remained dead.

Then slowly, his left leg began to twitch. His right leg started twitching shortly after, followed by his whole body. After several minutes of twitching, Plankton raised his head from the ground, and sat up. He looked down at his blood-covered tunic and sighed.

"Glad to have you back Plankton. Sir!" said Colin Gerbil.

Plankton wasn't too sure. He had a headache. After being stabbed in the chest with a nine-inch serrated dagger, most creatures would be quite happy to come out of it with just a headache. However, Plankton wasn't most creatures, and he wasn't.

"What's it like to be indestructible? Sir!" said Frank Gerbil.

"Awful." replied Plankton.

He slowly got to his feet and stared around. He still didn't know where he was.

This was actually perfectly normal for Plankton. He very rarely knew where he was. Being lost was as normal for Plankton as breathing. There had never been a single day as far as anyone could remember when he hadn't been lost at least once. It wasn't that he was stupid. He simply had no awareness of where he was, where he'd been or where he was going. That part of his brain was quite simply missing. He once got lost in his bed for three days.

All of this made him very depressed.

However, what depressed Plankton most of all, was that on top of all of this, some cruel twist of fate had also made him indestructible.

He had been run over by trains, electrocuted, fallen down ventilator shafts and buried under rubble. He had also now been stabbed to death on five occasions. Moreover, after each one it was the same depressing story - ten minutes of unconsciousness, followed by five minutes of twitching legs, followed by a terrible headache for the rest of the day.

173

Yet all this great power of being indestructible was completely wasted on Plankton. What's the point in being indestructible if you're a manic-depressive who can never remember where he is, where he's been or where he's going? Nobody realised this better than Plankton, and it made him very depressed.

In fact, it made him so depressed that he had thought of ending it all on several occasions. However, being indestructible meant this was not an option, which of course made him even more depressed.

Whilst the Gerbil Brothers and Plankton made their way across the road, Fuddlerook, Fligboge and Scorchington made their way into the great hall of The Natural History Museum.

They stood speechless. They had never seen a room so huge. It was enormous. The ceiling was a gigantic curved arch seemingly hundreds of feet high. The walls were lined with massive round stone columns reaching all the way to the roof. At the far end, a huge staircase with ornately carved balustrades ran across the hall from one wall to the other. Running down the sides of the hall were smaller archways leading off to other parts of the building.

However, as impressive and intimidating as the great hall was, it was what was in it that really stunned them.

Skeletons.

Gigantic skeletons, reaching all the way up to the ceiling of the great hall. Skeletons of strange creatures so big, they had to tilt their heads back to see the top of them.

Scorchington noticed that one in particular looked like a gigantic version of him. Well, a gigantic version of him minus the wings, T-shirt and carrier bag. As he walked off to take a closer look at it, Fuddlerook and Fligboge walked over to the other side of the great hall.

Scorchington looked up at the huge skeleton towering above him. It was standing on a large wooden plinth.

Several parts of it were held together with bolts and wire. Standing on the wooden plinth was a sign.

Diplodocus Dinosaur (Nickname Dippie).

It was taller than the tallest section of the underground and as long as an entire train. He walked down the length of it until he came to its head. It seemed to have a welcoming smile on its face.

As he pondered whether it really could be a distant relative, he farted loudly.

The fart echoed around the massive hall. It bounced off the walls, and drifted up to the ceiling getting louder and louder. It reverberated around the ceiling for a few seconds, before disappearing off to the staircases at the far end. A few seconds later, it bounced off those and came back to him.

He liked this. He liked it a lot. He farted again. Once more, it echoed loudly around the hall. This was fun. It was as if there were fifty Scorchington's all farting at the same time.

He clenched his claws, squeezed his bottom tightly and concentrated as hard as he could. His face screwed up into a grimace, as he tried to summon up the fart of all farts. A hall with such spectacular acoustics deserved a spectacular fart.

Unfortunately, he over did it. He squeezed too hard. Quickly covering his bottom up with his carrier bag, he shuffled off in embarrassment to clean himself up.

Whilst Scorchington had been amusing himself with the halls acoustics, Fuddlerook and Fligboge were looking at another sign on a wooden plinth.

Oviraptor Philoceratops.

However, standing on the wooden plinth was a very strange exhibit. It certainly wasn't the kind of exhibit you'd normally expect to find at a natural history museum, and it certainly wasn't '*Oviraptor Philoceratops'*.

It was a table. An old stone table. There was the faint aroma of sulphur, burnt fish and rotten eggs.

"Is that what I think it is?" said Fligboge.

"It's Wattage's table," replied Fuddlerook, smiling.

"The old turnip head was right then?" said Fligboge shaking his head in amazement.

They were so busy staring at the table that they didn't notice the three figures standing on the stairs at the far end of the great hall.

Ripperton, Woogums and Gobbit had certainly noticed them though. As Ripperton ran her fingers along the razor sharp edge of her dagger, she stared coldly and calculatingly at Fuddlerook.

Of all the Stobes, there was one she wanted to kill the most. Her hatred ran deep. It coursed through her bloodless veins like molten evil. She reached up and ran her black fingernails across the small tattoo in the nape of her neck.

She could wait though. She would catch up with her soon enough. For now, she would have to settle for the next best thing. Fuddlerook!

Ripperton studied him closely. The great warrior Fuddlerook certainly lived up to his reputation physically. She looked at his massive arms and legs and smiled. Maybe he would give her the challenge she was looking for. At least until she killed him. Reaching inside her leather jacket, she pulled out another dagger. With one in each hand, she turned to Woogums and Gobbit, and nodded. It was time.

Woogums didn't see her command at first. He was too busy chewing the stone balustrades. Gobbit was also too busy draining the last drops from a bottle of something ghastly looking to notice either. The sharp point of daggers pressing into both their throats soon attracted their attention.

Fuddlerook and Fligboge had finished examining the table, and were now looking round to see where Scorchington was so they could phone Wattage and let him know they'd found the table.

"I'll stay here and keep my eye on the table. You go and find Scorchington." Said Fuddlerook.

Fligboge walked off in the direction of the huge skeleton where Scorchington had last been. He muttered and cursed to himself as usual, as he made his way towards the dinosaur.

Ripperton smiled as she saw that Fuddlerook was now alone. They would be much easier to pick off now that they were separated. Gobbit started to make his way towards where Fligboge was heading, whilst Woogums began sneaking down the wall on the left in search of Scorchington.

Ripperton meanwhile homed in on her pray - Fuddlerook.

Stealth and surprise were not exactly the traits of either Gobbit or Woogums. In Gobbit's case, it was because he was almost permanently drunk. Woogums on the other hand, had the same level of intelligence as the piles of bricks he spent most of his time eating.

Concentrating hard, Gobbit managed to get almost within striking distance of Fligboge, but unfortunately, lost concentration at the crucial moment and walked straight into the one hundred foot long dinosaur he had failed to spot. One of the bones went straight in his left eye. His screams echoed around the huge hall.

Fligboge turned round, and ran back towards Fuddlerook. The screams alerted Scorchington, just in time. As he walked out from under one of the arches running down the side of the hall, Woogums leapt out in front of him.

"Kill the dragon, ha ha, kill the dragon!" he shouted as he hurled himself at Scorchington.

Scorchington managed to step back just as Woogums flew past him. As Woogums crashed to the floor, Scorchington ran across towards Fuddlerook.

With Gobbit and Woogums in full snarling chase, Fligboge and Scorchington ran as fast as they could.

Fuddlerook was so busy watching the trouble his friends were in, that he only realised the danger he himself was in when it was too late.

The second group of Cribbit Snocklers comprising Bodge, Rollo, Lug and Pratt arrived just in time to watch the action. They positioned themselves on the underside of the archway of the main door, and hung there in anticipation.

"Best seats in the house," grinned Bodge.

In a spectacularly athletic leap, Ripperton somersaulted across Wattage's table and sank a dagger deep into Fuddlerook's back. He span round in agony and tried to pull the dagger out, but before he could, Ripperton lunged at his throat with the other dagger. He put his arms up to protect himself. He roared in pain as the razor sharp blade slashed across his forearms.

As Fuddelrook dropped to his knees, Ripperton reached round and pulled the dagger out of his back. Fuddlerook winced in pain as blood poured from the wound. He collapsed onto the floor. Stepping back, she stood in front of him, daggers raised. She smiled coldly at him, and crouched down over him.

"You are such a disappointment to me." she sneered, tilting her head slightly to one side. "I thought you'd be much harder to kill than this."

Fuddlerook looked up at her.

"I am," he replied, as he hammered his right fist into the side of her. Ripperton's body buckled under the blow, and she let out a blood-curdling scream. As she dropped to the floor, Fuddlerook's left fist smashed into the side of her head.

As Ripperton lay on the floor, Fuddlerook slowly picked himself up and staggered away. However, as he stepped over Ripperton, she suddenly rolled back, swung round and, kicking both legs at him, delivered a fierce blow to Fuddlerook's stomach. He fell to the ground. In a split second, Ripperton leapt to her feet, and stood over him, clutching a dagger in her left hand. She reached up with her right hand and ran her fingers along the deep gash above her eye. Bringing her hand down again, she looked at her blood-covered fingers, and smiled.

"Not bad. Not bad at all." she whispered, wiping them across the front of his diver's suit. "But now I'm bored, and you must die!"

Just as she was about to thrust the dagger into his prone body, both Scorchington and Fligboge dived onto her back. All three of them fell to the floor.

Pushing Fligboge off her Ripperton snarled and began to lash out with her dagger. Scorchington managed to untangle himself just in time, as in a huge arc, Ripperton's dagger swung past him. It missed him by millimetres. His carrier bag was not so lucky. The blade slashed it open, spilling the contents onto the floor. He looked down and noticed that Ripperton's dagger had slashed through two loaves of bread.

Standing up, he let out a roar of anger, and breathed a huge jet of fire into the air.

"You've sliced my sliced!" He screamed. "Never ever mess with the bread!"

He turned round and proceeded to kick Ripperton repeatedly in the stomach.

Unfortunately for Fligboge, he was kicked several times too, as he tried to move out of the way.

Whilst Ripperton and Fligboge struggled to avoid Scorchington's frantic kicking, Fuddlerook pushed himself to his feet and started to pull Scorchington off them. Scorchington's feet were still lashing out as Fuddlerook finally carried him away.

In all the confusion, none of them noticed that Woogums and Gobbit were about to join in the fight.

While Woogums charged at Fuddlerook from the right, Gobbit decided to leap over the stone table, and come at him from the left.

He still hadn't fully recovered the sight in his left eye after running into the dinosaur earlier. As he ran towards the table, he tripped over the edge of the wooden plinth. Falling forwards, his right eye smashed into the corner of the table and he slumped to the floor.

Woogums, meanwhile, had been gaining ground quickly. As he got nearer, he started laughing and shouting.

"Ha ha kill the beardy man, kill the beardy man!"

Fuddlerook spotted him and swung round. Lifting Scorchington high in the air, he charged at him. Scorchington's legs were still kicking and lashing out as they collided.

Woogums head snapped backwards on his neck, as Scorchington's kicking feet slammed into his face. Dropping Scorchington to the ground, Fuddlerook turned and leapt on top of Woogums, grabbing him in a fierce headlock and wrapping his massive legs around his waist.

Woogums struggled to break free, but his strength was no match for the immense power of Fuddlerook. He held him tightly. The more Woogums struggled, the more Fuddlerook tightened his grip around his throat. A few moments later the struggling stopped. Woogums body went limp, as he fell into unconsciousness.

Ripperton meanwhile, landed a vicious blow to Fligboge's head as she kicked him away from her.

Picking up her daggers, she jumped up onto the stone table. She waited for Fuddlerook to push Woogum's body to one side and get up, before throwing one of the daggers at him. He ducked easily out of the way.

Screaming in frustration, Ripperton threw the other dagger at him. Once again, he dodged effortlessly out of the way as he walked towards her.

At exactly that moment, the Gerbil Brothers and Plankton walked into the great hall. Plankton let out a depressing sigh, as Ripperton's dagger flew through the air and went straight into his chest.

"Here we go again." he said as he fell to the floor.

"Look's like Plankton's dead again. Sir!" said Colin Gerbil.

"Affirmative Sir!" said Frank Gerbil, as Plankton landed on top of him.

Underneath the stone table, Gobbit started to come round. He pulled himself up using the top of the table, until he was leaning across it and staring directly at Ripperton's feet. He grabbed hold of them to pull himself up further, but instead knocked her off balance, and they both fell onto the table.

In the process, one of Gobbit's claws knocked the gold peg out its hole. He picked it up, looked at it, and then put it back in one of the other holes.

Ripperton kicked Gobbit away and, sneering at him, began to climb off the table. But before she could get off it, a loud bang came from the table, followed by a large explosion. The smell of sulphur, burnt fish and rotten eggs filled the air.

When the clouds of smoke cleared, Fuddlerook, Fligboge and Scorchington looked around. The table, Gobbit and Ripperton were no longer there.

At the far end of the hall, the Gerbil Brothers stood around the dead body of Plankton. Woogums meanwhile, was still unconscious on the floor behind them.

Scorchington picked up his ripped carrier bag, and looked down at his damaged loaves of bread and the rest of his belongings scattered on the floor.

He huffed and looked across at where Woogums was lying. Then he marched over and kicked him very hard, twice!

Walking back to the remains of his carrier bag, he bent down and picked up his phone. He scratched his head as he tried to remember the number to Spogworth's phone.

"Don't tell me," said Fligboge, "You've forgotten the number of Spogworth's phone?"

"No!" replied Scorchington still scratching his head. "I've just got an itch."

Fligboge raised his eyebrows, and sighed.

Scorchington dialled what he thought was Spogworth's number, and waited. Eventually someone at the other end answered.

"Yo Spog, the table was here, but now it's not."

"Who is this?" replied the voice at the other end.

"It's Scorchington, who's that?"

"It's Gino's Restaurant Italiano, and we have no tables as we are closed. Do you know what the time is? It's 1.30 am in the morning!"

"Stop messing about Spogworth and put Wattage on,"

"How about you stop messing about and go and prank call someone else?"

"Listen Spogworth, you stupid twazlet. Put Wattage on now and stop being a stupid Stobe!"

"Right that's it. You've done it now. I'm calling the Police. Just see if I don't. I'm getting sick to death of these prank calls!"

The phone went dead. Scorchington looked at it and shook it furiously. He then pressed the redial button.

"Gino's Restaurant Italiano," snapped the voice the other end again.

"Will you put Wattage on now?"

"Right. I've got your number," screamed the voice at the other end. "I'm definitely reporting you to the Police. It's like this every single night. If it's not someone trying to order a taxi, it's someone phoning for a plumber. And if it's not that, then it's someone complaining about their broadband connection!"

The shouting stopped. It was replaced by the sound of gentle sobbing. Then the phone went dead again.

Scorchington looked at the phone and started to whistle nervously. A sheepish, slightly worried expression spread across his face. He looked round to see Fligboge and Fuddlerook staring at him with their arms folded across their chests.

Fuddlerook reached down with the palm of his huge hand open.

"Give!"

Scorchington placed the phone into onto the palm of his hand and lowered his head. He then turned round, and as if nothing had happened, began picking up the contents of his carrier bag whilst whistling *Ace of Spades*.

"What are we going to do about him?" said Fligboge pointing at the unconscious body of Woogums.

"Well we can't leave him here," replied Fuddlerook. "We'll have to carry him back with us and dump him in the nearest tunnel, before going to meet the others at Earls Court."

Whilst Fuddlerook called Wattage to tell him what had happened, Scorchington finished repairing his carrier bag by tying lots of knots in it. He then followed Fuddlerook and Fligboge out towards the main entrance.

Plankton lay on the floor, his legs twitching, while the Gerbil Brothers climbed up Fuddlerook's legs and into his shoulder bag.

"Plankton should be undead in a couple of minutes. Sir!" said Colin Gerbil.

Sure enough, after a few more minutes of twitching, Plankton sat up.

"Are you alright?" said Fuddlerook.

"I'm very depressed," replied Plankton, pulling Ripperton's dagger from out of his chest. He looked at it for a couple of seconds, before throwing it to the floor, and pushing himself to his feet. "And I've got a terrible headache."

Fuddlerook picked up the dagger. As he studied it closely, he failed to notice that some of Plankton's blood was dripping off the serrated edge, and directly into one of the open wounds on his arms.

Wiping the remaining blood off the blade, he put it carefully inside his diver's suit, before picking up and throwing the unconscious body of Woogums over his shoulder.

Then together, they all walked out into the stillness of the night.

"I thought that was going to be a lot more violent?" said Pratt in disappointment.

"Where too now?" Said Bodge.

He had forgotten Neb's instructions, and looked at the others.

"Well?"

"Don't look at me," replied Rollo.

"I thought *you* knew?" said Lug looking at Bodge.

Bodge glared at him, and then looked at Pratt.

"What about you?"

Pratt looked blankly back at him.

"So *none* of us knows where to go next?" said Bodge, starting to get angry.

The others shrugged their shoulders.

"Well in *that* case, we'll have to head back to the Underground and wait there?"

Chapter Twenty Six

IN A TUNNEL, A FEW hundred yards down from the platform at South Kensington tube station, a dinted and battered supermarket trolley containing the unconscious bodies of Flem, Wobblett and Skerrett lay on its side in the middle of the tracks of the District Line.

Several miles further down the same stretch of track, the blurred shape of a ridiculously tall creature hurtled through the tunnels like a bullet. It moved so fast that a group of Topsider's working on the platform at Embankment never noticed it flash through the station.

As he sped past, Spoogemige suddenly realised he was heading down the District Line the wrong way. Instead of heading west down the District Line, and then south to Earls Court, he was travelling in completely the opposite direction. By the time he came to a halt, he was at Aldgate East, several stations further down the line.

Being able to accelerate from 0 – 70 mph in under two seconds and reach a top speed of over 170 mph was one thing. *Stopping* was another. Once he reached top speed, emergency stops were out of the question. The straps on his sandals simply couldn't handle the braking force. Therefore, he had to slow down gradually. This meant that he regularly overshot the station he was going too. Today was no exception.

Instead of simply going back the way he came, which anyone with even half a brain cell would have done, Spoogemige decided on a different route. He would cross over onto the Hammersmith & City Line, and then get onto the Metropolitan Line at Liverpool Street. He could then join the Bakerloo Line at Baker Street, and change onto the District Line at Paddington, then straight down to Earls Court. This was the equivalent of driving from Manchester to Birmingham via Norway.

Spoogemige set off once more at top speed. However, he somehow managed to overshoot Liverpool Street by four stations, and ended up at a dead end at Hammersmith, 3 miles away. Eventually, after getting lost once more, he finally found himself back where he had started, on the District Line at South Kensington.

The supermarket trolley was still on its side in the middle of the tracks, but now, Flem, Wobblett and Skerrett were starting to come round.

Spoogemige had no intention of hanging about, and sped off down the track again, this time in the right direction, narrowly missing a large dumper truck coming the opposite way. The Topsider driving it didn't notice him. He didn't notice the overturned supermarket trolley further down either. Flem, Wobblett and Skerrett struggled frantically to climb out, but it was too late. The dumper truck hit them.

Despite their screams, the Topsider never heard or saw them, as his truck pushed them down the track. It was half a mile and four stations later, before they managed to throw themselves free of the trolley.

Outside Earls Court station, Wattage, Spogworth, Hetty and the Mole in the Wall Gang started making their way down the road, which would hopefully lead to Cromwell Hospital. Eventually they reached a junction. They stared in stunned silence at the gigantic concrete building on the opposite side of the road. It was far from deserted.

Topsiders in brightly lit vehicles were coming and going, and the lights from the windows of the building lit up the area around.

Hetty didn't like it one bit. The oven mitts on her antlers were swinging from side to side as her antlers trembled. She fidgeted nervously with the frilly collar of her blouse, and kept trying to smooth creases out of her jacket, even though there weren't any.

Wattage watched her closely. Whilst there was a chance that he and Spogworth could sneak into the hospital, he wasn't sure about Hetty. A four-foot neurotic moose isn't the easiest of things to sneak into somewhere.

The Mole in the Wall gang sat in a row on the kerb at the side of the road. They were all studying a grid closely. Being experts at tunnelling, they automatically got to wherever they were going by digging a tunnel. Even if there was already a tunnel there, they would still dig another one.

Therefore, instead of simply walking across the road to get to the hospital, they were planning to dig a tunnel underneath it. The grid would give them a bit of a headstart. They all stood up and formed a circle round the grid. Then, using their razor sharp digging claws, they lifted the grid cover up, and carried it onto the pavement.

They were just about to jump down into the drain, when Spoogemige suddenly appeared from nowhere at top speed, tripped over the grid cover and fell head first down the drain.

"What are you doing here?" said Wattage.

Spoogemige pulled his head out of the drain and stood up.

"I overshot the station." replied Spoogemige, wiping the contents of the drain from his face.

"Well I suppose you'd better come with us now." said Wattage.

Wattage then turned to Spogworth.

"Call Vember, and let her know that Spoogemige is with us."

Chapter Twenty Seven

VEMBER, CRIBLEE, GERM AND THE Battenberg
Twins were already at Earls Court station when
Spogworth phoned them.

Being situated above ground, Earls Court was a very
exposed and dangerous place for Stobes, even in the early
hours of the morning.

As they waited for the others, at the far end of the
platform nearest to the tunnel entrance, Vember re-
dressed Nuggley Battenburg's wound. Meanwhile, Germ
was busy breaking into one of the waiting rooms to see if
there was anything worth nicking. Criblee, on the other
hand, sat quietly nursing the large bruise on the side of
his head.

They all felt vulnerable and exposed. Even Vember
was anxious. As they waited in the cold damp night air,
Vember heard sounds coming from inside the tunnel
behind them. She quickly jumped to her feet, and moved
silently towards the tunnel entrance, her body pressed
tight against the wall.

As she stared into the darkness, she could see four
figures making their way towards her. A smile spread
across her face, and she breathed a sigh of relief as the

familiar shapes of Fuddlerook, Scorchington, Fligboge and Plankton made their way towards the platform.

She rushed over to Fuddlerook and wrapped her arms around him, squeezing him tightly. She felt him wince. Pulling away, she noticed the blood stains on his diver's suit. Looking closer, she saw the wounds on his arms, face and chest.

Her eyes filled, and her body began to tremble. Fuddlerook looked down at her and smiled.

"Don't worry, I'm fine," he said reassuringly. "It's nothing that can't be sorted out by a well trained moose."

Vember hugged him tightly again and laughed, but tears still flowed from her eyes. She pressed her face tightly into his body so no one would notice. The thought of losing Fuddlerook was her greatest fear. It was something she doubted her heart could survive.

Fuddlerook had taken her under his wing during her difficult early years in the underground. Years of not knowing who she was or where she belonged. Over the years, he had become the father she had never known. He had taught her almost everything she knew. He had passed all his great skills as a warrior onto her. Her courage and bravery were all things she had developed under his attentive and protecting gaze. Fuddlerook had also taught her the importance of loyalty and kindness.

Fuddlerook pulled her gently away and opened up his shoulder bag. The Gerbil Brothers popped up one by one.

"Hello boys," said Vember.

The Gerbil brothers blushed and giggled. Like several other members of the Stobes, they thought Vember was the most beautiful creature they had ever seen.

"How are you Miss Vember, Sir?" said Seb Gerbil.

Vember bent down and kissed him softly on the top of his snorkel. His divers mask immediately steamed up, and the other two laughed and prodded him. He lowered his head in embarrassment, and slid back into the bottom of Fuddlerook's shoulder bag.

All of them then gathered just inside the entrance to the tunnel, and waited for Wattage's call. It was beginning to look like it was going to be a long and dangerous night.

Chapter Twenty Eight

AT CROMWELL HOSPITAL, THE DOCTORS and nurses milling around the main entrance didn't notice three small white luminescent sacks fly past them and into the main part of the hospital.

A junior doctor, coming to the end of yet another nineteen-hour shift, didn't notice them fly into the elevator behind him either.

As he opened up his file of papers, Dranoel, Pratt and Stubb hung above his head and studied them too. Dranoel kept glancing across at Stubb, to check he was still in control of his bowels.

When the elevator reached the third floor, he got out as a porter, pushing a trolley with an elderly patient on it, got in.

The elderly patient was lying on her back, with a drip fastened to her arm, and was staring straight up at the three Cribbit Snocklers.

"Did you know that your elevators have got creatures which look a bit like bats in them?" she said in a frail voice.

"Don't worry, we haven't," replied the porter. "It's just the effects of the anaesthetic. It'll soon wear off."

At that point, Stubb let out one of his long, wet, dribbling farts.

"And it can also affect your bowels too." Continued the porter.

"But that wasn't me," protested the elderly lady. "You actually do have bats in your elevators, and one of them has just broken wind."

The porter turned round and smiled at her.

"Don't worry; we'll keep it a secret between us."

The elderly woman continued to protest as the elevator reached the sixth floor, and the porter wheeled her out into a ward full of other elderly female Topsiders.

It was dimly lit and, apart from the occasional sound of snoring, very quiet. Dranoel, Pratt and Stubb flew silently across the room and landed on the underside of a fluorescent strip light, where they hung upside down and waited.

Back outside, across the road from the main entrance, Hetty had decided to go back to Brompton Road and wait for the Stobes to return. The outside world of the Topsiders was no place for a neurotic moose.

As Wattage, Spogworth and Spoogemige crossed the road, the Mole in the Wall Gang dropped down into the open drain next to the kerb and started to tunnel under the road.

By the time Wattage and the others had reached the other side of the road, the Mole in the Wall Gang had already surfaced and were waiting for them. A ridge of broken tarmac, along with several molehills of asphalt, stretched across the road behind them.

Hiding behind a small hedge just in front of the main entrance, the Stobes planned their next move. It was agreed that the Mole in the Wall gang would tunnel underneath the foundations of the hospital and get as near to the lift shafts as possible. The others would simply run as fast as they could through the main entrance and hope they weren't spotted. This was undoubtedly a high-risk strategy. However, it was their only one.

Spoogemige went first. The two Topsiders standing next to a vending machine felt a blast of hot air as Spoogemige zoomed past them. However, as they looked round, all they saw was a pile of papers from the reception desk fluttering in the air and a pair of doors further down the corridor swinging slowly back and forth.

As Wattage and Spogworth moved cautiously towards the entrance, there was suddenly a loud bang, and the hospital was plunged into darkness.

The Mole in the Wall Gang had tunnelled straight through the main electricity cable carrying the power supply to the hospital.

Taking advantage of the sudden darkness, Wattage and Spogworth ran inside, and down the corridor.

Down in the basement, the Mole in the Wall Gang surfaced in a cloud of smoke and burnt fur, just in front of the lift shafts. Two of them had been hit by the full force of the voltage in the electricity cable, and were in a bad way. The others tried to resuscitate them but it was no use, it was too late. They were dead.

This presented a problem. Under Mole in the Wall Gang tradition, all deceased members of the gang had to be buried in a certain way. This involved putting the deceased on a cardboard boat and floating it off into a sewer. Only when this ceremony had been completed would the rest of the gang continue.

The lights in the rest of the hospital suddenly came back on, as the emergency generators switched on and power was restored.

Wattage, Spoogemige and Spogworth hid in a broom cupboard opposite the lifts, and tried to figure out their next move.

They needed to get to the sixth floor. This was the floor that Wattage felt the table was most likely to appear, if indeed it did?

He had no scientific basis for this other than the fact there were six destinations the table seemed to be going to. It could just as easily appear on the ground floor. Then again, there was an equally good chance it could appear in the car park. However, he had convinced himself that the sixth floor was the most likely place. And once Wattage had convinced himself of something, then that was that. Right or wrong, they would do it that way.

Back down in the basement, the remaining members of the Mole in the Wall Gang were searching for a piece of cardboard. After much searching, the only thing they found was an old newspaper.

They stood in a circle round it, and tried to figure out if there was enough to make two boats. Burying them both on the same boat was not an option. Doing this would require the passing of a special resolution at the next council of members meeting. These meetings could only take place at Brompton Road Station, and could only be called by the most senior member of the council, after he had dug a double width tunnel and deposited a piece of pastry at the end of it. This then had to be retrieved by the youngest member of the council, and placed inside a special shoe.

The fact that it was the oldest and youngest members of the gang, who been fried on the electricity cable, was a further complication.

In the broom cupboard, Wattage, Spoogemige and Spogworth decided they couldn't wait any more. As Spoogemige carefully opened the door, Spogworth charged out towards the lifts. Not really knowing what a lift was, he had presumed that the doors would either already be open, or would open automatically when he reached them. They weren't, and they didn't. Spogworth slammed into the cold hard steel with a loud and painful thud.

As Wattage picked a stunned Spogworth off the floor, Spoogemige pressed one of the buttons. An arrow pointing down lit up. Spoogemige thought this was cool and started pressing the buttons to all the other lifts. He watched mesmerised, as all the numbers in the metal plates on either side of the lift doors began to light up one after the other.

Wattage glared across at him, and raised his eyes towards the ceiling.

"Leave then alone!" he snapped. "Can't you do anything right?"

Spoogemige lowered his eyes to the floor, and started fidgeting with the buttons on his cardigan. At the same time, his feet began to tap nervously on the floor.

"Now all the furtling lifts will come and attract attention," he continued.

First one lift, then two, then three, and finally all six lifts arrived. The arrival of each one, accompanied by a loud 'ding' as doors opened. The bright lights inside illuminated the entrance foyer.

Thankfully there were no Topsiders around, and Wattage quickly bundled Spoogemige and Spogworth, who was beginning to regain consciousness again, into the nearest one. He turned to Spoogemige.

"Press the button for the sixth floor." said Wattage angrily. "JUST the sixth floor, Spoogemige."

The lift doors closed, and the three of them ascended silently towards whatever was or was not awaiting them on the sixth floor.

Meanwhile, round the back of the hospital a black shadow, accompanied by the menacing shape of a five-foot rat, moved slowly and cautiously towards the building.

It was dark and deserted, apart from a couple of Topsiders doing some maintenance work on one of the vehicles. They slipped past them unnoticed and made their way towards a window round the corner and out of sight. A steel frame, containing a set of bars, protected the window.

Rodolp looked up at the shadow next to him and smiled. He rolled his head slowly from side to side, and as he did this, the bones in his neck clicked loudly. Leaning forward, he closed his massive gold teeth around one of the bars. There was a crunching sound as his teeth made contact with the cold steel. He squeezed his massive jaws even tighter around the bar, until there was a loud snapping sound.

Rodolp pulled his head back. The steel bar was now in two halves. Grabbing hold each side of the steel frame, he pulled himself up until he was standing on the bottom of the steel frame. The claws of one of his massive legs curled round the steel bar he had bitten through, and began to bend it downwards. There was a low groaning sound as the steel bent at right angles to the frame. He repeated this exercise on the bar on the left until there was a gap big enough for them both to climb through.

Rodolp climbed in first, and waited for the shadow to follow. When the shadow had climbed through, it straightened up and paused. A tall black shape stepped out from the darkness. It walked a few yards down the narrow corridor until it was underneath a light. Turning round to face Rodolp, it raised its head upwards and let out a low anguished groan.

Rodolp looked at the black shape, then back at the shadow it had stepped out of, and then back at the black shape.

Slowly, the black shape began to change, revealing the creature within.

The hairs on Rodolp's back stood on end. He shivered with a mixture of fear and anticipation. A few moments later, the black shape had completed its transformation. Rodolp lowered his head. His master had finally returned.

The tall sinister figure of Darl now walked slowly towards him.

No longer hidden behind his cloak of blackness, his appearance was even more frightening than Rodolp remembered.

The accident, in which everyone thought he had died, had left terrible scars. His large bald pointed head was covered in deep red gashes. The skin, which had always been a pale white colour, was now almost translucent. Dark blue veins were clearly visible, as if someone had drawn all over his head with a felt tip pen.

The huge pointed ears were slashed in several places, and the tip of the left one was held on by a single piece of dead looking skin. His large eyes were pure white and opaque, with tiny, almost non-existent black pupils. Running diagonally up from these were a pair of fierce black eyebrows, reaching high onto his forehead.

As he moved towards Rodolp, he raised his head into the air once more. His long thin pointed nose inhaled deeply, and the thin black lips of his mouth opened into a sneer, revealing a black hole devoid of any teeth.

Rodolp noticed he was limping. He also didn't seem to be quite as tall as before. He still towered over Rodolp though. As he got nearer, he reached inside one of the pockets of the long black overcoat, which completely covered his body, and pulled out a piece of bone.

He held it in his huge right hand. His fingernails, which were over three inches long, stuck up like a deformed claw. With his left hand, he reached down, and using his talon like nails, undid the bottom three buttons of the overcoat. Pulling it to one side, he revealed his left leg. It was encased in splints of wood, held in place by several dirty and tattered bandages.

Handing the piece of bone to Rodolp, he bent down, placed his hands on Rodolp's shoulders, and spoke.

"Remember, Rodolp," he paused, then started running his hands up and down the sides of Rodolp's shoulders. "You...are...my...Number...One!"

Rodolp held the piece of bone in his hand, and looked up at Darl.

"What's this?" he replied.

"It's for you. A souvenir,"

Darl closed his hand around the claw Rodolp was holding it in, and squeezed it tightly.

"It's my left knee," continued Darl, before turning round, and limping off down the corridor.

Rodolp looked down at the piece of bone, then at the dark figure of Darl limping off in the distance. Shrugging his shoulders, he followed Darl down the corridor.

Chapter Twenty Nine

BACK DOWN IN THE BASEMENT, the Mole in the Wall Gang had managed to make two boats out of the newspaper, and were now trying to find a sewer. They decided to tunnel out into the main part of the hospital in search of these two things. This was not an entirely sensible decision. Firstly, they had no idea of where they were going. Secondly, they were moles, and therefore had appalling eyesight. The chances of them being able to find anything that wasn't immediately in front of them in a tunnel was at best slim.

Nevertheless, they started to make their way out of the basement. By a complete miracle, they managed to find a door. Of course being moles, they couldn't open it. However, being moles meant they could certainly tunnel under it. A few minutes later, the tunnel was dug. Unfortunately, the two paper boats containing the bodies of their dead friends wouldn't fit through, so they had to widen it. After another few minutes, the two boats had been hauled through and they found themselves at the bottom of a stairwell.

It took them ages to haul the two boats up the stairs. On more than one occasion, the bodies fell out and tumbled all the way back down.

At the top of the stairs, they found a large trolley used for transporting patients pushed against a wall next to a door. The door suddenly opened, and a Topsider in green overalls walked in.

The Mole in the Wall Gang took the only course of action open to them. They jumped on to the bottom of the trolley, hauling the two boats after them, and waited.

The trolley began to move, as the Topsider wheeled it out into a brightly lit corridor. The Mole in the Wall Gang began to panic. However, what looked like a disaster, in fact turned out to be a blessing.

The trolley stopped outside a door, and the Topsider made his way through it. The Mole in the Wall Gang got ready to make their escape. However, just as they were about to jump off, the door opened and another Topsider walked out, and wedged a mop and bucket against the door to hold it open.

From inside the room, they could hear the sound of running water. This was what they needed. If there was running water, then it had to run out somewhere. It wasn't exactly a sewer, but it would have to do.

As the Topsider walked off down the corridor, the Mole in the Wall Gang lowered the corpses of their dead companions onto the floor then did the same with the two paper boats. They then jumped down themselves, put the corpses inside the boats, and dragged them into the room.

Down one side was a long white wall, with what looked like a river underneath it. Near the top of the wall, a series of small waterfalls trickled water down. The Topsider, who had pushed the trolley out of the stairwell, was leaning against the tiling and fiddling with his trouser region.

Down the right hand side of the room were a row of other rooms, each one with its own gigantic wooden door. The Mole in the Wall Gang noticed that none of the doors was the right size. There was a big gap between the bottom of the doors and the floor. *These Topsiders could certainly do with a lesson on how to build things properly,* they thought.

However, this gap was a great advantage for the Mole in the Wall Gang. They started to drag the boats across the floor. Fortunately, the Topsider was still rummaging about in his trousers, and didn't see them.

They quickly made their way through the gap under the door of the first room on the right, and found themselves looking up at a huge white structure. It towered over them. Maulwurfe leaned forwards and touched it. It was cold and smooth.

They waited for the Topsider to stop shaking whatever it was he was shaking in his trouser region, and watched as he stood up and down on tiptoe a few times, before finally walking over towards the far side of the room. The sound of running water could be heard, followed by what sounded like the whoosh of fast moving air.

A few moments later, they heard the footsteps of the Topsider walking across the floor and out of the door. Maulwurfe and the others gazed up at the huge white object in front of them, and pondered for a few minutes. After a while, Muldvar walked under the door and out into the middle of the room. Looking across at the wall on the far side, he noticed that the river below the long white wall with the waterfalls was a strange yellow colour. The water from the waterfalls ran down into it and then along it, before disappearing down a grid at the far end.

The grid was covered with a dome shaped metal cover. Peering down through it, he could see the water falling down a pipe, which vanished into the pitch black unknown. He sized it up, and worked out that it might just be wide enough to fit a mole – a dead mole. A dead mole fastened to a paper boat?

He signalled to the rest of them, and soon they were all standing in a line peering into the yellow river. Carefully, they pushed the boat carrying the first of their dead comrades into the river, and waited. The boat did not move, but just bobbed up and down, rocking gently from side to side. Maulwurfe, Muldvar and Mogra waded into the river behind it, and gave it a push. It moved a couple of inches and then stopped. Whilst the three of them tried to work out how to get the boat to float down properly, Muldvad, Talpa and Walter set to work on removing the dome shaped grid cover. It was messy work. It involved climbing into the smelly yellow river, and then reaching underneath the water, to try to prize the cover off. After a great deal of effort, they managed to release the cover, and lift it out onto the floor.

At the other end of the river, Maulwurfe, Muldvar and Mogra had reached a rather worrying conclusion. The paper the boat was made of was becoming saturated, and beginning to fall to pieces. The more they pushed the back of it, the more it started to crumple and collapse.

They all stood looking at the slowly disintegrating boat. Time was running out. Eventually Muldvar stepped forward and, loosening a small piece of thread from around his waist, pulled out the plastic tea stirrer, which the thread was holding in place. Several members of the Mole in the Wall Gang carried these for self-defence since they had seen a Star Wars poster at Leicester Square Station the previous year.

Making his way to the water, he climbed carefully onto the soaking wet and now decidedly yellow covered boat and, straddling the corpse of his dead comrade, lowered the tea stirrer into the water, and began to paddle.

Sure enough, the boat began to slowly pick up speed, and move nearer and nearer the grid at the other end.

The others shouted for him to jump off, but he didn't. He was determined to ensure his dead comrade got the traditional burial he deserved.

The boat moved faster and faster. As the water got deeper as it neared the grate, his comrades shouted even louder for him to jump off. But Muldvar kept paddling, until suddenly it was too late. The boat tipped over the edge of the grid and plunged   down into the darkness of the drain.

The rest of the Mole in the Wall Gang stood in silence, and lowered their heads in respect. Inspired by such a selfless, although, stupid and pointless act of courage, Walter, Muldvad and Eric pushed the boat, containing the dead body of their other comrade, into the yellow river. Eric pulled his tea stirrer out, and leapt onto the boat. Then with exactly the same display of stupidity as Muldvar, he paddled the boat, his other dead comrade, and himself down the drain.

Not wanting to be left out, the rest of the Mole in the Wall Gang all jumped into the river, and floated towards the grid. One by one, they all disappeared down the drain. A few seconds later, the room was silent apart from the trickle of water and the odd ghostly echo of screaming moles.

Chapter Thirty

IN A STRETCH OF TUNNEL somewhere near Holborn station on the Piccadilly Line, a rather nervous Hetty fiddled with the oven mitts on her antlers and looked nervously into the darkness of the tunnel beyond. She didn't like being away from the safe haven of Brompton Road. She *certainly* didn't like being all alone and away from the safe haven of Brompton Road.

Nervously adjusting the front of her jacket, and blouse, she continued on her lonely journey. The dim glow from the tunnel lighting cast eerie shadows on the walls. The distant sound of heavy machinery and Topsiders going about their nightly maintenance work, drifted through the labyrinth of tunnels in a muffled disjointed echo.

In another section of the underground, near Russell Square on the same stretch of line, six umbrellas were also making their way along the tunnel towards Holborn Station from the opposite direction. They moved together slowly, yet deliberately. Every now and then, the umbrella at the front would stop and look around, as if surveying the area.

Hetty made her way round a bend in the track and looked down towards the dim glow coming from Holborn Station. She approached nervously, and tried to remember exactly where the old metal door in the tunnel wall was, which connected to the narrow ventilation shaft that eventually led to Brompton Road. Staring at the brickwork and shattered tiling, she moved closer, her eyes widening as they penetrated the darkness.

Then the sound of a stone bouncing on the metal rails of the track distracted her. Turning round, Hetty stared into the tunnel beyond. Although she couldn't see anything, she could her hear what sounded like something scratching on the rails in the distance.

Further down the tunnel, the six umbrellas stopped moving. A feline head slowly peered out from behind the first umbrella, and stared down the tunnel. Her whiskers twitched. Arching her neck, she tilted her nose upwards to inhale the stale dusty scent of the air.

The oven mitts on Hetty's antlers started to wobble and shake as she became more anxious about what could be out there, and what was making that noise in the distance down the track.

She started rubbing her hoofs frantically against the tunnel wall, searching for the metal door. Pressing herself against the wall, she moved slowly deeper into the tunnel. She knew the door must be somewhere here, but where?

Back down the track, the six umbrellas were moving faster now, getting nearer and nearer to where Hetty was. As they got to the bend in the track, they stopped. One by one, the members of the Pussycat Brolls folded their umbrellas up and spread out across the width of the tunnel, and started to hiss angrily.

Hetty turned round and found herself staring at six sets of luminous green eyes. The glint of the sharpened metal tips of their umbrellas waved about in the half-light.

"Sssssstobe," hissed Scroat, the leader of the gang.

She looked round at the others, then with a growl charged at Hetty, now holding her umbrella like a javelin. The rest followed suit, all six of them bearing down on Hetty at alarming speed.

Just as the Pussycat Brolls got within striking distance, Hetty at last found the handle to the door. The heavy rusting door groaned as she pulled it open, and squeezed inside. Seeing her prey about to get away, Scroat leapt in the air whilst hurling her umbrella towards the door. Hetty just managed to get through and push the door closed as Scroat's umbrella, followed by Scroat, slammed into it.

As Hetty finally closed the door behind her, she could hear the sound of frantic scratching and clawing from the other side of the door. It was like a hundred fingernails being dragged down a blackboard at the same time.

She slumped to the ground against the door, her whole body shaking in fear. Reaching up to her antlers, she noticed one of her oven mitts was missing. Standing up, she looked round for it in the darkness. The scratching and clawing on the other side of the door had stopped. An eerie silence settled all around.

Turning round, she spotted her missing oven mitt. It was wedged in the door. Hetty was very attached to both her oven mitts, and the thought of leaving one of them wedged in the door was upsetting. However, it wasn't as upsetting as the prospect of what could still be lurking on the other side of the door. Reaching up, she gently stroked the oven mitt, before blowing it a gentle kiss. Then, with a heavy sigh, she made her way down the dark passageway towards an old disused ventilation shaft, which would take her to back to Brompton Road.

The Pussycat Brolls meanwhile, skulked off back down the tunnel hissing and cursing. However, Scroat was so angry at failing to capture Hetty that she suddenly turned round and, for no reason whatsoever, started hitting Scab with her umbrella. As Scab fell down onto the rails, Mank, Ferrel and Flap decided this was far too good an opportunity for a fight to miss out on, and wielding their umbrellas fiercely, leapt on top of Scroat. For the next ten minutes, accompanied by horrible screeching, hissing, growling and flying fur, the Pussycat Brolls proceeded to knock each other senseless.

Eventually the fight came to an end, and all five of them lay spread out across the track panting and groaning. Apart from a few superficial injuries such as missing whiskers, the tip of a tail, three broken teeth and a slashed ear, all five of them seemed relatively unscathed. This was more than could be said for their umbrellas, which were strewn across the floor of the tunnel, bent broken and snapped beyond repair, or in the case of Mank's, wedged fully open between two bricks in the tunnel roof.

Picking themselves up one by one, they skulked off back down the tunnel. Before they could go looking for any more trouble and mayhem, they'd need to go back to Finchley Central and replace their umbrellas!

Chapter Thirty One

ON THE SIXTH FLOOR AT Cromwell Road Hospital, the elevator arrived with a 'ping'. Wattage, Spogworth and Spoogemige stepped anxiously out of it, and looked around.

The large room contained many beds in which elderly Topsiders were sleeping. It was silent, apart from the occasional sound of snoring. Two strip lights at each end of the room gave off a dim 'half-light', which cast shadows across the walls and ceiling.

Hanging from the rail of a curtained screen next to one of the beds, Dranoel, Pratt and Stubb watched and waited. Stubb's bowels had still not fully recovered, and it wasn't long before a wet, dribbling fart interrupted the silence.

"Is that you Arthur?" said a voice.

"Who said that?" whispered Dranoel.

"There's some Imodium in the bathroom cabinet," continued the voice.

Dranoel, Pratt and Stubb looked at each other with puzzled expressions.

"I've told you not to eat prunes for supper..."

Dranoel looked down, and noticed that the voice was coming from an elderly Topsider in the bed next to them. She seemed to be fast asleep.

"...but you never listen do you, Arthur...?"

Dranoel watched in fascination, trying not to laugh as she continued to talk in her sleep.

"And don't forget it's Wednesday tomorrow... the bins need to go out."

On the other side of the room, unaware of the presence of the Cribbit Snocklers, Wattage, Spogworth and Spoogemige waited for something to happen.

They weren't waiting long.

A sudden bang, accompanied by clouds of smoke and the stench of rotten eggs, burnt fish and sulphur disturbed the peace.

When the smoke finally cleared, standing in the middle of the room was the stone table.

It wasn't alone.

Draped across it were the semi-conscious bodies of Ripperton and Gobbit.

The noise woke up several, though not all, of the elderly Topsiders.

"It's a bit early for the tea trolley." Said one of them.

"That kettle's over boiled if it is." Said another.

"That's not the tea trolley... and that is definitely not Nurse Rogers!" Shouted a third one, sitting bolt upright in her bed and pointing.

"Nurse! Nurse!" she screamed.

As the table sat in the middle of the room humming and vibrating, Dranoel, and Pratt flew across for a closer look. Wattage, Spogworth and Spoogemige were crouched down behind a desk, carefully watching every move.

"Oh no! Cribbit Snocklers!" whispered Wattage.

Dranoel and Pratt landed on the edge of the table just as Ripperton and Gobbit were regaining consciousness. As Ripperton slowly sat up, Pratt looked at the gold and silver pegs in the table. Tilting his head to one side, he reached out a stumpy leg and wrapped a claw around the gold one.

Slowly, he pulled and twisted it out of the hole, and lifted it up to his nose and sniffed it. He then began to put it back into the hole it came from, but at the last minute, decided to put it into a different one.

Just as he started dropping into the hole, Ripperton turned round.

"NO!" she screamed.

But it was too late, and the peg dropped into the hole with a 'clunk'.

The table immediately started to vibrate even more, and the humming got louder. Spoogemige, watching from the shadows, knew exactly what was going to happen next.

In an act of courage he was not renowned for, he leapt up and sped across to the table and threw himself across it, crushing both Dranoel and Pratt underneath him in the process.

There was a loud bang, followed seconds later by an explosion.

When the smoke eventually cleared, the table, Spoogemige, Dranoel, Pratt, Ripperton and Gobbit were no longer there. The smell of burnt fish, sulphur and rotten eggs hung in the air.

Stubb, not used to either being alone or having to think for himself, hung on the underside of the rail, doing a very good impression of an upside down meerkat. A few moments later, he decided the best course of action was to try to find Rodolp. Accompanied by a low grumbling fart, he flew across the room and out through an open window.

Wattage and Spogworth meanwhile, had moved across to where the table had been, and were pondering their next move.

This was decided for them when a large and fearsome looking nurse suddenly barged into the room.

"WHATS BEEN GOING ON IN HERE?" she bellowed.

Before the nurse could get to grips with exactly what had happened, Wattage and Spogworth made a run for the lift. However, whilst the nurse was large, she was surprisingly quick on her feet, and started to run after them.

The lift arrived, and Wattage and Spogworth rushed inside and pressed the 'down' button. As the doors began to close, the nurse hurled herself towards the rapidly closing gap and managed to jam her foot in between the doors just as they were about to shut.

Wattage kept pressing the close button, but every time the doors hit the nurse's leg they started opening again, accompanied by a loud pinging sound and a groan from the nurse.

After a few minutes of pinging and groaning, Spogworth decided to sort things out. Bending down, he bit the nurse's leg hard. He had expected her to pull her leg away, but she did the opposite, and started kicking her leg to try to shake Spogworth off.

Spogworth grabbed hold of her leg and bit her even harder. With a loud groan, the nurse kicked her leg upwards, slamming Spogworth into one of the doors. As Spogworth slumped to the floor in a heap, the nurse finally pulled her leg out from between the doors.

The doors closed, and the lift at last started to go down.

Down in a corridor at the back of the Hospital, Darl and Rodolp slowly skulked their way towards a stairwell. At the same time, Stubb noticed the two sinister shadows making their way upwards as he flew past. In a surprisingly aerobatic manoeuvre, he banked round and at the same time did an impressive loop-the-loop before coming to a graceful halt outside the window.

Looking up, he noticed that one of the windows on the next floor was open. He paused momentarily, as he was forced to empty his bowels yet again. Bowels attended to, he flew up and through the window and waited for Darl and Rodolp.

It wasn't long before the frightening black figure of Darl and the menacing bulk of Rodolp arrived.

Stubb had never met Darl before, and the sight made him tremble in fear.

"Well…?" said Rodolp threateningly.

Darl remained silent, and just watched. Stubb tried to speak, but nothing would come out. It was as if he was paralysed with fear. His tiny, stumpy claws were gripping the top of stair rail tightly, his whole body now frozen rigid.

"…I won't ask again!" continued Rodolp.

"I…I…er…I…t-t-thought you were dead?" Stubb finally managed to splutter.

"I might well be," replied Darl with an evil smirk.

Stubb, unable to control his fear any longer, farted loudly and then proceeded to empty his bowels all over the stair rail. This caused him to lose his grip, and slip round till he was hanging underneath the rail by one claw, with his wings flapping to try to keep hold.

Darl looked down at him and sneered. He then reached across and grabbed hold of one of Stubbs wings with the tips of his long nails. Raising Stubb high in the air at arm's length, he began to sway him from side to side.

Turning round to look at Rodolp, Darl grinned.

"Chicken?"

"I wouldn't know," Replied Rodolp. "Never eaten a Cribbit Snockler…but if you're feeling hungry, I suggest you give him a wash first. Even I wouldn't eat him in *that* state!"

"The…t-table…w-was…h-here," spluttered Stubb, trying to avoid being eaten.

"I suppose we ought to let him speak," said Rodolp.

"Yes, I suppose we should," replied Darl.

As Darl continued to hold him by his wing, Stubb relayed what had happened on the sixth floor a few minutes earlier.

When Stubb had finished, Darl looked over his shoulder at Rodolp.

"I assume you have a plan for what to do next?"

"Head back to the Underground, and wait for further developments," replied Rodolp, trying to sound more confident than he actually was.

Darl turned back to Stubb and, with a condescending sneer, threw him against the window. Stubb hit it with a thud and slid down the glass leaving a brown stain down the window. Darl and Rodolp then began to make their way back down the stairs.

Stubb picked himself up from the floor, pulled a crumpled wing straight and, relieved he was still alive, flew out of the window.

Over on the ground floor of the hospital, the lift containing Wattage and Spogworth arrived. Fortunately, the reception area was quiet, and they were able to sneak out unnoticed.

"We'd better get back to Earls Court as quickly as possible," said Wattage, as they made their way out into the still night air.

Chapter Thirty Two

AT EARLS COURT STATION, THE rest of the Stobes were waiting for news when Scorchington's phone rang. It was Spogworth, telling them what had happened at Cromwell Road Hospital, and that they would be there shortly.

As they waited, they noticed a couple of Topsiders coming down the far end of the platform. They hurriedly moved deeper into the tunnel entrance and pressed themselves tight against the tunnel wall. Fuddlerook raised his finger to his lips to tell them all to be silent. They waited anxiously as the two Topsiders made their way to the door of the main entrance, and proceeded to put what looked like a poster up on the door. When they had finished, the Topsiders walked back down the platform and out of sight.

Fuddlerook slowly made his way cautiously out of the tunnel and checked the coast was clear. He beckoned the rest of the Stobes. Keeping a watchful eye on the far end of the platform, he noticed two silhouettes slowly appear. He was about to herd the others back into the tunnel when he recognised who they were. Moments later, Wattage and Spogworth arrived.

"What shall we do now?" asked Fuddlerook.

"I think we need to get back to Brompton Road... very quickly," replied Wattage. "Hetty is there alone, and if there is a possibility that the Table has gone back there, then she is in grave danger. Also, the Topsiders will be starting about their business soon, and we can't take the risk of being seen up here." he continued.

Fuddlerook made his way over to where the rest of the Stobes were gathered round the main entrance, looking at the poster the Topsiders had put up.

"Looks like we're going to have the place to ourselves for the next two days." Said Fligboge.

The poster the Topsiders had put up said: -

TUBE STRIKE.

Due to ongoing disagreements with management over a number of issues relating to working conditions, redundancies and pension provisions, and despite concerted efforts by the Union to negotiate a fair and workable outcome, no agreement has been reached. Therefore, the Union is left with no alternative but to bring forward a planned course of action in protest to this, and the Underground will be closed for the next 48 hours, with immediate effect. We apologise for any inconvenience this may cause.

"That could be just as well...because I've got a feeling that all hell is about to break loose down there." replied Wattage.

With a sense of urgency and foreboding, the Stobes began their journey back down into the Underground, and whatever lay in wait for them.

Unfortunately, none of them noticed that one of them was missing. Down the platform in the opposite direction, Scorchington had decided to go for a walkabout in the world of the Topsiders.

However, back in the tunnel complex near Brompton Road, Hetty was about to find out exactly what was waiting for them.

She had finally finished tidying up the last of the mess in Wattage's study when there was a loud bang, followed by the sudden appearance of the table. Draped across it were the smoking bodies of Spoogemige, Neb, Dranoel, Ripperton and Gobbit.

The blast blew Hetty off her feet, a number of tiles off the walls, and several pieces of brick and rubble down from the ceiling. The stench of rotten eggs, burnt fish and sulphur filled the air.

Hetty stared through the clouds of smoke in the room and tried to get up. She couldn't. The blast had not only blown her off her feet but also blown her sideways across the room, and one of her antlers was now wedged in a small metal vent in the wall.

She struggled furiously to free her antler from the vent, but it wouldn't budge. She tried knocking it to one side with her hoof, but still it wouldn't move.

As Hetty struggled to free her antler, Ripperton slowly began to regain consciousness. As the smoke started to clear, she looked around the room with her coal-black dead eyes, until her gaze fell upon Hetty wedged in the wall. An evil grin spread across her face.

She tried to push the still unconscious bodies of Spoogemige and Gobbit off her, but they were too heavy. The pushing did however wake up Neb and Dranoel, who managed to squirm out from underneath Spoogemige and drop off the table onto the floor.

Neb shook himself and looked around the room. It wasn't long before he spotted Hetty.

"Nice twinset," he said sarcastically, before taking to the air and flying across to land on the antler that wasn't wedged in the metal vent.

"I thought oven mitts came in a pair?" he continued, as he looked down at Hetty.

Hetty started to struggle even harder to free her antler, but the more she struggled, the more jammed the antler became.

Meanwhile, Dranoel was feeling sick. The weight of Spoogemige had flattened his nose even more, and he was having difficulty breathing. One of his ears was bent across the front of his face obscuring the vision in his right eye, and his left wing was twisted.

He was about to stumble across the floor towards Hetty and Neb, when he felt someone grab him roughly by the throat, lift him up and start choking him. Turning his head round, he saw it was Ripperton.

"What have I done?" he gasped.

"Nothing." replied Ripperton coldly. "I just need to hurt someone."

"Well why don't you hurt *him*?" said Dranoel, pointing to the body of Spoogemige.

Ripperton turned her head slowly towards Spoogemige.

"Fair point," she scowled, and let go of Dranoel. He fell to the floor hitting it face first.

After picking himself up, he rushed quickly over towards Neb and Hetty before Ripperton changed her mind and tried to strangle him again.

Hetty was still no nearer to un-jamming her antler from the metal vent, and Neb was still no nearer stopping the insults.

"So what's with the suit and blouse? Are you thinking of going into politics?" mocked Neb.

"Furtle off you hideous little twazlet." replied Hetty, still trying to yank her antler out of the vent.

"That's brave talk for a jammed moose."

"Just you wait till I get my antler out. Then we'll see who's brave, you smelly, ugly little *thing*!"

"Well from where I'm standing, that's going to be some time…unless of course, you happen to have a crow bar in one of your pockets."

Neb then amused himself by kicking the oven mitt on her other antler back and forth.

"I have to say, these are seriously good quality... where did you get them from?"

Neb then grabbed hold of the oven mitt, pulled it closer to him and looked inside.

"You know, this would make a rather good Snockler sleeping bag,"

"Touch that oven mitt once more, and I'll knock you through the wall."

"Now given your current situation, that *would* be impressive," replied Neb.

Neb moved further down Hetty's antler and began to lift the oven mitt up and slide it towards him. However, his confidence in having the upper hand was about to be dealt a rather painful blow. Hetty may well have been jammed in a metal vent. She may well have been a short and not particularly agile creature. But when it came to anyone messing with her oven mitts, well, that was a different matter altogether. She'd already lost one, and had no intention of loosing the other.

As Neb slid the oven mitt nearer towards the end of her antler, Hetty managed to twist her body round, and in a fit of rage worthy of Miss Piggy from the Muppets, swung her right leg upwards and straight into Nebs face.

The blow knocked Neb clean off her antler and sent him flying through the air.

Dranoel, who up to that point had been too preoccupied trying to straighten his face back to normal, looked up in horror as Neb's body slammed into the wall with a dull wet thud and slid down in a crumpled heap on the floor,

Hetty looked over and noticed that Neb was still clutching her oven mitt in one of his claws.

"Grrrrrrrrrh!" she shrieked, and thrashing about wildly, like a shark on someone's leg, managed to wrench the jammed antler out of the metal vent.

She picked herself up and stormed over to Neb. Reaching down, she ripped the oven mitt from his claw then picked him up, threw him in the air, and dropkicked him across the room into the wall on the opposite side.

Dranoel ran for cover under the table and hid behind one of Spoogemige's legs, which were dangling down.

On the other side of the room, Ripperton was keeping one eye on Hetty, while still trying to push the dead weight of Spoogemige's body off her. After having spent several minutes strangling him, she was now punching him repeatedly. However, as he was already unconscious, this obviously had no effect.

Hetty looked across at Ripperton and glared at her. Under normal circumstances, Hetty would have been so nervous and frightened of the very sight of her that she would have run away. But a combination of the attempted theft of her one remaining oven mitt and the sight of Ripperton punching Spoogemige had made her so angry that she was ready to take on anyone.

Marching over to Ripperton like a school headmistress about to give the whole school detention, she climbed onto the table, and then jumped in the air and slammed her bottom down onto Ripperton.

Ripperton let out a muffled suffocated groan as the full weight of Hetty landed on her windpipe.

Climbing down off the table, she grabbed hold of Spoogemige's legs and began pulling him off the table. After several minutes of grunting, she managed to pull him off and onto the floor.

She knelt down beside him and stroked his cheeks. Still he didn't move. She tried rocking his head from side to side, but still nothing. Then she had an idea. Looking down at his enormous feet, she pulled one of his ancient sandals off and began tickling his foot. His foot started twitching and trying to push her hoof away. She carried on tickling his foot until finally he opened one eye, then the other.

She stopped tickling and smiled at him. She then took hold of his arm, and helped him to his feet.

Spoogemige stood up on slightly wobbly legs and looked round the room.

"What happened to the others?" asked Hetty.

"I don't know," replied Spoogemige. "The last thing I remember was diving onto the table at Cromwell Road Hospital."

"Well I hope they get back here soon, because I don't know long those two Darkenbads will be unconscious." replied Hetty.

Dranoel was still hiding behind the table, when he heard a low groan from the other side of the room as Neb started to come round. Pressing himself against the wall, he slowly started to sneak across towards Neb.

The sound of hiccups emerged from the table. Looking round, Hetty and Spoogemige noticed that Gobbit was starting to wake up.

On the opposite side of the room, Neb and Dranoel were planning their next move. Because a Cribbit Snockler can't really whisper or even talk quietly in fact, they had to communicate their plan by semaphore.

Neb pointed to the door. Dranoel didn't get it. Neb pointed to the door once more. Once more Neb didn't get it.

It was actually quite understandable that after being strangled by both Darl and Ripperton and then dropped on his face, that Dranoel's brain was possibly a bit foggy. However, Neb demonstrated that he did not intend to take this into consideration by poking him in the eye and flying off towards the door. Dranoel followed a few seconds later, but with restricted vision, only narrowly avoided a collision with side of the door.

As Neb and Dranoel escaped down the tunnel, Gobbit started to sit up on the table. At the same time, Ripperton started move.

"We'd better get out of here *fast*." said Hetty.

"We could use Criblee's lawnmower to wedge the door shut." replied Spoogemige.

"Is it near?"

"It's just next door, I think."

"Well hurry up."

As Spoogemige rushed out of the room to get the lawnmower, Hetty watched Ripperton and Gobbit nervously.

The sound of clanking and banging, followed by the rumbling vibration of metal on concrete came from down the tunnel. A few moments later, Spoogemige arrived pushing the lawnmower.

They pushed the door closed, and then together, heaved the lawnmower against it, jamming the top of it underneath the door handle.

"That should do it," panted Spoogemige.

"I hope so," replied Hetty.

"What shall we do now?" asked Spoogemige.

"Go down to the old platform and wait for the rest of them to get here." replied Hetty.

As he two of them made their way nervously down the tunnel, Hetty turned round to Spoogemige.

"I'll tell you something, young Stobe… I'm certainly not clearing up all the mess in Wattage's study *this* time."

Back inside the room, Gobbit and Ripperton were now fully conscious. Ripperton walked over to the door and attempted to open it. She turned round to Gobbit.

"I need you to do something for me."

"Shhertainly, and exshatly what do you want me to do?"

"I want you to open this door for me."

Gobbit swayed over to the door and tried to open it. The door moved about an inch, but no more.

"I think there's shomething jammed againsht it."

"I know. But I'm sure you'll be able to remove it for me."

She grinned at him, then kicked him violently in the stomach and sent him crashing into the door. The door burst open, sending Gobbit and the lawnmower flying into the tunnel wall opposite.

As Ripperton walked out of the room, she looked at down at Gobbit lying on the floor on top of the lawnmower.

"Thank you."

"My pleashure."

As Gobbit climbed to his feet, Ripperton noticed that the impact of Gobbit, the door and the tunnel wall had done considerable damage to the lawnmower. Looking closer, she noticed that the blades had become broken off one end and were bent and twisted.

Reaching down, she took hold of one of the old rusted blades and pulled it hard. It snapped off in her hand.

"Oh *yes*," she smirked, and pulled off two more.

She looked at Gobbit and smiled.

"You opened the door *and* made me some weapons at the same time… what a clever little smelly drunken thing you are."

Pushing the lawnmower blades into one of her pockets, she walked off down the tunnel. Gobbit straightened his puffa jacket, clutched his underpants to stop them falling down, and followed her.

Chapter Thirty Three

ON A STREET SOMEWHERE NEAR Earls Court, Scorchington stared up into the sky. Stars twinkled and a cool breeze blew through the night air. Feeling chilly, he reached into his plastic carrier bag and pulled out his hoody. It was ripped across the back, and there were stains of blood where Rodolp's claws had wounded him.

Pulling it over his head, he pulled out a loaf of bread and toasted about three slices, before munching happily and continuing on his way. He didn't know where he was going, but he felt a sense of excitement in this big wide world of the Topsiders.

Turning a corner he noticed there were some tall posts with coloured lights on the top of them. He watched as they started to turn from red, to yellow and then green. A few minutes later, they changed back to red. Walking nearer, he stopped right next to one of them. He stood there for several minutes watching them change colour. He started to tap his right foot and move his shoulders from side to side in time with the lights.

Reaching inside his carrier bag once more, he pulled out his latest iPod and, putting the earphones in, switched it on. A rush of music flooded his ears, and he started to dance in time to both the music and the lights.

After several minutes of this, he got bored, and set off walking down the street. As he turned a corner, he heard voices. Pressing himself tightly against the window of a shop, he leaned his head round the corner. Looking down the street, he noticed a group of about five Topsiders on the opposite side of the street. They were stood inside an illuminated shelter of some description. He could hear their voices and the occasional sound of laughter. One of the Topsiders then began to walk down the street. After turning round to wave back at the others, the Topsider continued down the street in Scorchington's direction. He looked around for somewhere to hide.

A few yards further down the street, there was a large wheelie bin. Slowly he sneaked down towards it, hoping the Topsider wouldn't spot him. As the Topsider on the opposite side of the street got nearer, Scorchington started to walk quicker. He just managed to get to the bin as the Topsider drew level with him opposite. He crouched down and hid in the shadows next to it.

He watched the Topsider walk past, and turn off onto another street. He was just about to stand up, when a black taxi pulled up a few yards down the street. A Topsider got out of it, and leaned through the window where the driver was sat. Whilst the Topsiders were distracted, Scorchington stood up and looked for a way to get into the bin. Clenching his carrier bag between his teeth, he stood on tiptoes and pushed at the top of it, it lifted up slightly.

Balancing one foot on the bottom of the shop window next to him and grabbing hold of a handle on the side of the bin, he pulled himself up until he was level with the top of the bin. Then he started to push the lid of the bin up. He managed to lift it up just enough to create a gap he could squeeze through. Throwing himself forward, he kicked his legs and wriggled his body until he dropped into the darkness of the inside of the bin. The bin lid fell shut behind him with a loud thud.

The Topsider standing next to the taxi looked down in the direction of the bin for a few moments, before turning back to finish paying the Topsider who was driving the taxi. The taxi pulled away and the Topsider made his way to a door, and let himself in.

On the opposite side of the road further down, Charlie, Wedge, Rod and Doreen had also heard the bin lid slamming shut, and stared down the road.

"Probably foxes scavenging for food." said Charlie.

"When's this bus due?" said Rod impatiently.

"I hope it comes soon," replied Doreen. "I'm starving!"

Wedge continued to stare down the street at the bin.

"I know foxes are clever, but I've *never* heard of one opening a wheelie bin," he said.

* * * * *

Back down in the underground in a deserted tunnel, Vember turned round to the others.

"Where's Scorchington?"

The rest of the Stobes looked round.

"SCORCHINGTON!" shouted Vember.

No one answered. She repeated herself, but still there was no reply. Fligboge was the first one to speak.

"I'll bet he's gone on a furtling walkabout up there," he said, pointing a finger upwards. "You know what a twazlet he is."

Vember looked across at Wattage, and then Fuddlerook.

"What should we do?"

"Leave him!" barked Wattage. "We can't go looking for him this time, he's just going to have to sort himself out. We have more important things to worry about right now."

Vember looked at Wattage in disgust, and then at Fuddlerook. Fuddlerook lowered his head slightly and sighed.

"Wattage is right Vember. We can't keep sending out search parties every time he decides to go walkabout."

He walked over to Vember and put a hand on her shoulder. Vember pushed it away and tossed her mane of raven hair angrily to one side.

"I'm not leaving him out there alone."

Wattage turned round and walked over to Vember and Fuddlerook. "We can't risk every other Stobe just because of Scorchington's stupid irresponsible behaviour."

Vember turned on her heels, and started to run off down the tunnel.

"VEMBER!" shouted Fuddlerook as he started to run after her.

He soon caught her up and gripped her tightly her round the shoulders. Vember tried to struggle free, but Fuddlerook was far too strong. He swivelled her round to face him and looked sternly into her eyes. He saw the look of disgust and concern on her face.

"He might be irresponsible. He might be a furtling twazlet. He probably deserves to get his comeuppance. But, he's still one of us, and we have to stick together." She said.

Fuddlerook had seen that look on Vember's face before, and knew that short of knocking her out, he was never going to persuade her to not go back to find Scorchington.

"Be quick, be careful and stay hidden," he sighed with resignation.

He reached inside his battered divers suit and pulled out his long screwdriver.

"Take this. You might need it."

Vember smiled at him, and then leaned forward and kissed him gently on the cheek.

"Thank you."

She then began to run off back down the tunnel. Fuddlerook watched in silence as she disappeared into the darkness. Turning round, he walked back to the others. Wattage was none too happy, and frowned at Fuddlerook.

"She'll be fine. I've taught her well," said Fuddlerook anxiously.

"I hope so, my friend. I certainly hope so." relied Wattage.

✳ ✳ ✳ ✳ ✳

Back inside the bin, Scorchington sat in complete darkness. The smell was rancid, and he appeared to be sitting on something very wet and cold. He breathed a jet of fire to light up the inside of the bin. This regrettably led to some of the rubbish catching fire. Scorchington frantically tried to stamp it out, but this only resulted in him sinking further through the rubbish and further down into the bin.

He tried blowing on the fire, but this just made matters worse.

On the opposite side of the street, Wedge was now taking a very keen interest in the bin, especially as there was now smoke coming out of it.

"Do foxes carry matches?"

"Not that I'm aware of," replied Charlie, sarcastically. "Why?"

"Well that wheelie bin over there appears to be on fire,"

They all looked down the street, to where smoke was now billowing out of the bin.

Inside the bin, Scorchington was leaping about trying to stamp out the various fires that were now blazing. Every time he stamped, he sank back down in the rubbish, until eventually he sank up to his neck. To make matters even worse, his carrier bag was now starting to burn.

Wedge loved nothing more than a good wheelie bin fire, and gleefully darted across the street towards the bin. As he got nearer, flames began to spit out the side of the lid of the bin.

Suddenly there was a boom, and the bin lid exploded up into the air covered in flames. Wedge managed to dive to the ground just in time as the blazing lid flew over his head and landed in the middle of the street.

Charlie, Rod and Doreen ran over to where Wedge was lying in the middle of the street. They helped Wedge get to his feet, and then all four of them stared at the wheelie bin. As they stared through the smoke and flames that were still billowing out of it, they heard movement coming from inside the bin.

Wedge started to move nearer to get a closer look. The sound of banging then emerged from the bin. The banging lasted for a few moments until out of the smoke and flames, Scorchington climbed out of the bin and threw himself onto the pavement. There was smoke pouring off him and his hoodie was in burnt tatters. He grabbed hold of his feet one at a time and blew on them.

"Ouch! Ouch! Ouch!" he panted.

He got up and, clutching the melted burnt remains of his plastic carrier bag, walked a few feet down the street before slumping down onto the floor in a shop doorway.

"Oh my God, it's some kind of monster!" screamed Wedge.

Scorchington had been called many things, but at barely three feet tall, a *monster* wasn't one of them.

"I think it must be some kind of alien!" said Rod nervously.

Scorchington looked up, "I'm a Stobe actually."

"It can *speak*," said Charlie.

Scorchington looked at them, tutted, and started rummaging around in what was left of his plastic carrier bag.

Wedge, Charlie and Rod stood speechless as they watched Scorchington pull the burnt remnants of a carpet slipper, and then a completely burnt loaf of bread out of the bag. He then pulled a couple of slices of the burnt loaf out of its melted plastic wrapper, and started to eat them.

"IT'S HIM!" Screamed Doreen as she finally joined the others. "Look... it's him... I wasn't imagining it... it's the orange dragon...!"

Charlie and Rod turned round and looked at Doreen. Wedge, however, continued to gawp in disbelief at Scorchington.

Doreen then pushed Wedge to one side and moved over until she was directly in front of Scorchington.

"Recognise *me*?"

Scorchington looked up at Doreen with a slightly puzzled expression on his face, before returning to check the damage to the contents of his carrier bag.

"Well...do you?" repeated Doreen. "Let me jog your memory... West Brompton Tube station...*yesterday*." she continued.

Scorchington looked up at her and scratched the side of his head.

Charlie, Rod and Wedge meanwhile were still standing open mouthed and speechless. Charlie was the first to speak.

"Please tell me that I'm not the only one who can see this?"

"No, you're not," replied Rod.

"Well, we're either all suffering from a group hallucination, or we *really* are looking at a small orange dragon who's just set a council wheelie bin on fire, and who is now having a conversation with Doreen...who has *apparently* met him before?" continued Charlie.

Scorchington looked down at what was left of his plastic carrier bag, then tossed it over his shoulder into the shop doorway. He then pulled what was left of his hoodie over his head and threw that into the shop doorway too. He suddenly felt very naked and very alone. He looked up at Doreen and smiled pathetically at her.

Doreen looked down at him. His small orange body was covered in black smoke stains. His black t-shirt was covered in burn marks and holes, and there were bits of burnt rubbish from the wheelie bin stuck to various parts of his tiny body. Instead of being angry, Doreen suddenly felt very sorry for him. She reached out a chubby hand and smiled at him. Scorchington took hold of her hand, and pulled himself to his feet.

"Where do you come from?" she asked him softly.

Scorchington pointed to the ground.

"Down there."

"Down where?"

"Down there in the underground. That's where we live,"

"We? You mean there are more of you?"

"Yes, many more,"

"And are they all like you?"

"No,"

Charlie, Wedge and Rod made their way over to Scorchington and Doreen. They looked at Scorchington, still not able to believe their eyes.

Over to the left, the wheelie bin was still burning, lighting up the street with its bright orange glow.

"I think we'd better get out of here," said Wedge. "The police or fire brigade will be here any minute, and I don't want to be around when they do. And I doubt you do either." he said pointing down at Scorchington.

With his track record of setting things alight, and a pending court case regarding the incident with the wheelie bin at Asda, it was understandable that Wedge did not want to be found next to another blazing wheelie bin.

"What's your name?" said Doreen as she led Scorchington away by the hand.

"Scorchington."

"I'm Doreen."

The five of them made their way back across the street, passing the still burning bin lid in the middle of the road.

When they reached the other side, Scorchington let go of Doreen's hand and smiled at her. "Thanks, but I've got to get back to Earls Court Tube station. The rest of the Stobes could be in a lot of trouble, and I need to get back to them."

"Stobes?" said Wedge.

"That's what we're called," replied Scorchington. "But there are also the Darkenbads and the Cribbit Snocklers too. But I shouldn't be telling you any of this. If Wattage and the others find out I've been seen by Topsiders, I'm in big trouble."

"Topsiders? Who are they?" said Charlie.

"That's what we call you...all of you who live up here." replied Scorchington.

"Do you know where you're going?" asked Rod.

"Not really." replied Scorchington.

"Well in that case, we'll give you a *Topsider* escort back there," smiled Rod.

Wedge took of his jacket, and put it around Scorchington's shoulders.

"I'm not cold." said Scorchington.

"It's not to keep you warm. It's to try and disguise you," replied Wedge.

Scorchington smiled and pulled the jacket around him. Then the five of them made their way slowly and cautiously down the street. Wedge stopped momentarily and looked back at the wheelie bin, which had now burnt down to just the wheels. The pavement was covered in melted plastic and charred rubbish. Miraculously, the fire had avoided the shop immediately behind.

In the distance though, he could see blue lights flashing, then the unmistakable sound of a fire engine siren echoed round the deserted streets.

"We'd better get out of here, and a bit quick too!" he shouted to the others.

They all started to run down the street. Scorchington's short legs were struggling to keep up the pace, so Charlie and Rod both grabbed him under his arms and picked him up. Even though he was being carried, Scorchington's legs still continued to run, much to the amusement of Doreen who was huffing and puffing to keep up.

Eventually they rounded a corner, and in the distance the neon glow of the tube station sign came into view. When they arrived at station, it was still deserted.

Charlie and Rod lowered Scorchington to the ground and took a few moments to catch their breaths. Doreen followed by Wedge moments later.

"Are you OK?" said Charlie looking at Doreen's purple face.

"I'm...fine...thanks." she panted.

Scorchington headed towards the entrance to the platform.

"How are you going to get in, it's closed?" said Wedge.

"We have our special ways." smiled Scorchington.

"Before you go, can I take a selfie of us all?" said Doreen.

"What's a 'selfie'?" said Scorchington.

"It's a photograph," replied Charlie.

Scorchington smiled. He knew something the Topsiders didn't, and it amused him.

"Sure."

The five of them huddled together with Scorchington in the middle, and Doreen held her phone out at arms length.

"Smile," she grinned. "One more for good look." she continued.

"Want one with flames?" said Scorchington.

"Pardon?" said Doreen.

"Just take the picture and I'll show you," grinned Scorchington.

As Doreen started to take another picture, Scorchington blew a big jet of fire up into the air.

"Now that is seriously cool!" said Wedge excitedly.

Scorchington smiled, and walked over to the entrance. Charlie, Rod, Wedge and Doreen were distracted by the sound of another siren along with flashing blue lights, as a police car hurtled down the road passed them. When it had disappeared out of sight, they turned back round.

Scorchington had gone.

They walked towards the locked entrance and looked around, but all they found was Wedge's jacket on the floor.

A muffled voice echoed from somewhere on the other side of the locked entrance.

"See you around Topsiders!"

After a few moments, Charlie, Rod and Doreen started to walk back down the road. Wedge stood in front of the entrance and continued to look around. *There must be a way to get in,* he mumbled to himself.

Over on the right was a big poster sign on the wall of the station. In between that and the entrance was a drainpipe. Wedge began to climb up it. After much grunting and struggling, he reached a small flat roof. At the back of this was a line of metal railings. He carefully climbed over these and began to lower himself down the other side. He managed to get his toes onto the roof on the other side, but in the process his sweater had snagged on the top of one of the railings. He tugged at the sweater, but it wouldn't budge. The more he struggled the more his sweater snagged.

In a last effort, he managed to rip his sweater off the railings, and fell backwards onto the roof. He looked down onto the platform below. In the distance at the far end, he saw Scorchington walking towards the tunnel entrance.

Just as he reached the entrance, the tall slender figure of Vember walked out of the tunnel. Wedge sat motionless on the roof watching.

He watched as she reached down and slapped Scorchington hard on the top of the head, then pushed him into the tunnel and gave him a kick up his backside.

"See you around Scorchington!" Shouted Wedge.

Vember turned round and looked in his direction. Wedge stood up and waved at her. Vember didn't wave back, but turned round and headed into the tunnel.

"Have you *any* idea what you've now done?" she snapped at Scorchington.

Scorchington decided silence was the best form of defence, and continued to walk sheepishly down the tunnel.

Wedge couldn't wait to tell the others, and tried to vault back over the metal railings, this time snagging his jeans on them. By the time he caught up with Charlie, Rod and Doreen, he looked like he'd been in a fight with a pack of wild animals.

"I've just seen another one," he panted. "There are more of them. This is just so exciting! I mean come on, we've proved there are strange creatures living in the underground... I knew there was. And we've got proof. Doreen lets look at the pictures you took?"

Doreen took out her phone and opened the selfies she'd taken of them all.

They all huddled round Doreen's phone and looked at the pictures. Whilst they clearly showed Charlie, Rod,

Wedge and Doreen, there was no sign of Scorchington in any of them.

"How can that happen?" said Rod.

"Where is he?" said Doreen.

She reloaded the pictures just in case there was something wrong with her phone. Still there was no Scorchington. However, on the third picture, there was a big jet of flame visible. It started about three foot above the ground and finished about six feet above Wedge's head.

"This is now beyond weird," said Charlie.

Doreen looked at the pictures once more and smiled.

"*Boy your lovin' is all I think about,*" she whispered.

"What?" said Wedge?

"Oh, nothing." replied Doreen.

Slowly they all walked off down the street, each one of them deep in their own thoughts as to just what had happened.

Chapter Thirty Four

ON THE LONG ABANDONED PLATFORM across from the disused line of track near Brompton Road, Hetty and Spoogemige waited nervously in the shadows. Further down another tunnel, Ripperton and Gobbit were heading for the same platform.

"They might not come back this way." said Spoogemige.

"I think they will at this time of night," replied Hetty. "It's the quickest and there won't be any Topsiders to worry about."

Spoogemige looked at Hetty, and for a moment, tried to work out how much she weighed. He knew if things got bad, he could run away to safety. But what about Hetty? Could he carry her weight on his back if he needed to?

Hetty looked at Spoogemige, and pondered the same thing. Could Spoogemige carry her on his back? She looked down at her short fat body, and breathed in to try and make herself look slimmer. Reaching up to her antlers, she pushed a hoof inside her oven mitt and pulled it towards her, gently rubbing it against her cheek. A look of sadness spread across her face as she remembered the *other* oven mitt.

Spoogemige stared into the tunnel. *Where were they?*

The sound of footsteps started to echo from behind them. They weren't coming from the tunnel at the end of the platform. They were coming from somewhere behind them – *very* close behind them.

Spoogemige and Hetty climbed down onto the track and moved a few yards into the tunnel. The footsteps got nearer until it seemed they were only a few yards away. Then they stopped.

Hetty and Spoogemige held their breath and tried not to move or make a sound.

Ripperton looked around the platform, then down onto the tracks. Reaching inside her leather jacket, she pulled out one of the old lawnmower blades. Running a long black fingernail along the edge of it, she continued to look around. As she did, she started to tap her fingernails on the blade, in a slow deliberate way, *tap...tap...tap.*

After a few moments, she stopped tapping the blade. Spoogemige didn't know how much longer he could hold his breath for. Hetty too was struggling. The air was filled with a menacing silence.

Spoogemige leant back and closed his eyes. He could feel Hetty pressing against him. He put an arm gently around her and pulled her closer too him. They both waited for something to happen.

It did.

A faint sound from deep inside the blackness of the tunnel began to ripple in waves towards them. Slowly and steadily it got nearer, and louder.

It was the sound of footsteps – several footsteps, all heading in the direction of Spoogemige and Hetty.

Ripperton heard them too. She walked over to the platform edge, and stared into the tunnel. Spoogemige and Hetty pressed themselves tightly against the tunnel wall.

At the back of the platform, Gobbit was leaning against an old faded poster stuck on the old cracked tiling of the platform wall. He clutched his underpants tightly in one claw, whilst with the other he picked his nose. He pulled out a large piece of snot, and looked at it. He moved his claw towards his mouth and stuck his tongue out to taste it. He was about to eat it, when he suddenly hiccupped.

Ripperton span round on her heels and glowered at him. She turned back and slowly climbed down onto the track. *Stobes or Darkenbads?* She thought to herself.

Spoogemige and Hetty knew the answer before she did. Spoogemige let out a huge sigh of relief as familiar shadows came into view from round the bend.

Ripperton heard his sigh too.

With a sinister glint in her eye, and a lightening quick flick of her arm, she hurled the lawn mower blade into the tunnel. It ricocheted of the tunnel wall just next to Hetty. She screamed as it smashed into her antlers, before bouncing off them and landing with a metallic echo on the tracks.

The shadows down the tunnel heard this, and immediately started to run. Spoogemige and Hetty started to run towards them waiving their arms.

Ripperton scowled and lashed out her right foot in frustration, before climbing back onto the platform.

"*Stobes.*" she snarled, as she walked back across the platform and into the tunnel behind. Gobbit clutched his underpants and followed her.

Fuddlerook was the first to arrive. He'd recognised the silhouette of Ripperton from down the tunnel, and jumped onto the platform to try to catch her. He made his way into the tunnel behind the platform and stared into the darkness, but there was no sign of her.

He made his way back onto the platform where the others had now arrived.

Scorchington was so pleased to see them, especially Criblee. He gave him a big hug. They all climbed onto the platform.

"Where's Vember?" said Spoogemige.

"She's gone back to try and find that little orange twazlet," replied Fligboge. "He decided to go walkabout out there." he continued, pointing an arm upwards.

"She's gone alone?" said Spoogemige anxiously.

Fuddlerook walked over to Spoogemige and put a hand on his shoulder.

"She'll be alright, don't worry."

Hetty, meanwhile, was busy explaining to Wattage that the table was now back in his study, and that it had been accompanied by two Darkenbads *and* Two Cribbit Snocklers.

Wattage walked over to Fuddlerook and grabbing him by the arm, pulled him over to the far side of the platform.

"We need to get back to my study. The table is apparently there. But we don't know whether there are also any Darkenbads there."

"I'll take Spoogemige and Criblee with me, and we'll check it out. If there's no one there, I'll send Spoogemige back to tell you," replied Fuddlerook.

"We'll be there too. Sir." said Colin Gerbil as he poked his head out from Fuddlerook's shoulder bag. The heads of Seb and Frank Gerbil closely followed.

"No. I'm coming with you," said Wattage.

Wattage walked back to the others and told them.

"Wouldn't it be better if we all stayed together?" said Hetty.

At that moment, the sound of movement back down the tunnel interrupted them. Fuddlerook jumped down onto the track, and stared down into the tunnel. He motioned the rest of them to be quiet.

Slowly through the darkness, he could make out two shadows heading towards them. He turned and smiled at the others as the tall figure of Vember accompanied by the much shorter figure of Scorchington came into view.

Vember smiled at Fuddlerook and hugged him. Scorchington though, walked sheepishly past him and climbed onto the platform. The rest of the Stobes stared disapprovingly at him.

"Nice one twazlet," mocked Fligboge. "Been making *friends* with Topsiders then?" he continued sarcastically.

Scorchington looked down at his feet, and felt himself begin to turn red – well as red as it's possible for something orange to actually turn red.

"Where's the Mole in the Wall Gang?" said the Battenberg Twins.

Of course, nobody heard them.

"WHERE'S THE MOLE IN THE WALL GANG?"

"Ssshhhhh," said Hetty.

"Sorry."

"The last time I we saw them, they were tunnelling into Cromwell Road Hospital," replied Wattage. "But I think they might have hit one of the main power cables, because all of the lights suddenly went out. And I've a horrible feeling something bad must have happened."

"Oh dear. I hope they're OK."

"Did you actually meet any Topsiders?" said Criblee crouching down next to Scorchington.

Scorchington didn't say anything. He was in enough trouble as it was. To admit to not only meeting some Topsiders, but also having his picture taken with them, would guarantee more trouble than even *he* was used to getting into.

Wattage and Fuddlerook started to make their way towards the tunnel at the back of the platform.

"Come on," they said to the rest of them.

They all slowly filed across the platform and into the tunnel. Fuddlerook led the way, with Vember bringing up the rear. As they crept down the tunnel, the familiar surroundings of what was their home did little to calm their fears.

They eventually reached the corridor leading down to Wattage's study. Whilst the rest of them stayed where they were, Fuddlerook and Wattage went ahead. Soon they were level with Wattage's study. Everything seemed silent. Wattage looked down at his study door lying on the floor on top of the old lawn mower. Slowly Fuddlerook inched his way forward. He reached into his divers suit for his screwdriver, but then remembered he'd given it to Vember.

He paused and looked back at Wattage. He then looked back at the rest of the Stobes. They were all in a line, next to the wall of the corridor. They looked like they'd all been lined up for a firing squad.

Fuddlerook lifted the flap of his shoulder bag. The Gerbil Brothers' heads popped up. He pointed to the study, and then raised two fingers to his eyes and pointed to them, and then pointed to the study.

The Gerbil Brothers climbed out of the bag and dropped to the floor. Rolling onto their stomachs, they started to wriggle their way towards the entrance. It wasn't long before they disappeared out of sight and into Wattage's study.

There was a pause of a few seconds, before Frank Gerbil reappeared in the doorway.

"All clear and secured. Sir!"

Wattage pushed his way past Fuddlerook and ran into the study. He looked round at all the mess, and then he saw what he was hoping for. There in the far corner stood the table. It was humming and vibrating. He walked over to it and sighed with relief. Fuddlerook walked into the room after him, and turned round to the Gerbil Brothers.

"Good work men. Now scout out the kitchen and the rest of the rooms."

"Affirmative. Sir!" Replied Colin Gerbil.

As the Gerbil Brothers set off down the corridor to check the other rooms, Vember and Spoogemige followed them.

Fuddlerook walked back into the study to where Wattage was leaning over the table looking at the gold and silver pegs. Although he wanted to keep the table and explore what it could do, he knew he couldn't. The table was dangerous. It spelt trouble. He knew what he had to do!

He reached out and grabbed the silver peg. Pulling and twisting it, he lifted it out of its hole. The table stopped vibrating. He did the same with the gold peg. The table fell silent. He looked at the two pegs in his hand, and closed his long wrinkled fingers around them and squeezed them tightly.

Walking out of his study, he made his way down the corridor towards the metal door at the far end. Reaching up he slowly pushed the two pegs through the mesh grill in the door. The two pegs fell silently down the void of the lift shaft on the other side of the door. He waited to hear them hit the bottom, but the lift shaft was so deep that he heard nothing.

The Gerbil Brothers, Vember and Spoogemige had finished checking out all the other rooms, and found no traces of either Darkenbads or Cribbit Snocklers. However, in one of the rooms they did find something else?

Sitting in a row, very wet and exhausted were the Mole in the Wall Gang.

"You're all safe?" exclaimed Vember.

"Not all of us." replied Muldvar mournfully.

"Two of our comrades have gone to the big mole hill in the sky," said Mogra.

"Oh I'm so sorry," replied Vember. "What happened?"

243

"Moles and electric cables don't get on very well," said Muldvar. "Our eldest and youngest both died valiantly though, and now we must appoint a new leader,"

"We need to do this in private, if you don't mind." Said Talpa walking towards the door.

"Of course," said Vember.

"Permission to show respect and leave the Mole in the Wall Gang to find their new commander. Sir!" said Frank Gerbil to Vember.

The Gerbil Brothers stood in a line and saluted Talpa, before making their way out of the room. Vember and Spoogemige followed. As Talpa began closing the door, Spoogemige turned round and noticed that Mogra was carrying some bits of pastry, and Walter was holding a shoe. The door closed, and soon the sound of digging could be heard.

Vember, Spoogemige and the Gerbil Brothers made their way back to the kitchen, where the rest of the Stobes were now gathered and waiting - apart from Fuddlerook - who was still in Wattage's study staring at the table.

As Wattage walked back in, Fuddlerook turned to him.

"Are you sure it's now safe?"

"I think so. Without those pegs, it's just a table."

"And you're sure of this?"

"As sure as I can be? The problem is, the Darkenbads and Cribbit Snocklers don't know that?"

"You know they're going to come back for it don't you? And this time, it will be *all* of them."

"We're certainly in *grave* danger. I don't know how long it will be before they come, but *come* they will!"

They both headed off towards the kitchen. The rest of the Stobes needed to know about the storm that was coming.

Chapter Thirty Five

ON A STREET IN EARLS Court, the Topsiders in the bright red fire engine had finished putting out the wheelie bin by the time PC Meredith and PC Walton arrived. As one of the firemen was removing the bin lid from the middle of the road, the others were busy coiling up their hoses.

PC Meredith looked at the burnt out wheelie bin and sighed. *Will I ever get to investigate a proper meaty crime?* He thought to himself. PC Walton, on the other hand, was more than happy to not be doing so. Idiots mowing other people's lawns at three in the morning, stolen supermarket trolleys burnt out wheelie bins - these were the kind crimes he liked. All the nonsense with the stone table the previous day had been too much for him. He didn't need any more excitement this year.

He headed over to PC Meredith, who was looking around the area next to the wheelie bin, desperate to find something interesting.

"Obviously some kids messing about." he said.

"Maybe," replied PC Meredith. "But you never know – especially after what we witnessed and experienced yesterday."

"Oh God, you're not trying to make a connection, are you?"

"I don't know."

"Look, it's obviously some youths who set fire to it for a laugh. It won't be the first time. That one at Asda the other week, for instance?"

PC Meredith walked over to the shop doorway next to the remains of the bin. "Well, what have we got here?"

He bent down and picked up a ripped and burnt hoodie, and the melted remains of a plastic carrier bag.

"This hoodie's got blood on it... look!"

PC Walton looked at the hoodie. It did indeed have what looked like blood on it. It was slashed open across the back too. He then pulled out the charred remains of a loaf of bread, a single burnt carpet slipper and what looked like the melted remains of an iPod. "Tramp?" said PC Walton.

As PC Meredith examined the items, he suddenly had a thought.

"You remember yesterday, when we were at Baker Street? Well remember that bloke who was there, you know, the one who was also at that garage I got taken to on that damn table? There was a girl with him, you know, a bit on the fat side..."

"Yes I do, but what has that got to do with a melted plastic carrier bag and a burnt out wheelie bin?"

"...Well...if you recall, she said she'd seen some kind of a small orange dragon like creature earlier... remember?"

"Oh you *believed* that, did you?"

"If somebody told you what happened to us yesterday, would you believe them? Probably not, but that doesn't alter the fact it *actually* happened."

"True. So what are you trying to say?"

"She said that it wore a black t-shirt."

"That's a hoodie."

"…Yes it is. But she also said it was wearing carpet slippers, listening to music and eating toast. So what are these?"

PC Meredith waved the burnt loaf of bread, then the singed carpet slipper and finally the melted iPod in front of PC Walton.

"Oh, bugger!"

"Exactly!"

Chapter Thirty Six

IN A DIMLY LIT TUNNEL, with a floor full of foul, sticky grunge and an awful smell, seven Cribbit Snocklers had returned from their journey into the world of the Topsider's, and hung from the roof on their tiny stumpy claws.

Dranoel's face was still looking odd and slightly twisted, Neb had a large lump on his face that was rapidly turning a violent shade of purple, and Stubbs's bowel problems were even worse after his run in with Darl and Rodolp.

Pratt, Bodge, Rollo and Lug were no longer on speaking terms, and there was an even more depressing atmosphere than normal in the tunnel. The Cribbit Snocklers expectations of being able to witness carnage and mayhem were not fulfilled.

No one was more frustrated and disappointed than Neb. He didn't like being disappointed. It made him angry. He needed to find a way to create some serious havoc to compensate for this. *I wonder if those Stobes know something that I don't?* He thought to himself, before deciding to go and find out.

The rest of the Cribbit Snocklers were, for once, not remotely interested in where Neb was going as he flew off down the tunnel. Instead, they continued sulking with each other. Except Stubb, whose bottom was in the process of making its way noisily over to another part of the tunnel to increase the amount of grunge on the floor and make the smell even worse?

* * * * *

Down in another part of the Underground, most of the Darkenbads had also eventually made their way back to the abandoned platform where they lived. Ripperton was still furious with what had happened and was brutally kicking the remains of the old ticket office and snarling very unpleasant things about what she was going to do to various members of the Stobes.

Gobbit on the other hand had found a half-empty glass bottle of something on his way back, and was slumped against one of the walls with a silly smile on his face. Woogums was sat cross-legged on the floor chewing a brick, and Wobblett was punching the plasterboard wall, which ran down the centre of the platform.

At the far end of the platform, Grizthrop had returned from whatever he'd been doing whilst the rest were up in the Topsiders world. His welders mask was all steamed up and there were even more blood stains on his sledgehammer.

The creaking of the old heavy metal door at the opposite end of the platform slowly opening, distracted the Darkenbads. Rodolp walked onto the platform. He was followed a few seconds later by the tall black menacing form of Darl.

Silence fell as he limped slowly down the platform, staring at each one of the Darkenbads in turn. They all lowered their heads in deference to him. He stopped when he reached the old ticket office where Ripperton was. He slowly leant his head to one side and let at a long, almost tortured sigh.

Ripperton stared back at him and a beam spread across her face. She rushed over and embraced him. Darl flinched slightly, unused to physical contact or affection. He didn't seem to know what to do, and hesitantly closed his arms around her.

"You're *dead.*" she whispered into one of his long pointed and horribly scarred ears.

"Not completely, it would seem," he replied, an almost soft tone to his voice.

Rodolp stood in the middle of the platform, lifted his nose upwards and loudly inhaled the stale air.

"Last night was not one of your finer moments." He said condescendingly.

Darl pulled away from Ripperton and walked over to him.

"There's still the chance for them to redeem themselves my friend."

* * * * *

Meanwhile, Neb had arrived at the ventilation shaft that led up to tunnels near Brompton Road where the Stobes lived. He paused for breath. The lump on his head appeared to be expanding, and he had a thumping headache. He grabbed hold of an old iron bar sticking out of the wall with his feet and hung upside down. Looking down into the darkness below, he noticed something shiny lying in the dust and dirt at the bottom of the shaft.

He dropped down to the bottom of the shaft and landed next to the shiny object. Picking it up in a stumpy claw, he raised it up to his face to look closer. It was a gold peg. It was heavy and smelt strange. He flew back up the shaft until he reached a small metal pipe. He didn't want to carry the gold peg with him, so he placed it carefully in a gap between two bricks so he could come back and collect it later. Squeezing and squirming his way through the pipe, he dropped out of the other end into the tunnel – the tunnel where the Stobes lived.

Flying quickly and silently, he soon reached Wattage's study. He could hear the sound of voices from further down the tunnel. Banking left, he glided into Wattages study and came to rest on a metal shelf on the far wall. He looked across the room and smiled. Standing in the corner was the stone table.

"Oh yesss!" he hissed.

Taking to the air, he flew as fast as he could out of Wattages study and down the tunnel. All he had to do now was tell Rodolp, and the carnage and mayhem he wanted so badly was now guaranteed to happen.

Taking a different route out of the tunnel, he completely forgot to collect the gold peg he'd hidden in the ventilation shaft.

* * * * *

In the kitchen, Wattage and Fuddlerook told the rest of the Stobes what was almost certainly going to happen.

There had been many skirmishes and battles in the past. But after the last big one - The Battle of Bakerloo - things had been relatively calm. There had still been muggings and other minor attacks, but with the demise of Darl at Bakerloo, things had not been too bad.

However, as the Stobes began to prepare themselves, none of them knew that Darl had returned. Or that he hadn't died in the fight with Fuddlerook, which saw him dragged under the wheels of the 10.52 to Elephant & Castle.

They didn't know it, but what they were about to face, was going to be a lot worse than what they were planning for.

Chapter Thirty Seven

NEB MADE HIS WAY THROUGH the labyrinth of tunnels and ventilation shafts until he was in the deepest levels of the Underground. As he approached an old rusting metal door, the hairs on his tiny body began to tingle and stand on end.

On the other side of the door was the one creature in the Underground who unnerved Neb like no other. He suspended himself upside down on the top of the lintel, knocked on the door and waited. A few moments later, the door creaked and groaned open. Standing in the doorway was Rodolp.

"Oh look. It's Meals on Wings," he said with a glint in his eyes. "I'm presuming you have something really interesting to tell us? Or do you just want to jump straight into my mouth now?" he continued sarcastically before opening his mouth wide.

Neb just hung there in uncharacteristic silence, and stared over his shoulder down the platform.

"What? No pithy comeback? No sarcastic retort? I do so enjoy our occasional banter," said Rodolp.

Neb remained silent. His eyes fixed on the hideous dark figure, which was now making its way down the platform towards him and Rodolp.

Rodolp reached up and flicked Neb on the nose with his claw, but there was still no reaction.

'Has a Pussycat Broll got your tongue?" continued Rodolp.

Neb tensed up, his whole body rigid as the figure of Darl finally reached the door.

Darl held out his arm and smiled menacingly at Neb.

"Take a seat."

Neb reluctantly dropped down onto Darl's outstretched arm and wrapped his claws into the course fabric of Darl's overcoat. As Darl walked back down the platform, he reached across and ran a long dirty fingernail across the lump in Neb's head.

"Been in the wars, have you? I know exactly how you feel."

When he got level with the old ticket office, he stopped, and with remarkable gentleness, lifted Neb onto the top of the counter. The rest of the Darkenbads slowly gathered round.

"Now, please tell me that the table is still with the Stobes, or if it isn't, that you know where it is. Because anything else will most certainly result in you becoming elevenses for my dear friend Rodolp!"

Neb looked up at Darl, and at last managed to choke some words out of his mouth.

"Aren't you dead?"

"You know, you're not the first to ask me that. In fact I'm beginning to wonder myself."

Darl looked down at his hands and the long claw like nails protruding out of his fingers. He then looked down at Neb and sighed deeply, before suddenly slamming his fists down onto the counter inches away from Neb.

"As much as I'd like to catch up on what we've both been up to since we last met, I'm afraid I haven't got the time right now." he snarled. "So tell me where the table is."

To emphasise his point, Darl then poked a long fingernail into the bruised purple lump on Nebs head.

Neb flinched in pain, before speaking once more.

"The table is still in Wattage's study."

Darl reached down and gave him a condescending pat on the head before turning round and walking off down the platform. Rodolp and the rest of the Darkenbads followed obediently behind.

When he got to the door Darl turned round and shouted down the platform to Neb.

"We can catch up on things later if you like. And make sure you get that lump seen to."

Rodolp was the last one through the door. As he stepped through it, he looked back down the platform at Neb.

"You're most welcome to join us, you know. I find a blood-soaked battle always gives me an appetite."

Neb flew down the platform and out of the door, before making his own way back to the rest of the Cribbit Snocklers.

Meanwhile, the darkenbads began their journey to Brompton Road, and a long overdue battle with the Stobes. For Darl, Rodolp and Ripperton however, it was much more than that. It was personal. There were long overdue scores to settle, and revenge to be taken.

Chapter Thirty Eight

THE UNDERGROUND WAS VERY QUIET compared to normal. Thanks to the Tube Strike, there weren't millions of Topsiders rushing about frantically from one station to another. Even the Topsiders responsible for maintaining the Underground were on strike.

Station entrances remained padlocked, ticket offices lay silent, and escalators stood stationary. Lift doors remained closed, and trains sat motionless on their subterranean tracks.

Most of the lighting was off and the whole place had a peculiar atmosphere to it, as if it had been suddenly evacuated.

In the tunnel complex next to the long abandoned station of Brompton Road, the Stobes waited anxiously. They had all armed themselves with whatever they could find. Fuddlerook was convinced that the best course of action was to move to Brompton Road Station itself. Brompton Road gave them more space, and more opportunities to surprise the Darkenbads compared to the restricted and claustrophobic confines of their own tunnels.

And so it was, that a plan was hatched. Fuddlerook and Vember would remain as bait, whilst the rest of them moved to Brompton Road. Fuddlerook and Vember would then lead the Darkenbads to Brompton Road, where the rest of the Stobes would be lay in hiding ready for a surprise attack.

It was a dangerous plan. Fuddlerook and Vember were the strongest and most skilled fighters. If anything were to go wrong and anything happened to them, then the chances of the rest of the Stobes being able to survive a Darkenbad onslaught were slim.

It was with great reluctance that Wattage left Fuddlerook and Vember behind, and began to lead the others to Brompton Road.

"Please be safe, my friend." Said Wattage.

"Of course we will." Replied Fuddlerook.

As they filed off down the tunnel, Fuddlerook turned to Vember and smiled.

"Are you ready for this?"

"Yes."

"Remember everything I've taught you. You will need it all today...and more. I wish your father were here to see you. He would be so proud of what you've become.

"You *knew* my father?"

"Yes. I knew him well, very well."

"Why have you never told me about him?"

"I was waiting for the right moment...but somehow never found it...until *now*."

"Tell me about him. What was he like? Who was he?"

"He was very special. Strong, yet gentle. He always looked for the good in someone. Unfortunately, he looked for the good in the *wrong* one. A good that was *never* there, and it cost him his life."

"How did he die?"

"You don't need to know that. It would serve no purpose. All you need to know is that he died protecting what mattered most to him. You."

"Tell me what happened. I need to know."

"It was a long time ago, Vember. And those wounds don't need opening again."

"Tell me!"

"Your father...well, he was my brother. His name was Nazzeroth. He fell in love with a beautiful Stobe called Miras... your mother. Unfortunately, there was another who was also in love with her - a Darkenbad. A Darkenbad, who couldn't bear the thought of her loving someone else. After you and your sister were born..."

"My *sister*?"

Straight way Fuddlerook realised his mistake. He'd never meant to tell anyone *that* secret, certainly not Vember.

"I have a *sister*?"

Fuddlerook quickly tried to stop things going any further.

"You did have. But she died a long time ago."

Fuddlerook knew this was a lie. But it was a lie for the right reasons. He could not risk Vember finding out who her sister was. It was a secret he'd promised to carry to his grave. Sworn to his brother as he lay dying in his arms.

He could never reveal the truth. The truth that the Darkenbad in question was Darl. That it was Darl who had killed her father - his brother, and her mother too. That it was Darl who had then tried to steal both Vember and her sister. That Fuddlerook had only been able to save one of them, and that he had chosen Vember.

"Who is my sister?"

The sound of movement coming from the far end of the tunnel suddenly interrupted them.

They're here!" whispered Fuddlerook.

"Who *is* my sister?" continued Vember.

"Now is not the time or place, Vember. We will continue this later. Right now, we have some Darkenbads to deal with."

Vember kicked the tunnel wall in frustration. Then both of them made their way down the tunnel to meet the Darkenbads and put the first part of their plan into action.

Suddenly the huge figure of Grizthrop came charging down the tunnel swinging a large sledgehammer around in circles. The hammer smashed into the walls of the tunnel knocking bricks and tiles to the ground. As he got nearer and nearer Fuddlerook and Vember could only turn back, and start running. Behind them, the sound of the metal head of the sledgehammer smashing into the walls echoed violently. In front of them lay the bricked up wall at the end of the tunnel.

As Grizthrop was about to bring the sledgehammer down on top of them, Fuddlerook grabbed Vember. They both dived sideways into Wattage's study just as the head of the hammer came crashing down, missing them both by millimetres.

Grizthrop stopped, turned round and charged into Wattage's study after them, still swinging the hammer wildly around his head.

Back down the tunnel, Rodolp and Darl had been watching in amusement.

"He isn't the most subtle of creatures," said Rodolp. "But he is very effective."

Fuddlerook and Vember ran over and crouched down behind the stone table. Grizthrop stopped swinging the sledgehammer, and stood in the middle of the room breathing heavily. His boiler suit was covered in what looked like bloodstains, and his welders mask was now completely steamed up. Sweat was dripping off the bottom of his red beard, which poked out from behind the mask. He let the sledgehammer drop down to his side and, lifting a massive gnarled and calloused hand up to the mask, tried to wipe the glass clean.

Behind the table, Fuddlerook and Vember were trying to figure out their next move. *Was Grizthrop alone, or were the rest of the Darkenbads waiting back down the tunnel?*

Fuddlerook decided to try to take on Grizthrop. He stood up from behind the table. As he did, Vember suddenly jumped out from behind the table and ran across to the other corner of the room to attract his attention.

"NO!" shouted Fuddlerook.

It was too late. Grizthrop grabbed his sledgehammer in both hands and started walking towards Vember, slowly swinging the sledgehammer round in circles over his head. Just as Grizthrop got with striking distance, Vember dived to the ground, did a forward roll and rushed back to join Fuddlerook behind the table.

Grizthrop turned and rushed at them. As he got within a few feet of the table, he lifted the sledgehammer high above his head, and with a muffled yet blood-curdling roar brought the hammer crashing down. Fuddlerook and Vember managed to leap backwards just in time as it missed them and instead smashed into the table. A loud cracking noise came from the table. Grizthrop raised the hammer in the air once more, and was just about to bring it crashing down for a second time when there was another loud cracking sound from the table, followed by a huge flash of light.

Fuddlerook and Vember turned to face the wall and covered their eyes as bolts of light flashed from the table filling the room. Grizthrop let out a loud scream as one of the bolts of light hit him in the head, shattering the glass on his welders mask. He slumped to his knees and let go of the sledgehammer. Another even louder cracking sound then came from the table, followed by huge explosion, as the table suddenly disintegrated into a hundred pieces.

Bits of table ricocheted across the room. Fuddlerook and Vember threw themselves to the floor and pulled their arms around each other for protection. Eventually an eerie silence fell on the room.

Vember turned round and noticed Grizthrop was still slumped on his knees in front of where the table had been. He was clutching his welders mask and groaning. His was covered in dust and small fragments of table. One pointed piece of table was sticking out of his chest, and a steady trickle of blood ran down from the wound. The sledgehammer lay next to him on the floor. Vember ran across to him, picked up the hammer and then swung it fiercely at his head. The hammer slammed into his welder's mask and knocked him onto his back. He let out a low anguished groan, and then nothing.

Fuddlerook walked over and took the sledgehammer from Vember's hands.

"Is he dead?" she asked.

"I don't know," replied Fuddlerook. "But we're not going to hang about to find out."

Down at the far end of the tunnel Rodolp and Darl had seen the bolts of light and heard the explosion. They waited to see who would come out of the room - if anyone.

Fuddlerook and Vember were still in a precarious position. They didn't know who was waiting at the end of the tunnel. If they could sneak down to the room where Spoogemige and Criblee slept there was a doorway, which opened onto a passageway that led to the old abandoned platform of Brompton Road. However, even if they could get to it, how would they then be able to lure the Darkenbads to the ambush waiting there?

The solution to their problem however, was about to come from the most unlikely source - The Cribbit Snocklers.

Whilst Fuddlerook and Vember had been battling with Grizthrop, Rodolp and Darl along with the rest of the Darkenbads had been watching from the far end of the tunnel. The Cribbit Snocklers had also been watching proceedings from the tunnel roof.

None of the Darkenbads noticed Neb fly into Wattage's study. Even Fuddlerook and Vember failed to notice until he spoke.

"He's going to struggle to get a new piece of glass for that welders mask."

Fuddlerook and Vember looked up at the ceiling of the room from where the voice was coming from.

"Mind you, it looks like that could be the least of his problems." continued Neb, looking down at the prone body of Grizthrop lying on the floor.

Fuddlerook lifted the sledgehammer in the air, and moved towards Neb.

"I know what you're thinking, but believe it or not, although hitting me with that might seem a sensible thing to do, it probably isn't – that is, it isn't, if you want to get out of here without being torn to pieces by the gang of Darkenbads waiting for you at the end of the tunnel." said Neb.

Fuddlerook stopped and let the hammer fall to his side.

"Yep, that's right. They're all waiting for you down at the far end of the tunnel -including..." Neb paused in order to get maximum effect for what he was about to say next. "...A Darkenbad you probably weren't expecting even in your worst nightmares!"

"What do you mean?" replied Fuddlerook, now beginning to take a very keen interest in what Neb was saying.

"Does the name *Darl* ring any bells?"

Fuddlerook let go of the hammer. It dropped to the floor with a thud.

"He's dead. You'll have to do better than that if you want to scare us." said Vember, moving closer to Fuddlerook.

"Unfortunately, I can assure you he isn't," replied Neb. "He is most horribly alive, and take it from me, even more hideous and frightening than before."

Fuddlerook stared at Neb, a look of fear beginning to take hold of the features of his face. Fuddlerook wasn't scared of any creature in the Underground - except Darl. He had watched him go under the wheels of the train. He had seen him dragged onto the track. He had seen the flash as Darl's battered body hit the 'live' rail. *How could anyone – even Darl - survive that?*

Vember could see the effect the mere mention of Darl's name had on Fuddlerook. She also now knew why he felt such hatred for him.

"You've seen him?" she said; trying to hide the anxiety she too could feel building up inside her.

"Seen him? Oh yes," replied Neb. "And trust me, there's something even more sinister about him than before. He certainly gives me the willies."

Fuddlerook began to compose himself. He certainly did not intend to let a Cribbit Snockler see how worried he was.

"So what have we done to deserve your help? And what makes you think we'd trust you in the first place?"

"Let's just say that, at this moment, it suits me better for you to stay alive,"

"And if we were interested, exactly how do you plan on helping us?"

"Quite simple really. I'll fly down there, and tell them that you were both killed when the table exploded."

"And you think they - Darl – will believe you?"

"Why not? I mean who would lie to someone like Darl? Could you think of a more stupid thing to do?"

"So you're going to be stupid, just to save our necks?"

"It would appear so,"

Neither Vember nor Fuddlerook trusted Neb. Nobody trusted the Cribbit Snocklers. Trusting a Cribbit Snockler would be like trusting a politician. However, at this moment, Fuddlerook and Vember didn't have any other option. They were between a rock and a dark place.

"By the way," continued Neb. "Where are the rest of the Stobes?"

"You honestly think we'd tell you that?" said Fuddlerook.

"Why not?" said Neb.

"So that you can fly off and tell the Darkenbads?" replied Vember.

"Why would I do that?"

"Because you're a Cribbit Snockler?"

"Fair point."

"I tell you what," said Fuddlerook. "You get us out of here, and *then* we'll tell you where the rest of the Stobes are."

Vember looked at Fuddlerook and frowned.

"How can I trust you?" said Neb.

"You'll have to," replied Fuddlerook. "In the same way that we'll have to trust *you*."

"Touché." smiled Neb.

Neb then flew down from the ceiling, out of the room and down the tunnel towards the Darkenbads.

"You trust him?" said Vember?

"Of course not," said Fuddlerook. "The minute we tell him where the rest of the Stobes are, he'll tell the Darkenbads."

"So why are you going to tell him?"

"Because we *want* the Darkenbads to know where the rest of the Stobes are, don't we? He only wants us alive so we can tell him where the rest are hiding, so he can then go and trade that information with the Darkenbads."

"Why doesn't he just tell the Darkenbads we're here?"

"Because he knows that we would rather fight and die, than tell the Darkenbads anything."

"But what about Darl? That changes everything."

'It changes *something*, but not everything. We still have to do this. If Darl is alive, he won't rest until he's got his revenge. He won't stop until *we* stop him."

"But can we?"

"I honestly don't know."

Vember smiled softly. "Maybe this hammer might come in useful?"

"If a train can't kill him, I don't know what use that hammer will be."

At the far end of the tunnel, Neb settled himself uneasily on the roof a few feet above the razor sharp teeth of Rodolp, and the dark figure of Darl.

"Is this a social call, or have you got something I might be interested in knowing?" said Rodolp sneeringly.

"What do you want first, the bad news, or the bad news?"

Rodolp's tail flicked from side to side, as he let out a deep and unsettling sigh.

"The bad news?"

"Well, your friend in the welders mask is out of action for the foreseeable future." replied Neb, anxiously watching their every move.

"And the bad news?"

"The Stobes no longer seem to be here. Looks like they've gone into hiding."

"What about the table?" asked Darl?

"Oh, I forgot about that. It's bad news though."

"Before you tell us, can I ask you a question?" said Rodolp.

"Sure."

"After coming down here and giving us not one, but three pieces of bad news, what do you think the odds are of you still being alive in five seconds time?"

"Probably not brilliant, judging by the expression on your faces."

He let out a nervous laugh, which was immediately wiped from his face by a withering look from Darl.

"Choose your next words very carefully, Neb. They may well be your last." he said coldly.

"So why did you bother?" continued Rodolp.

Neb shifted from one stubby claw to the next, and tried to disguise the fact that his heart was now beating faster than the snare drum of an angry heavy metal drummer.

"I'm beginning to wonder that myself."

Darl pushed Rodolp to one side and moved directly underneath Neb. He looked up with piercing white eyes. The thin black lips of his mouth parted slightly. He reached up with his hand, and pushed a long curved fingernail into the skin of his bald pointed head. Then slowly he pushed harder, until the nail pierced the white translucent flesh. He then dragged the nail across the side of his head tearing the skin. A black liquid started to ooze from the wound.

"I'll ask once more. Then it will be your pathetic flesh that this nail rips through. The table?"

"It exploded. It didn't seem to like being hit by your friend's sledgehammer. It's now nothing more than a five thousand piece jigsaw."

"*Aaaaarrghhh!*" roared Darl, and slammed a clenched fist into the tunnel wall.

The sound of Darl's roar of anger echoed down the tunnel. It seemed to go on forever. Fuddlerook and Vember heard it. So did the rest of the Stobes in hiding at Brompton Road. The roar seemed to create an icy chill, which swept through the Underground.

"Find out where the Stobes are in hiding," demanded Darl. "If you don't then I suggest you find a way of living up there with the Topsiders, because there will be no safe haven for you down here anymore. You will be nothing more than a dead Cribbit Snockler walking – correction, flying!"

Darl turned quickly on his heels and made his way over to where the rest of the Darkenbads were waiting out on the deserted platform.

Rodolp, however, remained and continued to stare up at Neb. He wasn't sure he was telling the truth. Whilst it is almost impossible to tell when a Cribbit Snockler is lying, Rodolp had a feeling in his gut.

"Don't disappoint him," said Rodolp, before turning away, and following after Darl.

Neb swallowed hard, before flying off back down the tunnel to Wattage's study where Fuddlerook and Vember were still hiding.

"I've done my part, now tell me where the rest of the Stobes are?"

"Did they buy it?" said Fuddlerook.

"Yes!"

"Meet me at the ventilation shaft at end of the tunnel in two minutes."

Neb flew back to the rest of the Cribbit Snocklers. Fuddlerook and Vember waited until they saw them all fly back down the tunnel, and then slowly made their way out of the study and down the tunnel to Spoogemige and Criblee's room.

"Go to the others, and tell them what has happened. I'll be along in a few minutes,"

While Vember opened the small door behind a set of bunk beds in the room and quietly sneaked down the narrow tunnel on the other side, which led to Brompton Road, Fuddlerook walked cautiously to meet the Cribbit Snocklers at the ventilation shaft.

They were already there, hanging from the tunnel roof.

"Well?" said Neb.

Fuddlerook looked round to make sure there were no Darkenbads.

"The disused station at Brompton Road."

"All of them?"

"Yes."

Behind the wall round the corner on the platform, Rodolp heard every word. His hunch was right. He would deal with Neb later.

He slowly moved across the platform and climbed down onto the tracks. In the distance he spotted the Darkenbads.

As Neb and the rest of the Cribbit Snocklers flew off, Fuddlerook dashed back down the tunnel and into Spoogemige and Criblee's room. Squeezing through the small door, he ran down the narrow tunnel to catch up with Vember and the rest of the Stobes at Brompton Road.

"This might work." He whispered to himself.

Chapter Thirty Nine

PREDICTABLY, IT TOOK NEB LESS than five minutes to break his word to Fuddlerook, and tell the Darkenbads where the Stobes were in hiding.

A broad smile spread across Darl's face. Rodolp too seemed very happy. He had a long, overdue score to settle with a certain small orange dragon.

At Brompton Road, the Stobes prepared themselves. The news that Darl was alive cast a black mood over everyone. Even without Darl, they knew that this battle was going to be hard one. But the presence of Darl would make things even worse.

Vember pulled Fuddlerook to one side.

"Tell me more about what happened to my Father and Mother."

"After the battle. We need to prepare."

"But you will tell me?"

"Yes. After this battle is over, I will tell you everything."

"You promise?"

"You have my word."

Vember smiled and squeezed his arm gently, before kissing him softly on the cheek. She knew that Fuddlerook always kept his word.

The Stobes began to find places to hide in the darkness of the old abandoned station. In one of the tunnels, there were some old bunk beds fastened to the wall, relics of when the Ministry of Defence used Brompton Road as an emergency shelter during the Second World War. The old woollen blankets were still in place, and there was a stale musty smell to them.

The Battenberg Twins, Gerbil Brothers and Mole in the Wall Gang all found hiding places there.

Fuddlerook walked into the corridor to check everyone was OK. The Gerbil Brothers stood to attention on the top bunk.

"Ready to commence covert guerrilla ambush. Sir!" said Colin Gerbil.

"Locked, loaded and ready. Sir!" said Frank Gerbil.

"Stealth position engaged. Sir!" said Seb Gerbil.

Fuddlerook smiled at them. He had a real soft spot for the Gerbil Brothers.

In another longer tunnel, Spoogemige, Criblee and Hetty crouched in the darkness against the wall behind an old generator. At the end of this tunnel, a flight of steps led down to a metal door. On the other side lay another tunnel. It was covered in decades of dust. Halfway along it, two semi circular metal grills on either side overlooked the stretch of tunnel of the Piccadilly Line between Gloucester Road and Knightsbridge. Here, Scorchington, Spogworth and Fligboge concealed themselves as best they could.

In order to conceal himself even more - even in a dimly lit place, orange tends to stand out - Scorchington rolled on the floor and covered himself in grey dust. For once, it actually worked. When he stood next to the grey walls of the tunnel, he really was almost invisible.

At the far end of this tunnel, another flight of steps led down to another tunnel running parallel to the Piccadilly Line. A big section of the tunnel wall had been removed so that it opened up onto the track. Fuddlerook, Vember and Wattage positioned themselves there, as it seemed the most obvious place the Darkenbads would come into the station.

Down another tunnel leading to where the ticket office used to stand, Plankton and Germ wandered around aimlessly. Plankton, as usual, did not know where he was and was, as usual, depressed. Of course, it didn't matter whether he hid or not. Being indestructible means you don't have to worry about things other creatures do - such as getting killed. Germ on the other hand, being the spineless coward he was, had no intention of getting involved, and was instead using the opportunity to see what he could knick.

Brompton Road stood silent, as the Stobes hid the shadows and waited for the Darkenbads to arrive.

"I thought the last battle might have been the last?" said Wattage woefully.

"After the fire, before the war." replied Fuddlerook solemnly.

Chapter Forty

PLANKTON WAS THE FIRST ONE to be unaware that the Darkenbads had arrived as a rusted lawnmower blade flew out of the darkness and punctured his rib cage. He let out a despondent sigh as he slumped to the ground. *Here we go again.*

Ripperton strolled casually over to Planktons body, rolled him over and pulled the lawnmower blade out of his tiny chest.

"Haven't I killed you before?" she said in a matter-of-fact way to Plankton's corpse. Plankton didn't answer.

Germ, watching from behind some old bags of cement, did what he did best and quietly slithered away down the tunnel to hide.

In an old ventilation shaft, seven Cribbit Snocklers flew down into the blackness until they reached an opening where a metal grill had once been, leading out onto the stretch of the Piccadilly Line, which led down to Brompton Road.

As they made their way along the tunnel roof, they saw the shadows of four Darkenbads walking down the middle of the track in the distance. Neb immediately recognised the tallest of the shadows.

Darl, Gobbit, Flem and Wobblett approached the section of tunnel wall that was missing, and where Fuddlerook, Vember and Wattage lay in hiding. Meanwhile, Woogums and Skerrett were making their way into Brompton Road via one of the other staircases.

And down at the bottom of another flight of steps, the solitary figure of Rodolp moved slowly closer to the tunnel Scorchington was hiding in.

Ripperton made her way down the tunnel and turned into the section where the Battenberg Twins, the Gerbil Brothers and the Mole in the Wall Gang were hiding. The Battenberg Twins were the first to spot her, and crawled further under the blanket they were hiding under on the bottom bunk.

On the second bunk, the Gerbil Brothers lay on the top of their blanket in sniper positions. The fact that their guns were only plastic, and they were about to come face to face with a ruthless cold-blooded killer, didn't seem to bother them at all.

On the top bunk, the Mole in the Wall Gang had also spotted Ripperton coming slowly towards them. They all quietly lined up against the wall and waited for her to get nearer.

As Ripperton moved closer to the bunk beds, she noticed two tiny little lumps slowly moving about under the blanket of the bottom bunk bed. Reaching inside her leather jacket, she pulled out a long metal skewer in one hand and a rusting lawnmower blade in the other. Then, in a blink of an eye, she pounced onto the bottom bunk and started stabbing the metal skewer through the blanket where the lumps were. Nuggley and Doodie Battenberg wriggled frantically under the blanket to avoid the skewer. It stabbed repeatedly through the blanket, narrowly missing them each time. Doodee eventually found his way over to where Nuggley was curled up in a frightened ball. He climbed on top of her to protect her as the skewer continued to stab through the blanket.

On the bunk above, the Gerbil Brothers had wriggled over to the edge, and were looking down at Ripperton wielding the skewer at the Battenberg Twins.

"Time to save the Battenberg Twins. Sir!" Shouted Colin Gerbil.

"Affirmative. Sir!" Replied Frank Gerbil.

"Primed and ready. Sir!" Joined in Seb Gerbil.

Ripperton stopped stabbing the metal skewer into the bottom bunk, and stood up so she was level with the Gerbil Brothers. She looked at them with a mixture of amusement and annoyance.

"Ready?" said Colin Gerbil.

"Aim?" said Frank Gerbil.

"Fire!" said Seb Gerbil.

They all pulled the triggers on their plastic toy rifles at the same time. Of course nothing happened. They were plastic toys. However, this didn't seem to bother the Gerbil Brothers, because as they pulled their triggers, each one of them made the sound effects of a gun.

"Ddddddddddddddd!" shouted Colin Gerbil.

"Bratatatatatatatatat!" shouted Frank Gerbil.

"Taka Taka Taka Taka Taka!" shouted Seb Gerbil.

After about five seconds of this, Ripperton got bored. However, just as she was about to batter the Gerbil Brothers to death with the lawnmower blade, the Mole in the Wall Gang leapt at her from the top bunk.

The Mole in the Wall Gang may have been small, but they were moles, and they had very sharp claws.

"Ouccccchhhh!" Screamed Ripperton, as Muldvar dug his claws into the top of her head. Maulwurfe Mogra and Muldvad did the same to her neck. Talpa, Walter and Eric were also busy scratching her face.

As hard as she struggled, Ripperton could not shake the Mole in the Wall Gang off. They clung on with their razor sharp claws like limpets. As Ripperton staggered backwards frantically trying to brush them off, the Battenberg Twins wriggled out from under the blanket on the bottom bunk, and jumped down onto the floor. Nuggley landed badly and twisted his ankle, but Doodee managed to pull him under the bunk to safety.

Ripperton grabbed hold of Eric and threw him brusquely off her. His tiny body hit the wall with a sickening crunch before falling to the floor where it lay motionless. The rest of the Mole in the Wall Gang saw this, but continued clawing and scratching Ripperton. Soon, however, her strength and ferocity became apparent. Walter was the next to fall victim as she brushed him off her neck then kicked him twenty yards down the corridor.

The rest of the Gang, realising things were only going to get worse, jumped off and ran for cover. The Gerbil Brothers followed suit.

"Tactical withdrawal. Sir!" shouted Colin Gerbil, as they dropped down onto the bottom bunk, and then the floor, to join the Battenberg Twins hiding against the wall under the bottom bunk.

Ripperton would have normally hunted every one of them down, but she had more important prey on her mind.

Wiping the blood from the scratches on her face, she walked down the tunnel and down the flight of steps at the end.

* * * * *

Down in another part of Brompton Road, Spoogemige, Criblee and Hetty were now facing their own problems. Woogums and Skerrett stood in the middle of the dark tunnel just a few yards away from them.

"I smell Stobes," said Skerrett.

Woogums giggled and started punching the air.

Spoogemige wasn't about to let them make the first move. He started running on the spot.

"What are you doing?" whispered Criblee. "They'll hear you."

"They might hear me," replied Spoogemige. "But they won't *see* me."

In a breathtaking explosion of speed, Spoogemige dashed down the tunnel in the direction of Skerrett and Wobblett. His speed was so great, that by the time Skerrett and Wobblett caught a glimpse of the blurred shape hurtling towards them, Spoogemige was already travelling at well in excess of a hundred miles an hour. As he approached them, he stuck both his arms out to the side.

He caught both of them in the throat as he sped past, knocking them both over like skittles in a bowling alley. Unfortunately, as usual he had completely misjudged his speed and his stopping distance. As he attempted an emergency stop, he suffered a double blow out in his sandals, and went crashing down the stairs at the other end of the tunnel.

Hetty and Criblee, unsure of exactly what had just happened, rushed off down the corridor after him. Passing the unconscious bodies of Skerrett and Wobblett, they arrived at the top of the stairs to see the crumpled heap of Spoogemige at the bottom.

*****

Meanwhile, the hulking shape of a five-foot rodent began to walk down the tunnel where Scorchington, Spogworth and Fligboge were.

Every few steps he stopped and raised his head upwards, sniffing in the stale air deeply and savouring it. Further down the tunnel, the sound of a fart broke the silence.

"Ooops," said a small orange dragon.

"Furtling typical!" whispered Fligboge. "Trust that orange twazlet to do something like that."

"How do you know it was him?" replied Spogworth, in a whisper, which was a bit too loud to be a whisper.

"Who else do you know who constantly farts?" replied Fligboge.

Rodolp had heard the fart, and could now also smell it. He began to move down the tunnel in the direction of the bottom that was responsible for it.

While Fligboge and Spogworth slowly tried to inch their way further down the tunnel, their backs pressed tight against the wall, Scorchington remained stationary. He could see Rodolp heading towards him, but was convinced that his grey dust camouflage would do the trick.

Rodolp however didn't need to see Scorchington. He could smell him. His long tail whipped up clouds of dust from the floor as his pace quickened. Fligboge had no intention of hanging around. Three against one counted for nothing, when that *one* was Rodolp. He ran off down the tunnel as fast as he could. Spogworth, who was never mentally prepared to think for himself, followed him.

In any other circumstance Rodolp would have chased after them, but this time he had some very personal business to attend to.

As Rodolp got closer, Scorchington held his breath and tried not to move. He just hoped his bottom would do the same. Soon Rodolp drew level with Scorchington. His dark crimson eyes stared closely at the wall. Saliva dripped from his jagged gold teeth. He stopped and sniffed the air. Scorchington remained motionless, his eyes closed. After a few moments he started to move again. Scorchington felt him walk away, and risked opening one eye. Sure enough, Rodolp was walking away. He let out a small sigh of relief, but unfortunately at the same time so did his bottom.

Rodolp span round and stared directly at Scorchington.

"Hello, my little orange friend."

Scorchington remained motionless as Rodolp began walking back towards him. Then, just as Rodolp was almost next to him, he leapt out from the wall and breathed a jet of fire at Rodolp, followed immediately by another one.

"Aaaarrrggghhhh," screamed Rodolp as the two jets of fire swept across his chest. He staggered backwards patting his chest with his claws to stop the flames. He now had two horizontal burn marks resembling a # to go with the two vertical burn marks from his last fight with Scorchington.

Rodolp roared in anger, and ran at Scorchington. Scorchington turned round and started running down the tunnel as fast as he could. With each yard, Rodolp was gaining ground on him as his huge back legs powered him down the tunnel. Scorchington just managed to reach the ventilation shaft at the end of tunnel and dive into it as Rodolp's claws came scything down on him. He fell down the shaft head first, faster and faster. He somehow managed to grab hold of an old iron ladder on the wall of the shaft and came to a halt level with another ventilation shaft running off at right angles. He hung from one claw and looked up the shaft to see Rodolp starting to descend the ladder.

"*Time to die!*" screamed Rodolp as he climbed down towards him.

Scorchington pulled himself up and into the smaller ventilation shaft and began to crawl down it, constantly looking to see how far behind him Rodolp was, and to blow jets of fire. Scorchington crawled faster and faster, but Rodolp was gaining. Realising he couldn't outrun him, Scorchington stopped, turned to face him, and waited until Rodolp was almost on top of him before unleashing a huge jet of fire. Rodolp screamed as the flames engulfed him till he was a huge rodent fireball. Scorchington kept breathing fire until he had none left. The burning shape of Rodolp slumped to the floor of the shaft, and he lay there groaning and smouldering. Then he stopped moving. Scorchington turned round and started crawling down the shaft again. Soon the ventilation shaft opened out onto another much bigger vertical shaft. He heard a sound coming from behind him and turned round. What he saw made him shudder in fear. The now badly burnt figure of Rodolp was once more crawling towards him.

An old rusting and derelict steel bridge with mesh grills on the bottom led across to the other side of the shaft, where another ventilation shaft disappeared into the far wall. Scorchington threw himself onto the bridge. The bridge creaked under his weight and started to vibrate and wobble on the ancient bolts fastening it to the wall. He looked down at the gaping void below his feet. The bridge suddenly shook and tilted over to one side as one of the anchors snapped out of the rotten crumbling brickwork.

Scorchington was thrown over into the side rail and only just managed to stop himself falling into the abyss below. Regaining his balance, he nervously moved across the bridge. Suddenly one if the mesh grills he was standing on gave way, and he fell through the floor of the bridge. He grabbed hold of next one as he fell, until he was left dangling from his short little arms. The shaft was so deep that he never heard the mesh grill that had fallen hit the bottom.

Rodolp emerged out of the shaft opposite and looked down at Scorchington hanging from the bottom of the bridge.

"Well, well, well. Now isn't *that* a sight to fill your heart with happiness."

As Rodolp lowered himself onto the bridge, Scorchington tried to pull himself up, but he couldn't, his arms were not strong enough.

"The bridge isn't strong enough!" he shouted across at Rodolp.

Rodolp just smiled down at him and started moving across the bridge towards him.

"You'll kill us both!"

"That's a risk I'm prepared to take."

The bridge started to creak and groan even louder under their weight. The metal bolts on either side started to pull out of the wall. Scorchington struggled frantically to try to pull himself up as Rodolp got nearer and nearer.

Scorchington knew he could not hold on much longer. Rodolp was now only a couple of feet away from him. He felt his tiny claws start to loose their grip. His legs peddled wildly in the air. One of his claws lost their grip. He was now hanging from just one claw. He looked up at Rodolp. He was grinning. He looked back at the one remaining bolt, which was holding the bridge to the wall on that side. It was slowly pulling out of the wall.

Scorchington could no longer hold on, and realised he was about to fall to his death. His tiny claw finally lost its grip and he started to fall. He closed his eyes and waited for the bottom of the shaft to end his life.

But instead, he felt something grab his arm. Looking up he saw Rodolp's claw wrapped round it. Rodolp looked down at him and then lifted him powerfully back up onto the bridge.

Rodolp sat down on the bridge opposite him. While Scorchington caught his breath and tried to understand why Rodolp had saved him, Rodolp just stared at him.

His body was badly burnt. His face had horrible deep red burn marks all over it, and his fur was singed black all over. His breath came in short painful gasps. One of his eyes was melted closed. His huge gold teeth still glinted in the half-light of the shaft though.

Then he spoke.

"I've seen things you Stobes wouldn't believe. Trains to High Barnet stuck off the shoulder of Archway. I watched steel beams glitter in the dark near Lancaster

Gate...All those moments will be lost in time...Like tears down a drain."

He paused, looked over his shoulder at the bolt finally pulling out of the wall behind him, and then turned back to Scorchington.

"Time...to...die!"

The bolt ripped out of the wall, and the bridge started to collapse. Scorchington span round and scrambled his way up the bridge as it fell and swung towards the far wall. Moving faster that he had ever moved in his life, he kept moving. The bridge slammed into the wall, but Scorchington held on. He looked down to see Rodolp falling silently into black void below.

The bridge finally stopped swinging, and with his last ounce of strength Scorchington managed to climb to the top and pull himself into the safety of the shaft above. He slumped down exhausted. After a few minutes he picked himself up and, still shaking began to make his way along the ventilation shaft and find a way back to the others in Brompton Road.

* * * * *

Fuddlerook, Wattage and Vember had been waiting for what seemed ages at the open tunnel parallel to the Piccadilly Line. They had no idea what had been going on in the rest of Brompton Road.

Little did they know, that a few yards down the track, Darl, Gobbit, Flem and Woogums along with seven Cribbit Snocklers were about to pay them a visit.

* * * * *

A barefoot Spoogemige, Criblee and Hetty were now slowly working their way through the other tunnels in search of the rest of the Stobes. They had heard the echoes of fighting coming from a variety of directions. Turning into the tunnel where the bunk beds were, they made their way cautiously down it. Eventually they spotted the Mole in the Wall Gang in the middle of the tunnel. They were standing in a circle around the bodies of Eric and Walter. Slowly they raised the bodies of Eric and Walter onto their shoulders, and in a funeral procession carried them down the tunnel.

When they reached Spoogemige, Criblee and Hetty, they stopped.

"We need to bury them," said Muldvar sadly, his head bowed.

"I'm so sorry," said Spoogemige.

Spoogemige, Criblee and Hetty bowed their heads in respect, as the Mole in the Wall Gang filed off down the tunnel.

They were about to continue their search when they heard footsteps. Pressing themselves up against the tunnel wall, they waited to see who it was. Then they heard voices. It sounded like the Mole in the Wall Gang talking to someone. Finally, the unmistakable voice of Fligboge drifted towards them.

A few moments later, Fligboge and Spogworth headed down the tunnel.

"Shame about what happened to the Mole in the Wall Gang." said Fligboge, in a typically insincere manner.

"Where's Scorchington?" asked Criblee.

"Don't talk to me about that little orange twazlet," replied Fligboge. "His flatulence nearly got us killed by that big rat Rodolp."

"So where is he?" said Hetty.

"Last time we saw him, he was being chased by Rodolp. We weren't hanging about to find out though." continued Fligboge.

"*What?* You left him alone to fight Rodolp?" Glowered Criblee.

"And?" said Fligboge, shrugging his shoulders defiantly.

"You really are a coward, aren't you?" said Spoogemige.

"And what about you?" said Hetty to Spogworth.

Spogworth dropped his head in embarrassment. "I panicked."

The sound of movement coming from near to the bunk beds distracted them all, as first the Gerbil Brothers, and then the Battenberg Twins slowly appeared from under the bottom bunk.

"You're all safe?" beamed a relived Hetty.

"Affirmative. Sir!" said Colin Gerbil.

"Correct. Sir!" said Frank Gerbil.

"Who's that? Sir!" said Seb Gerbil. He couldn't see anything because he had cracked the glass on his snorkel mask when he jumped to the floor earlier.

Nuggley Battenberg limped across the floor holding on tightly to Doodee.

"We're so glad to see you," they both said at the same time.

Nobody heard them.

"WE'RE SO GLAD TO SEE YOU!"

"Oh great!" said Fligboge scathingly, clutching his ears. "Every Darkenbad down here will have heard that."

"Sorry."

The sound of something heavy, being dragged across the floor coming from the end of the tunnel then attracted everyone's attention.

They watched and waited to see what it was. The sound came closer and closer. They all rushed over to the bunk beds and hid behind them.

Eventually the sound stopped at the end of the tunnel. Everyone held their breath. Then the sound started again. A few seconds later, it stopped again. Spoogemige leaned his head out to see who it was. He could just make out a short figure in a bowler hat. He sighed with relief.

"It's Germ."

It was indeed Germ, dragging a large bag of cement behind him.

"What are you going to do with that?" said Fligboge.

"Sell it!" replied Germ.

"To who, you stupid twazlet?"

"To her," replied Germ, pointing to Hetty.

"And exactly what would I want with a bag of cement?" said Hetty, her hooves folded across her chest.

"Rat and Gravel Pie mix."

"I've got more than enough of that thank you. And anyway, I wouldn't buy it from you even if I didn't,"

"I can do you a good price. In fact, if you carry it back, I'll give you a discount."

Hetty tossed her antlers in the air and turned away. Germ sat down on his bag of cement, took his hat off, and wiped a big drop of sweat off the end of his long pointed nose.

"What do we do now?" said Fligboge.

"Find the others." said Criblee.

They slowly started to make their way out of the tunnel. Germ, having been unable to cut a deal with Hetty, reluctantly abandoned his bag of cement and followed them.

* * * * *

Down by the Piccadilly Line, a tense silence hung in the air. Fuddlerook didn't mind the fighting; it was the waiting he didn't like. The waiting set him on edge.

Seven Cribbit Snocklers appeared out of the darkness and positioned themselves in a line on the tunnel roof directly above where Fuddlerook, Vember and Wattage were hiding.

"Best seats in the house." said Neb.

Fuddlerook looked up at Neb.

"Make the most of this, because it's your last one." he snarled.

"I wouldn't be too sure of that," replied Neb arrogantly.

Suddenly, Flem and Woogums leapt from nowhere over the wall and pounced on Wattage. Fuddlerook jumped up and dived across to help him, but at the same time, Gobbit threw himself on top of Fuddlerook. His sharp claws ripped through Fuddlerook's divers suit and he winced in pain.

Vember was about to help him when she felt a hand grab her round the throat from behind. She grabbed the hand and tried to pull it away, but it was too strong. The hand tightened round her throat. As she kicked and struggled to break free, she looked across at Wattage. He was lying on his back, and Woogums was straddling his chest punching him repeatedly in the chest and face.

"Ha Ha, kill the turnip man!" he shouted as he battered Wattage.

Flem meanwhile had moved over to join Gobbit, who had wrapped himself round Fuddlerook's back. Flem charged at Fuddlerook and rammed the barbed fin on his head into Fuddlerook's stomach. Fuddlerook reached down and grabbed hold of the barbed fin, slicing his hands in the process on the razor sharp edge.

Vember felt the breath being squeezed out of her as the hand round her throat held her effortlessly. Suddenly the hand let go, and she dropped to the floor.

Clutching her throat and trying to get her breath back, she turned round and saw Darl staring down at her. He was smiling coldly.

He reached down and grabbed her by the throat again. His long nails dug through the surface of her skin. Her body started to go limp again. He pulled her up until she was inches from his face.

"Things could have been so different," he said, staring deep into her eyes. He raised his other hand into the air, and clenched his fist. His nails crunched and splintered with the force. "But none of that matters now."

He was just about to bring his fist down onto Vember's face, when another hand grabbed it from behind, and stopped him.

"Leave her. She's mine."

Darl pulled away, and out from behind him stepped Ripperton.

She looked down at Vember, rolled her head to one side, and then kicked her visciously in the stomach. Vember's legs jacked up into her stomach as she reeled in pain. Ripperton kicked her again, only this time even harder.

Fuddlerook watched as Ripperton circled Vember's prone body. He let out a huge roar and threw himself backwards into the wall, crushing Gobbit against it. Reaching down with his hands, he grabbed hold of Flem's head in a fierce headlock, and started lifting him up and down in the air. The bones in Flem's neck made horrible crunching sounds, until with one huge effort, Fuddlerook lifted him high in the air, and at the same time twisted his neck ferociously to one side. Flem let out an agonising scream as the bones in his neck finally snapped. His lifeless body slammed into the floor as Fuddlerook let go. Turning round, Fuddlerook pushed Gobbit up against the wall, and repeatedly punched him in the face and stomach with his huge powerful fists until Gobbit stopped moving. Fuddlerook let go, and Gobbit slid to the floor.

The sound of clapping echoed round the tunnel. Turning round Fuddlerook saw Darl smiling at him.

"I see you haven't lost any of your prowess."

Fuddlerook stared at him coldly, and walked towards him. As he came nearer, he looked down at Woogums, who was still punching Wattage on the floor.

"Excuse me." he said to him.

Woogums stopped punching Wattage, and looked up at him.

"He's my friend, and I think it's time you said goodbye."

He then kicked Woogums in the face with such force that the few remaining teeth he had in his mouth flew out in all directions. As Woogums fell sideways to the ground, he kicked him in the face once more.

He knelt down next to Wattage. He was badly injured but thankfully still breathing.

"Hang on in there, my dear friend." he whispered softly.

Ripperton stared across at him and licked her lips, and then turned to Darl.

"He's good, isn't he?"

"He always has been," replied Darl. "But there's good, and there's *good*."

Whilst Ripperton and Darl had been watching Fuddlerook, Vember had caught her breath and had picked herself off the floor. She tapped Ripperton on the shoulder.

"Remember me?"

As Ripperton turned round, Vember punched her hard in the face. Ripperton fell back onto the floor.

At the same time, Fuddlerook moved closer to Darl until they were only a few feet apart.

"I didn't think I'd have to kill you for a second time."

"Prepare to join your brother, Fuddlerook."

Fuddlerook threw a fierce punch at Darl but he grabbed his fist effortlessly, stopping it inches from his face.

"You'll need to be quicker than that."

Fuddlerook threw another, but once again Darl blocked it easily. Before Fuddlerook could throw another punch, Darl launched his knee into Fuddlerook's stomach. He buckled forward in pain, and as he did so, Darl socked him in the face. The force sent Fuddlerook flying backwards onto the floor.

In an astonishing display of speed and agility, Darl leapt on top of him. Soon they were both rolling about on the floor. Fuddlerook tried to avoid Darl's punches, but he seemed to have developed reactions and reflexes that were so quick Fuddlerook didn't know what to do.

And then there was his strength. Fuddlerook had never known anyone have so much strength.

All he could do was soak up the blows. His body winced and writhed in pain as Darl rained down blows on him.

Behind them, Vember and Ripperton were locked in their own deadly fight. They exchanged punches and kicks relentlessly, neither prepared to give in. Ripperton swung round, grabbed Vember from behind in a headlock and rammed her against the tunnel wall. Vember could feel Ripperton's hot breath on the back of her neck as her face was pushed into the tiling of the wall.

"I've waited so long for this moment." whispered Ripperton into her ear.

Vember struggled to break free, but Ripperton held her firmly and powerfully.

Ripperton increased the pressure round Vember's neck. "Such a pretty little neck it is too." Then she noticed the small tattoo of a cross on the back of Vember's neck. "Where did you get this?" she hissed.

Vember felt her grip relax slightly. She pushed back against her and brought her feet up onto the wall. Then, with a spectacular piece of athleticism, she somersaulted over Ripperton's head and, grabbing her from behind, got her in a headlock before ramming her face first against the wall.

Vember then whispered into Ripperton's ear, "Why are you so interested?"

Ripperton reached back with one hand, and pulled her own hair to one side. There, on the back of Ripperton's neck, was an identical tattoo.

Vember let go of Ripperton and stepped back. "*Sister?*"

* * * * *

Behind them, Darl was straddling and methodically punching Fuddlerook all over. Blow after blow hit

Fuddlerook's body. Then, without warning, Darl stopped. He raised his nose high in the air, and inhaled deeply.

"I love the smell of dying Stobes in the morning."

Fuddlerook, summoning the last ounce of strength in his body, threw a punch. It hit Darl in the side of his head and sent him sprawling to the floor. Fuddlerook picked his battered body from the ground. Darl picked himself, raised both arms in the air and let out a blood-curdling roar. Fuddlerook charged at Darl, and grabbed him round the waist in a rugby tackle. Together they both fell over the low wall and down onto the track of the Piccadilly Line.

As Fuddlerook and Darl lay on the track, Spoogemige, Criblee, Hetty and the rest of the Stobes appeared out of the far end of the tunnel. At the same time, a rumbling sound from deep inside the Piccadilly Line grew closer and closer.

Fuddlerook picked himself up and stood in the middle of the track swaying from side to side. The sound got louder. Fuddlerook then realised what the sound was. It was a train. He looked back at the rest of the Stobes standing in the tunnel opposite. Lights shone out of the tunnel.

"Get out of there!" screamed Vember. "The power's back on!"

Fuddlerook started to climb up from the track, but just as he was about to pull himself to safety, Darl got up and grabbed him.

"Oh no you don't. You're coming with me."

Vember rushed towards the track to help him. She threw herself onto the edge of the track and held out her arm to Fuddlerook. Darl looked at her and smiled.

"Too late, I'm afraid."

Vember managed to grab hold of the sleeve of Fuddlerook's diver's suit. Her eyes bore into his, willing him to survive.

"Don't die on me." She pleaded with him.

Fuddlerook tried to pull away from Darl but he was spent. He had nothing left.

Vember could only watch in horror, as without taking his eyes off her, Darl calmly placed his foot onto the live rail of the track, just as the train came rushing at them.

The tunnel flashed blue as thousands of volts of electricity ripped through Darl and Fuddlerook. Seconds later, they disappeared under the wheels of the train as it sped past.

Vember only just managed to get her arm in time. She knelt on the side of the track, and looked down at her hand. It held all that was left of Fuddlerook - a small piece of his diving suit.

She let out an anguished cry as her heart broke into a thousand pieces.

The rest of the Stobes stood in tearful silence. Spoogemige, with tears streaming down his face walked over to her. Bending down, he held her gently in his arms. He felt her cling tightly to him as her whole body shook in pain and grief.

Ripperton, who had still been standing against the tunnel wall, slipped away silently to deal with her own loss - if it's possible for a Darkenbad to feel loss - and the discovery that she and Vember might have more than just a tattoo in common.

Criblee and Hetty went to help Wattage up from the floor. He was drifting in and out of consciousness. He grabbed Criblee by the arm and raised his battered face towards them.

"Fuddlerook?"

Criblee turned away to try to hide his tears.

"He didn't make it." said Hetty tearfully.

"Oh no. Not my friend. Not my *dear* friend!"

With the help of Criblee and Hetty, he managed to get to his feet. He looked around the tunnel.

"Where's Scorchington?"

"I'm here." said Scorchington as he rushed out of the other end of the tunnel.

Everyone breathed a sigh of relief - even Fligboge.

Scorchington looked around, and noticed someone was missing. He also noticed Vember sobbing in Spoogemige's arms.

"Not Fuddlerook? Please don't tell me something's happened to Fuddlerook.

Vember looked over Spoogemige's shoulder at Scorchington. Through her own tears, she saw the tears starting to fill Scorchington's eyes. She dropped down from Spoogemige's arms, and walked over to him. Crouching down, she put her arms around him and hugged him tightly.

"I'm so sorry, Scorch." She sobbed.

Scorchington rested his head on her shoulder and gripped her tightly. It was then that he noticed seven Cribbit Snocklers hanging from the tunnel roof.

He pushed Vember away, and walked over to the edge of the track.

"Enjoy the show?" he shouted up at them.

"The best we've ever seen," replied Neb. "It'd get a five star rating, even in the London Evening Standard."

"Well try this for an encore." replied Scorchington.

With a roar that was far too loud to come from such a small dragon, he breathed an enormous jet of fire at the tunnel roof.

"It's getting a bit too hot down here, boys." shouted Neb to the others.

Whilst it was seven Cribbit Snocklers who flew away, it was only six who managed to escape the fire from Scorchington's mouth. Lug only managed a couple of seconds of flight before being turned into a flaming bat kebab. As his burnt body fell to the track, Neb looked back.

"Either the Stobes have got some Chinese lanterns, or Lug's just copped it."

Not bothered either way, they flew off into the darkness.

A strange eerie quietness fell on the tunnel, as everyone stood deep in their own private thoughts. It was Hetty who finally broke the silence.

"Home?"

Everyone nodded, and slowly they made their bruised and battered way back to what they hoped would be safety.

Chapter Forty One

IN THE DOG & TRUMPET, Charlie, Rod, Wedge and their new friend Doreen were sitting quietly at a table having a beer. In the background behind the bar, the TV was on.

None of them paid much attention to it. They were too busy trying to get their heads round what they had seen the previous night.

"I still keep pinching myself to see whether or not it's a dream." said Wedge.

"I know what you mean," said Doreen. "But we all know it wasn't."

"Another drink?" said Charlie.

The others nodded an agreement. Charlie walked to the bar and ordered. As he waited, he watched the TV. The sound was very low, but he could just about hear it.

As the barman put the four pints on the bar, a news item came on about the Tube Strike.

"Can you turn that up?" said Charlie.

"Sure," said the barman.

Charlie watched the TV. There was a reporter stood outside Earls Court Tube Station. Charlie rushed over to the others.

"Look at this."

Rod, Wedge and Doreen followed Charlie back over to the bar and listened as the news reporter spoke.

"I can confirm that the forty-eight hour Tube Strike has been called off. But we have reports coming in that there have been some unusual events in the Underground in the last twenty-four hours. There are no further details at present, but according to my sources it includes reports of sightings that are currently being termed as unexplained activity. I can also confirm that at present, Earls Court, Knightsbridge and Gloucester Road Tube stations are closed until further notice."

A tingle ran down Wedge's spine as he looked at the others and smiled.

They headed back to their table, and sat down. They each took a long drink of beer. Charlie was the first to speak.

"Looks like we might not be the only ones who have seen *them*."

"Sssshh," said Wedge. "People might be listening."

"Well, one thing's for sure," said Doreen. "Our lives are probably never going to be the same again."

"A toast," said Wedge. "To new friends, new adventures…and a very special secret shared!"

* * * * *

At Gloucester Road tube station, PC Meredith and PC Walton waited at the ticket office. The place was swarming with official-looking people. It was a peculiar atmosphere.

Three gentlemen in immaculate suits walked over to them.

"PC Meredith and PC Walton?" said the tallest of the three.

"Yes," replied PC Meredith.

"My name is Inspector Gudgeon from Special Branch, and this is Mr Proudfoot from the Home Office and Mr Doyle from MI5."

PC Walton looked nervously at PC Meredith.

"If you don't mind, we'd like to ask you a few questions about certain events that have transpired over the past forty eight hours. In particular, at the locations of St Stephen's Church, Johnson Pratt & Livingston and an address in Knightsbridge, where I believe you might have witnessed something... shall we say... out of the ordinary?"

"There's more than that," said PC Meredith.

"Yes," replied Inspector Gudgeon. "I do believe there probably is."

Chapter Forty Two

IN A DIMLY LIT ROOM off a disused tunnel near to the abandoned tube station of Brompton Road, the Stobes sat in silence around the old metal door propped up on bricks, which they used as a table.

The mood was sombre. Not even the arrival of a copious quantity of Hetty's rat and gravel pies could raise even the slightest of smiles.

Scorchington tried to toast some bread, but he couldn't. His flames would not come, unlike his tears, which dropped from his eyes forming small pools on the metal surface of the table.

Hetty brushed her oven mitt across the top of his head. Looking up at her, he tried to smile, but he couldn't.

He looked round the table. Criblee, Spogworth, Fligboge, Germ, the Battenberg Twins, the Gerbil Brothers and the remaining members of the Mole in the Wall Gang. There was not a dry eye in the place.

Vember came into the room accompanied by Spoogemige, who had his arm around her shoulder protectively. She made her way to the empty space where Fuddlerook usually sat. Reaching into her gown, she pulled out the piece of red diver's suit and kissed it softly. Then her eyes flooded with tears, she laid it down gently on the table.

"Sleep well," she wept.

Further down the tunnel in his study, Wattage stared at the floor. The remains of the table lay scattered around in tiny pieces. Now he would never know exactly where it came from, or why. He noticed some broken glass and a piece of bloodstained blue clothing at his feet. There was also a clump of what looked like red hair. It too had blood on it.

However, none of this was important anymore. He had lost his oldest friend, and the Stobes had lost their bravest and strongest warrior.

He walked slowly and painfully down to join the others. His injuries at the hands of the Darkenbads would take time to heal. But heal they would, unlike hearts, which sometimes never do.

He knew this only too well as he entered the room. They had won the battle against their greatest enemies, but the price had been high, too high. Now they faced an uncertain future.

"What about the remaining Darkenbads?" asked Spoogemige?

"They will have gone into hiding, especially now Darl and Rodolp are dead." replied Wattage.

"Where's Plankton?" asked Criblee.

"Not even he'll know that?" replied Fligboge. "He'll turn up sooner or later. It's not like he's in any danger of getting killed."

For the briefest of moments, there were smiles instead of tears.

But as they sat round the table, the Stobes were unaware, that behind the metal grill in the door of the old ventilation shaft at the end of the tunnel, a dark crimson eye was observing their every move from the shadows.

Waiting. Plotting.

THE STOBES TRILOGY

Book Two

The Assassinator.

Chapter One

SCROAT DIDN'T FEEL ANYTHING BEFORE the bones in her neck were crushed against, and then severed her spinal nerve.

She didn't feel anything afterwards either.

The grip around her neck loosened, and her body slumped to the ground. It lay motionless in a pool of oil-covered water. Next to it, equally motionless, lay her umbrella.

A dark figure moved out of the shadows. The distant light from the platform at Finchley Central briefly revealed its identity, but there was no one else to witness it.

Reaching down to pick up the umbrella, the figure moved back into the shadows again. Striding over Scroat's dead body, it walked off into the darkness of the tunnel.

TO BE CONTINUED...

ABOUT THE AUTHOR

NJ Rayner grew up in Mellor in Cheshire, and now
lives in Kent.
He is married and has one son and two step children.
He spent his career working in advertising
for a number of leading agencies, before finally deciding to
follow his dream of becoming a writer.
He firmly believes that Douglas Adams was right
when he said the Earth is a giant computer programme
run by mice.
The Time Table is his debut novel, and the first book
in The Stobes Trilogy.

33895624R00183

Made in the USA
Charleston, SC
26 September 2014